"Terry Bisson looks at things from unique and persnickety angles—out of a shoulder hunch, up from under, sideways, down, and with a cockeyed clarity that transfigures, whether the world or our own nearsighted take on it, if not both."

—Michael Bishop

"Terry Bisson has always been unique—in the best sense of the word. He writes stories and novels which simply could not have come from anyone else. And I'm delighted to say that his new book, *Pirates of the Universe*, is a perfect example. It has all his familiar strengths: affection, imagination, and energy, combined with an obliquely evocative use of language. It's also wildly funny—and poignant as well, as his all-too-human characters shamble into glory. God send that his work will be with us for a long time."

—Stephen R. Donaldson

"Terry Bisson's work has everything: originality, humor, charm, passion, and underneath it all, a deep river of seriousness and sweetness. Only a blockhead wouldn't love this book."

—Paul Park

"Filled with Bisson's unusual perspectives, including a mini-civilization of microscopic machines. This is a novel that will appeal to SF traditionalists as well as those who prefer a more modern approach to the field."

—*Science Fiction Chronicle*

Tor Books by Terry Bisson

Bears Discover Fire
Pirates of the Universe

PIRATES OF THE UNIVERSE

Terry Bisson

A TOM DOHERTY ASSOCIATES BOOK
NEW YORK

This is a work of fiction, set in an imagined future. All the characters and events portrayed in this book are fictitious, and any resemblance to real people or events is purely coincidental. All presently existing corporations or other entities that appear in this novel are used fictitiously.

None of the presently existing corporations or other entities mentioned in this book has in any way authorized or endorsed the book or any of its contents.

PIRATES OF THE UNIVERSE

This book is printed on acid-free paper.

Edited by David G. Hartwell

A Tor Book
Published by Tom Doherty Associates, Inc.
175 Fifth Avenue
New York, NY 10010

Tor Books on the World Wide Web:
http://www.tor.com

Design by Nancy Resnick

Library of Congress Cataloging-in-Publication Data

Bisson, Terry.
Pirates of the Universe / by Terry Bisson.
p. cm.
ISBN 0-312-86295-4 (pb)
I. Title.
PS3552.I7736P57 1996
813'.54—dc20 95-30050
CIP

First hardcover edition: April 1996
First trade paperback edition: April 1997

Printed in the United States of America

0 9 8 7 6 5 4 3 2 1

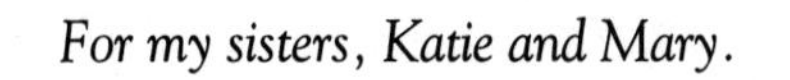

For my sisters, Katie and Mary.

PIRATES OF THE UNIVERSE

ONE

It was the dream itself enchanted me.
—William Butler Yeats

You have seen pictures. Who on Earth hasn't?

But no matter how many pictures you may have seen, they never prepare you for the real thing, in the flesh, so to speak; in the glory; swimming up out of the darkness in which the stars themselves swim.

Gun missed the approach, usually his favorite part, when the Peteys first appear as a blur of light, dimmer than the farthest star; then as the ship closes, glow brighter and brighter; until it is at last clear that what you are seeing is no faraway galaxy, or nebula, or gaseous cloud, but something altogether other, something entirely undreamed of until now, something new in the universe. . . .

Three of them. In formation.

Gun missed it but he had seen it before, for this was (with luck) his next to last hunt. This time he had drawn setup, and setup had to be done right. When you are about to pull eight hours on a rail, you don't fool around. By the time Gun got to the Nittany Lounge, racing weightless through the long halls, the triad was already close, filling the big windows, its glow painting the dark room rose.

The door slid shut behind him as silently as a prayer.

The lounge was empty, as he knew it would be. The other Rangers were either suiting up, or sleeping, or eating, or checking their mail, or emptying their bowels for the long pull in high vac. The Sierras were already pulling away in their blunt yachts, or on the bridge of the *Penn State*, waiting for showtime.

Gun left the lights down. He had at most twenty minutes before he had to suit up, and he wanted to be alone; solitude is rare in space.

Every time he saw them was like the first time. Like an old lover, always new.

The *Penn State* was well inside the orbit of the Moon, but already, there they were: closer than usual to the Earth, swooping in like moths to a flame. The Peteys were "upright" to the ship's plane like three mountains or towering clouds (even though a hundred times as big). The ship was on a long fall angling across the "front" of the triad, and as Gun watched, the *Penn State* and the Peteys seemed to be turning together, like dancers. Gun pushed off the doorway and drifted toward the window, holding his breath all the way, enjoying the complicated waltz made by his movement, the Peteys', the ship's, and the slow spin of the universe itself—all joined into one movement as wide and smooth as the foam on the turn of a river, moving and yet never going anywhere.

The Peteys' molecule-thick skin shimmered like an oil slick, a faint rose rainbow. Occasionally a star glittered through it; or was it a reflection? a refraction? It was said that their inner atmosphere tied light in knots.

The lounge smelled like Chinese food. Every part of a spaceship has its own stink.

Reaching the high curved glass, Gun lodged with one knee under the bar that circled the window. The landing gave him a small but sweet pleasure: zero/g comes more naturally to some than to others, and his own easiness contrasted with the awkwardness he had felt on Earth since he was a child. His first week at Academy, when the others were throwing up, he had thought: *This is more like it!*

Suddenly, as if reproaching him for letting his thoughts wander, a star ignited in the near distance. That would be the Sierra yacht, the *John James*, Shorty's new command, course-correcting with a bright blue benzine streak.

Gun watched with a special, almost proprietary interest. Shorty had been a Ranger until only a few months before—one of the old-timers who had trained both Gun and Hadj, Gun's partner. Now Shorty was wearing the blue and gold.

Under the interim Protocols, the Sierras got the first look at every triad: for the communication attempt (a formality), for scientific research (ostensibly) and of course, for the pictures—on old-fashioned chemical film, since Peteys did funny things with light and their images were impossible to digitize. It was chemical photographs that presented the images seen around the world, the magnificent holos in *National Geographic* and the four-color trading cards that started boys dreaming of becoming Rangers.

There were no girl Rangers; just as there were no pictures of what Rangers actually did.

* * *

There was a bright, brief scratch, as if someone had struck a match on the side of the universe. The *John James* was turning. The Sierra yacht's brief burn trail provided perspective, and the Peteys that had seemed, to Gun, almost nearby, once again seemed as large as three continents and as far away. Gun watched as the *John James*, now a blinking light, dropped into the rose-lit canyon between two Peteys and disappeared.

A few minutes later, the blinking light reappeared, behind but higher, and seemingly brighter: the curious optical effect of the Peteys' atmosphere. Then the *John James* disappeared again in a crackling of silvery light as a storm broke inside the sunward Petey. It left a silver blue haze, a cloud within a cloud. The other two were flashing now, shoulder to shoulder, "top" to bottom. The Sierras insisted they were involuntary electrical discharges, but Gun preferred to imagine that the Peteys, awakened, were giving the alarm. Shouting in colors.

"Hard to believe, ain't it?"

Gun turned, startled and a little irritated, though he tried not to show it. It was Hadj, come to fetch him for suit-up.

Gun made room on the rail at the window, but Hadj remained floating, stationary, with the perfect zero/g ease of the eight-year veteran. His short hair was black, his eyes bright blue, and his moustache was gray, as if he had been assembled from parts of different men.

"Hard to believe what?" Gun asked.

Hadj, who had learned English from movies, spoke with a Texas/Germanic drawl:

"Hard to believe we're going to kill one of those mothers."

* * *

Hadj was from Syria, or from that part of the Quarter that used to be Syria, and he once told Gun that he actually saw the Peteys when he was a kid. From Earth. The atmosphere was clearer in those days, especially in the desert where it almost never rained; and one October night when Hadj was nine, his uncle, a tanker driver on the Assad-Baghdad run, pulled over to the side of the highway and sat with him on the warm, ticking turbine cover of the Ossian-Peugeot and helped him pick out what he called "the visitors" from the forest of stars and satellites.

Gun was from K-T, cloud-locked even then, and he saw his first Petey in one of the stacks of *National Geographics* his father and uncle, Ham and Hump, kept in the attic of the house portion of the Ryder family compound ("Stately Visitors from the Depths" NG:539:89:9). Gun was only five but Gordon had already taught him to read before disappearing underground.

The first Peteys (or PDs—*Psioraimen Directicii*) were picked up in 538 by the optical early warning array at Houbolt Moon Base. Three 1820-kilometer-long, faintly luminous, elongated "soap bubbles" were clocked entering the inner solar system across the orbit of Mars, at an inclination of 13 degrees to the plane of the ecliptic, traveling at a velocity relative to the Sun of 118 kps, or twice the speed of a comet.

The information was received and logged by PanAsia, the insurance consortium that had financed and then operated the unmanned array to track irregular asteroids after the near miss of "Big John" in 521 had run insurance projections off the scale.

The problem was, the series of wars later known as the Three was then raging, and Houbolt had been unmanned for almost twenty years. PanAsia was well into Chapter Twenty and no one was reading the files. An alarm went off unnoticed, then another. It was left to another electronic array, the orbiting oral history project known as Biogens Historicum to notice the incursion and gain the interest of astronomers; or, at least, of those astronomers who, through political disloyalty or disinterest or ill-health, were uninvolved in the fighting, which was then confined to Southern Europe, the American Northwest, Indonesia, and Low Earth Orbit.

Within a week, over a hundred astronomers had picked up the intruders on telescopes on mountaintops and in the backyards of the war-darkened cities. It was hard to clock the course of the PDs, as they were then called, since it kept changing. Defying scientists' predictions (and apparently the laws of special relativity as well) the three giant shapes slowed as they penetrated deeper into our sun's gravity well. They stayed in the same formation, a line, even as their trajectory changed. They grew either more luminous or more reflective as they approached the Sun.

By the time they had crossed Earth's orbit, and were passing within .007 AU or a million kilometers of the Earth, they had slowed to a speed of 55 kps and were visible with a three inch refractor and had revived the dead science of optical astronomy. Invisible to radio, they were beautiful on film and in the lens. The Peteys' special and strange luminosity was a mystery, defying spectroanalysis at first and later showing that they were empty, more than empty (or, rather, less than empty), crammed full of emptiness, as it were; so empty as to make space itself seem a rain forest of particles and semi-particles, leptons and quarks. They were filled with an altogether new kind of nothingness.

Because of their mysterious reversal of speed and their at least quasi-phototropic behavior, the questions on the mind of every astronomer (and boy) were: Where are they coming from? What do they want from us? These were the questions that decorated the fronts of the Petey trading cards of Gun's youth.

The first three Peteys passed within .2 AU (half the orbit of Mercury) of the Sun and with a 35 percent change of direction, were off again, picking up speed and losing luminosity as they left the solar system. By the time they again crossed the orbits of the Outer Planets, their magnitude had dropped until they were visible only to deep sky telescopes, and was red-shifted to show an incredible speed of .2c, the fastest velocity known for any nearby heavenly body. Then they were gone.

For weeks this data was digested and discussed in the tabs and on the Net; then as the Three raged on, and the tabs went under and the Net shattered, it was forgotten. Almost. Then, two years after their first appearance, the Peteys were back.

This second triad was first sighted just outside the asteroid belt, and passed within half a million miles of the Earth. They were visible with binoculars from blacked-out London, Melbourne, and even, in a grainy newspaper photo, from Bloomington, Indiana. For a solid week they stopped the Three (and some say they slowed the wars and began their long decline).

The third triad of Peteys, eighteen months later, snuck up on the Earth. They apparently never crossed the Outer Planets at all but appeared on the far side of the Moon as if they had come up from a hole. They were found lurking in the Moon's stone shadow like the nesting bats that were even then in K-T being called "wing meat" by people who were war-hungry but not ready to eat *anything*. These were the Peteys Hadj saw, or thought he saw (Gun always suspected it was in fact the league-long orbiting teardrop of Overworld). They drifted out of hiding, toward the Earth—and then suddenly red-shifted away—apparently without ever leaving the vicinity of the Moon.

Gun was a boy that summer. Just learning to read and shoot.

Another three came the next year, and the following year. They came in threes, appearing and then disappearing between Earth and the Moon, blue-shifting in and red-shifting out of existence, as though coming and going through a new hole in the Universe. They came and went without crossing space as we knew it. They came and went like weavers working a shuttle that was our world, weaving several new religions, and unraveling a war.

Their approaches were seen only by scientists, but their departures were watched by more millions than any other natural phenomenon since the last of the elephants.

It was obvious that the Peteys were attracted to the Earth. Was it the water? The nitrogen? Since they now appeared and disappeared within the orbiting shadow of the Moon, there were those who speculated that it was the Moon and not the Earth that attracted them.

The Sierras wanted to protect them. Disney-Windows wanted to exploit them. The Fundamentals wanted to worship them (with fire, of course). But with space travel impossible because of the war, there was no way to reach them.

The Peteys were as inaccessible as the stars.

Some even credited the Peteys with ending the Three, though in fact the Three had been slowing down for several years. Just as it had been noticed some thirty years earlier, that there was war raging on every continent, without anyone actually knowing why or when it had begun; so it was noticed by the mid-540s that in almost every part of the world some kind of rough order, if not justice, was in place; and that except for the robot bombs and leftover mines, there was little actual killing going on.

On the surface, that is. Automated war in orbit went on, as if death had taken on a life of its own. The self-replicating defense and maintenance systems built into the orbital war platforms had learned to defend themselves against their makers, and were unapproachable. Overworld, Disney-Window's 80K-long orbiting theme park, had been abandoned, though it was still there, shining like a smeared star every morning and evening. Someone or something was keeping the lights burning.

When the Peteys started lurking around the Moon, it was agreed (by Disney-Windows and the Sierras at least) that someone needed to get a closer look. What were they? What did they want? The problem was, the few spaceships that had not been destroyed in the Three, or "cracked" in the one of the many ceasefires, were orbiting. And without some kind of peace agreement there was no way to get into orbit.

Soon competing dispensations were being scripted and cobbled together in Rome, Orlando, Belig and Singapore. The Protocols allowed liftoff and Disney-Windows was the first to successfully retrofit a shuttle. Reclaiming Overworld (which no one else wanted, or could reach) D-W spent the winter sealing off the sections still controlled by the renegade nanobots and their progeny, and refitting the *Penn State*, the cislunar space ship left over from the abortive attempt earlier in the century to mine the Moon for helium-three.

The twin purposes of D-W's first mission the next year were video (unsuccessful, of course, since something that is not quantum cannot be digitized) and communication (unsuccessful). The Peteys were gone before the *Penn State* even left earth orbit. The next two years were spent making the deal with the Sierras that resulted in the Ranger Corps, and retrofitting the two yachts that were to become the Sierra fleet. Perhaps because they were smaller, perhaps because they were prettier, the Peteys let the yachts approach, and a new era in history began.

Gun was a teenager that summer, just learning to unhook Donna's bra with two fingers of one hand.

D-W claimed that the first kill was an accident, the result of a misguided spectroanalytic probe attempt. Two Rangers were lost but much was gained. In addition to the pictures that graced the cover of the *National Geographic*, the *Penn State* brought back something Earth didn't even know it needed—a gift from beyond (or so we then thought) the stars; a fabulous (literally) item of exchange that created a new banking system, and reanimated a weary world's ravaged economy.

Not to mention providing jobs in space for those lucky enough to draw a Disney-Windows ticket; for, as the old timers might have said, a happy, happy few.

TWO

Learn to hold loosely all that is not eternal.
—A. Maude Royden

Bring us down a little," said Hadj.

"Down a little," said Gun. Jiggling the benzeners.

Space this close to anything this big had an "up" and a "down." In toward the Petey was down. Steadying the roll with delicate puffs, Gun let the rail drift down. The almost-planet-sized creature below looked dark, solid (even though Gun knew it wasn't) and strangely inviting.

"This is close enough," said Hadj.

"Close enough." Gun drifted down a little closer.

"Hold her steady here," said Hadj. "Guess what I saw today?"

"Steady," said Gun: unnecessary words in answer to unnecessary words, but he knew that Hadj liked to hear the sound of voices, especially when he was on a rail, in a coffin suit, a speck in the emptiness. Hadj claimed it was his Bedouin background, the genetic answer to the emptiness of the Quarter; and he pointed out from his reading (he had an Associate's Degree in English from Harvard Riyadh) that Melville's sailors talked a lot. Gun was, historically, the exception, though he didn't mind listening. He also felt the need for a little chatter especially when they were alone, the two of them, in high vac on a benzene-powered rail.

The Ranger boats were called "rails," after the auto drag racers of a previous century. Take a single, twenty-meter beam, and place on the front a two-man open pod, and in the back a benzene/operzine engine. No environmentals—only an electrical connection for the coffin suits. That was it, but it was enough; for some people at least. Disney-Windows was a lottery job, but Rangering was self-selective, since only one person in three could tolerate zero/g for long periods of time, and only one in ten (one regular person™ in five) could last eleven hours in a coffin suit.

The coffin suits were a cross between space suits and small ships. There were no legs, just arms. They came with a bathroom (of sorts) and the arms could be pulled in to scratch an itch or pick a nose. Still, eleven hours was a long time, even though men had been known to live in them for twenty-two hours while awaiting rescue after the foundering of the first helium-three mining boat, the *Bradford Angier*, back in 519.

At least that was how long it was assumed they had lived, when the bodies were found.

"This is close enough," said Hadj. "Guess what I saw today?"

"Roger. Close enough. What?"

Gun held the rail steady at a thousand meters. That's as close to a Petey as you wanted to go. As solid as the mass below looked, Gun knew that it wasn't. Objects that got too close got "winked" and disappeared. It had happened to two Rangers on the first encounter.

"I saw a gen," said Hadj. "Hold it steady here."

"Steady," said Gun. "I thought gens weren't allowed off Overworld."

"This one was. I saw her on the *Penn State*, and guess who she was with?"

"Shorty," Gun said.

"How'd you know?"

"Because he's a Sierra now, and they're not allowed to speak to Rangers, and he's the only Sierra you know."

"I wonder if she's with him on the *John James*," said Hadj. "Why are you getting so low?"

"I'm not," said Gun. "I'm holding at three hundred meters. They're not allowed on the yachts."

"Well, pull up a little," said Hadj with a yawn. "We have to be high enough to see them come over the horizon. You keep talking about what's allowed. She's already off Overworld, on the *Penn State*. So what's to keep her off the *John James?*"

Gun pulled up a little. He didn't like these kinds of conversations. Hadj was always wanting to talk about something new.

"Funny how they whisper," Hadj said. "Just watch and ask questions."

It's not funny, Gun thought. It's just what they do.

"Funny how they look like girls. Speaking of which, why are we shimmying?"

"There's a wiggle in the jets." Gun could feel an oscillation in number four's directional. It was the directionals (electrically operated) that were the weak point in the rails. By comping he was able to keep the wiggle down. It was an easy adjustment, like driving a boat against the current back home in K-T.

"Hold there," Hadj said, yawning. "Speaking of girls, how's it going with what's-her-name?"

"Who?" But Gun knew who.

"Timpany?"

"Tiffany," said Gun. "I don't know. OK, I guess."

"Has she taken you to her Upper Room?"

"I don't know. She's copy-protected. I don't remember."

"You would remember," Hadj said. "This is our spot! Can you hold us right here?"

Gun nodded. The trick was to keep a comfortable distance from that mysterious, not-quite-real surface, and yet stay close enough so that when the hard-light equipped *Yankee* came over the horizon and started its cut, Hadj would be able to pick up the skin along with the other rails. Even though they were not visible, Gun knew the other three rails were just over the horizon, one behind and two to the "east." As soon as the *Yankee* started its cut, all four would lock on with their gather lights and begin the pull. Meanwhile, the word was wait.

At this point they were out of radio contact; they would have to guess where and when the *Yankee* and the *Henry David* (its escort) would show. There was no radio communication near the Petey's surface. Signals were unpredictable; they might show up an hour or even a week later. They had even been known to show up before they had been sent.

"We can hold here for a while," said Hadj, who was in command. He checked his FauxRolex analog, the only kind of watch that worked near the Petey's surface, where Time seemed to flutter in sheets. It had been his uncle's, or so he claimed. "Maybe I'll catch a little shut-eye."

"Go ahead. I'll watch for the dawn."

The *Yankee's* approach would show up in the Petey, as faint as the first hints of dawn—reversed so they came in the "ground" instead of the sky.

Gun knew dawns. As a kid he had spent hours in the Ryder compound attic looking through Ham's and Hump's piles of *National Geographics*. That old magazine, heavy enough to be carried as ballast, like china in clipper ships, was as much about sky as Earth, and Gun knew what dawn looked like in every part of the world. Dawn was the great equalizer. In her rosy hands central Massachusetts was as grand as the Monument Valley; Indiana as wild as the northern reaches of Labrador; New Jersey as awesome as the Tien Shan.

The Petey has its own dawn: the dawn of death. While Hadj snored on, Gun watched and waited for it. It was hours since he had peed. The pain in his bladder reminded him and he knelt in the suit to relieve himself. The Petey below was as dark from three hundred meters as a universe without stars.

Somewhere above, lost in the swarming stars, was the *Henry David* with its Sierra observers. The *John James* would be long gone now, heading back for Overworld with its photos—and maybe even a gen, if Hadj's guess was right. Who knew, these days? Gun didn't like to think about it. Everything was always changing. He emptied his mind and fell into the Ranger's watch that looked, to those not in the know, like sleep. Or like thought.

Like the dawn in the Hindu Kush, or in southern Indiana, the first light of the Petey, or the "wake up" as the Rangers call it, is the most beautiful part of the job. What had been as dark as the ocean at night becomes, gradually, lighted. Flashes of rose, cracklings of reds and violets and oranges . . . all the Peteys' colors were from the same end of the spectrum, but it was Gun's favorite end.

"A quaker," said Hadj, alert. The surface was rolling below

them in great half-kilometer waves, lit from below. The quakers were the Peteys with the brightest show; the ones that hated dying the most. *We are watching the beginnings of death,* Hadj once said, *and who knows, maybe the birth of consciousness.*

There was a flash just over the horizon that seemed to rock the rail. Another flash, this one just underneath, bleeding off on three sides, all crackling spines like lightning. Right behind the quake, which moved down the hemisphere like a school of waves, was a slow light, reds and roses impossible to imagine back on Earth where all the light was flung from one paltry sun.

"There she blows!" Hadj.

First the *Henry David* came over the horizon. The escort. Like its twin, the *John James*, it was streamlined for visual effect. Disney-Windows had built the two yachts in the golden days of Overworld, to ferry passengers around the Moon, those who could afford the trip. Below and in front was the *Yankee*, an angular workhorse riding ahead of its cut, so it was always over pure idaho (the dark, unmarked Petey, or potato, as the older Rangers called it), the hard-light beam dragging along behind like a stinger.

First Gun saw the Petey's flashes, then the *Henry David*, then the *Yankee* and the hard-light. He didn't have to look back to see what Hadj was doing. Hadj was twirling his gather-light beam, fishing for skin.

"Back up," said Hadj, suddenly in command again.

"Back," said Gun. He comped straight back a thousand meters, then several hundred to the "east" without being told. This was the easy part, where he didn't have to think. The ship felt like part of his suit, and his suit like part of his body, his body like part of the universe.

"Got it!" said Hadj. Now for the first time the other rails were visible, two of them at least, flashing faraway lights, anonymous and indistinguishable in the electrical storm of light and dark. A third was far behind, pulling the seam open before it closed in on itself. They were dark spots, less than dots, visible only because Gun knew where/when they should be.

Hopefully, they were all latched on.

"Now close in," said Hadj.

Without a word, for the talking was over, Gun dropped the rail to within a hundred meters of the glowing, flashing surface and flew skimming like a crop duster behind and to the left (or "west") of the *Yankee* almost a kilometer ahead. Even at this distance the hard-light hurt his eyes; and even seen indirectly, the glow from the Petey pulled at him. They were catching up to the Sierra yacht and its great, grand, glorious, light-giving wound. The light from inside seemed to pull at Gun's eyeballs, as if to call them out of his head, as if to set them, like jewels, in some as-yet-undreamed-of glorious . . .

"Closer," said Hadj.

Gun touched a lever and the rail drifted to the left, pulling the skin away from the opening seam. Technically, according to some physicists, the radicals who believed the Peteys were other universes, the Petey's skin did not "exist" until it had been peeled from the Petey's great sailing-onward soul.

Whatever it was that Hadj's gather-light had seized, they held onto it. The *Yankee* was straight ahead of them now, a little to the west or right, its hard-light laser like a buzz saw; and moving behind it, just after the cut, was the seam, opening like a door into—well, Gun looked away. There was nothing, less than nothing in there. He felt a fear that predated even life, the fear of matter for unbeing that predates existence itself.

"Closer," said Hadj.

It was the end of the pretty part of the kill and the beginning of the work. The job now was to follow the seam and find a way to pick up the skin. The *Yankee* was in the safest spot, ahead of the cut. The *Henry David* was above and behind. The only danger was down here, close to the seam. Too close, and you could get *winked*, Gun knew.

"Closer."

The *Henry David* headed down while the rails followed, two of them visible by now, although it was hard to tell in the strange time distortions near the Petey's surface. Light signals, like radio, were unreliable.

The cut continued. Below, to the rear, the colors were gone. The strange light of the seam still spilled straight up to heaven but Gun knew not to look. Beyond it and behind were the other three rails.

"Back off," Hadj said.

The trick was to pick up the two sides at once and pull the skin back lest it curl down into the seam and disappear. Eat itself. It had been known to happen.

"What the hell's that?" Gun asked. He saw a light where a light shouldn't be, sailing toward them, over the cut.

"Hold steady!"

"Somebody has lost it. A rail . . ."

But it wasn't a rail. It was the *John James*. The sleek Sierra yacht that should have been already tied up at the *Penn State*'s exitway was dropping, eerily lit by the dark-light spilling out of the 10K long wound. "What the hell is Shorty trying to do?"

"He's trying to go to Heaven," Hadj said, alarmingly matter-of-factly.

"Heaven?"

How can they get so close to the seam? Gun wondered. Were

they trying to take a photograph of the inside? The strange light spilled straight up bathing the *John James* in a weird glow.

"He's going too low!" said Gun.

Suddenly the controls kicked in Gun's hand, as if a load had been let off the ship, and he saw with horror that Hadj had dropped his corner of the skin. It was the Ranger's one unpardonable sin.

A shadow flew out and up, like a cloak falling across the Universe. "You lost it!" cried Gun. The *John James* sailed on. The skin peeled up and flapped in the starlight and started to waft inward, on itself.

"Shorty, pull up!"

Hadj didn't say anything. Gun realized he hadn't said anything since the disaster had started to unfold. There was nothing to say. The skin snapped in on itself, and the *John James* went with it, turning downward in a stately, deliberate arc, flipped sideways as if hit—then dove straight into the shimmering unlight of the cut.

And disappeared.

THREE

Death never knocks. Death just walks through the door.
—Tennessee Williams

It was like waking from a dream. Except it hadn't been a dream.

Gun could feel the *Penn State* shudder as it went into a braking burn. Soon they would be docking at Overworld. He closed his eyes and tried to sleep again, listening to his own internal *booms*. Rangers carried an aural-crystal block in the carotid to give the heart something to push against in zero/g. But the booming that usually put Gun to sleep wouldn't work tonight, because every time he fell asleep he saw the *John James* falling into the blazing light of the Petey's opened seam, over and over. . . .

Waking brought no comfort, either. Gun's eyes opened wide, and still in his mind he saw Shorty's first command turn sideways and then over and then dive—

The two remaining Peteys, the rest of the triad, had redshifted away, as always, disappearing into whatever it was they disappeared into. As always, when one was killed, all three were gone.

They had left behind no wreckage, no bodies, no *John James*, no Shorty. . . . All that was left was the skin, what remained of it, being shepherded hurriedly into the *Penn State*'s open hold by the rest of the Rangers. It would continue shrinking until it got into oxygen, which meant that the four-hour return to Overworld had to begin immediately.

Hadj had stayed behind with the *Henry David* for the search. The space they were searching wasn't really space; it was less than vacuum, at least for the first hour or so until the electron-rich vacuum of "normal" space rushed in; it was just a dark spot against the dark.

Gun had left with the *Penn State*, the skin and the rest of the Rangers, none of whom were friends. "It wasn't your fault," Gun called to Hadj in parting. It hadn't sounded convincing even to himself.

Another short burn—and the light leaking into the hallways meant they were sliding into high earth orbit. Gun gave up trying to sleep and went to the Nittany Lounge to watch. The first sight of Overworld was almost exciting as first sight of the Peteys. It was a kind of dawn, too.

Overworld in darkside was just more stars: stars in rows and stars in arcs; stars that slid and stars that rotated; near stars and far stars. Bright and dim, white and colored stars. Approached from sunside, Overworld was more dramatic: coming into view suddenly out of the terminator, like a city leaping into light: not sketched in slowly, as are cities in Earth's leisurely dawns, but bursting instead into existence, fully formed: first the Muir Geophysical Observatory, closed down for years; then the wobbling torus of the High Hilton, once a luxury hotel and then a military base; then the Academy campus (Gun's year), a subassembly of

Harvard Orbital and now a ruin, lighted and heated only to keep it from being claimed by the Tangle, the self-repairing labyrinth that had sealed itself off during the Three.

After Academy came the lit sections of the shuttle shops (cheaper to fix up here, where old parts could be cannibalized off the station itself); and then the sunlit, outer arc of abandoned parts, modules, sections, and half-burned ships with bodies still inside them. For it had been a Pearl Harbor, that first day of the Three, even though it was still unclear which of the three sides had started it—or if, in fact, any of them had.

All this Gun had seen many times before, coming in from the Petey range on the *Penn State*, or up from Orlando on the shuttle. But he never tired of it. The still-occupied Cinderella; the abandoned sections such as Muir, Mao, Dover Beach, Raj Eye, Jai Kaileipoea; even the forgotten sections had all been united under the doomed First Dispensation and cobbled together into an eighty kilometer arc, which had been further linked in apparent and nonapparent ways by a more recent accretion.

For around, between, underneath and over it all, darkening Overworld like a runaway vine, like a child's scribble over a color photo, was the Tangle.

Overworld was all colors, but the Tangle was all gray. It was a gray gray, a gray that repelled rather than drew the eye. It was hard to see from the outside, with its annihilating unsheen, woven (it was rumored) from a fabric in which every third particle was anti-matter. The Tangle had been created—or rather, created itself—during the Three when the different sections of Overworld had been attacked by the rocket bombs of all three warring parties. The bombs of course had no politics, no religion, but the maintenance and defense nanounits activated by the attacks had a politic: Repair and Seal, and a religion, Unite and Grow. The result was that every time Overworld was hit, the Tangle grew in size and complexity, until its actual shape and size was unknown to any but the nanobots that created and modified it. And they didn't "know" anything except Repair and Seal and Unite and Grow. Connected and yet unconnected to Overworld, the Tangle grew over and around it like a vine, a crust, a cancer. The Three ended, but the nanobots set fires to activate the alarms, altering themselves, evolving not randomly as with evolution, but deliberately within the shifting parameters of fuzzy logic, so that the changes they made would have astonished even their creators, had they any but themselves.

No one knew what the hell was in there.

An expedition was sent when Overworld was reoccupied, equipped with air, water, food, and guns—those four staples of expeditions everywhere. They had returned a half day after they had left, more than half mad, remembering only that the Tangle smelled like fire, was painful to look at, and impossible to remember. The nanobots had learned to replicate the "mobys," the neonewtonian möbius knots developed by a physics team at Harvard Seattle just before the Three. Only approved as a cleaning device under the Protocols, the mobys had been developed in the Tangle into a slip connector that was flexible in both space and Time, enabling the nanobots to create a noneuclidean space that was unmappable and often incomprehensible. And therefore unconquerable.

Since the Tangle was at least partially extradimensional, flickering in and out of ordinary space, it was impossible to photograph. But to Gun it was fun to look at, even beautiful from an approaching ship, spreading into and around over the sun-washed colorful squares and tubes of Overworld like a grapevine on a barn.

Boom.

Clunk. Then groans as the *Penn State* with its precious cargo was secured to Overworld. The good thing about spending a few days in space was that it made high orbit seem like home again. It was home to Gun, since he spent half his life up here. The other half was about to begin, though. His tour was over and he would be taking the shuttle down to Orlando in just a few hours. His other life, with Tiffany, would begin.

Meanwhile there was Hadj to worry about. And Shorty. How would the accident affect the hunts? The Fundamentals were clamoring to call them off. Gun hoped it didn't happen before he at least got a chance to draw for "Pirates," Disney-Windows' flagship live-in theme park in Orlando Proper. With a little more luck . . .

But rather than dream about it, which was the same as worrying about it, Gun decided to lock on through to Overworld and check out the Glass Slipper. He pulled on the polarized sandals that would allow him to tread the static strips (just in case security was around, since floating was illegal without a helmet on Overworld) and pushed off down the long hall toward the main lock.

Two Sierra Marines with empty holsters—Overworld was a no-fire zone—waved Gun through from the *Penn State* into the larger halls of Overworld. Gun readjusted his breathing as he passed through. It wasn't a pressure differential: Cinderella had started as an amusement park, and it still smelled like puke.

Only a little of course; all that was fifty years ago.

Gun was hoping to find some of the other Rangers in the

Glass Slipper, but the lounge was empty. He nuked a tube of herb tea, found a terminal that was working, and scrolled through "Headlines and Happenings." The incident—the accident—Shorty's death—wasn't on the menu. Gun wasn't surprised. Under the interim Protocols, news was withheld until its impact on the economic, religious and military situation was evaluated, and the review procedure often took several months. And it had been less than a day.

Gun scrolled through "Hollywood Hall." There were one hundred and sixteen movies on the menu, one hundred and four of them remakes, most of which he had seen in both versions. He didn't like movies anyway; he preferred dreams, when he could afford them.

He didn't bother with "World of Sports." Nothing on "Wild Kingdom" but dingoes eating zebras. Nothing on "What They're Wearing" but celebs at a party in Malta. There was a rap concert and a bluegrass festival on "Soundz!" and a five hundred miler on "Gentlemen, Start Your Engines," but it was all dull stuff, especially the auto race; nobody wanted to watch electrics, and the bootleg gas engine contests had dried up long ago, with the gas.

Nobody went off world for the entertainment. After a few months it wasn't even entertainment. It was filler, debris, like daily life. Gun had been off planet for almost a year. Was it surprising that there was nothing left he wanted to see?

As a last resort, he logged onto "Rain, Sleet, Snow." He only got one letter a year, from Gordon, and he hadn't read this year's. It was already six months old, but mail from somebody doing life in prison could hardly be urgent. Plus he knew it would be a lecture.

This would be a good time to read it, Gun decided. While there was nothing else to do.

Surprise. There was mail. Other mail.

The mail icon was reminiscent (Gun supposed) of the days of rural mail delivery. The little round-topped door was closed, which meant it contained mail, which he had expected. But instead of a "1" (Gordon's annual lecture) it now had a "3."

Three letters? Another lecture from Gordon? An alarm from Iris? She had promised to write if Ham, his father, got worse. Gun didn't even know anyone else who would write. Certainly not Tiffany, and Donna had written only once, when he was at Academy. It was the letter he had never answered.

The mail could be identified for free; opened and read for a fee; and for a larger fee, printed out. The first step was to see who it was from.

Gun wished he had never logged on. He hated mail. It was never good news. But there was no turning back now. He swallowed hard, as if he were stepping out of an airlock, and clicked on the mailbox door. To his surprise it didn't open.

He clicked again. Nothing.

He was partly relieved. And partly curious.

He clicked on *query* and got another surprise. The frowning icon of a cop in an old-fashioned (like the mailbox) leather-brimmed hat came up. His arms were crossed and he was frowning. Gun clicked on his potato nose and a deep voice said:

"I'm sorry but the mail belonging to" [another voice] "Ranger Gunther Ryder" [back to the original voice] "cannot be released while the authorized recipient is" [still another voice] "Administrative Hold."

Administrative hold? Gun clicked on *query* again but all he got was the same voice:

"Administrative Hold."

Oh, well. There was no way of knowing what it meant, and nothing to do about it anyway. It was probably one of the glitches that often turned up in Overworld's communications system. Gun was relieved. The last thing he wanted to do was read his mail.

He scrolled through "Hollywood Hall" again but how many times can you watch Bette Davis play Queen Elizabeth? Or even watch *Bonnie and Clyde* or *Miracle Mile*, remake or original?

He heard a movement behind him and he turned, hoping to see another Ranger; maybe even Hadj, returned from the Petey range. But it was a Sierra.

"Is the *Henry David* back?" Gun asked.

The Sierra nodded.

"Any luck?"

The Sierra shook his head and looked away. They hated to talk to Rangers; they resented being forced to share a lounge with them.

Gun put the Sierra out of his misery by leaving. He pushed off through the lens-shaped door and headed down the observation hall to Sleepy, Cinderella's Ranger dorm. The glass-walled hall was dark, its handrails gleaming in the thin light from the million stars. It was creepy. Gun hurried, wondering why people found looking at the stars restful. They were watching the Universe burn down.

The dorm was still empty but Hadj's hammock was up, stretched tight across the bulwarks. There was a package in it, wrapped in brown paper and tied with string. Gun couldn't help noticing because paper, not to mention string, was such a rare commodity on Overworld.

Careful not to touch it, he pulled close and read the note scrawled on the paper: "Joe at the Littlest." Gun didn't recognize the handwriting but he recognized Shorty's signature—the s with the circle around it. For some reason Gun had never understood, a lot of the regular persons™ affected western brands.

Had Hadj left the package? Or had someone else left it for Hadj to deliver? Where was Hadj? Why had he stretched his hammock? The shuttle was leaving soon and he was supposed to be on it, with Gun.

Gun checked the analog over the door. There were still a couple of hours to kill. No point trying to sleep: he knew that if he closed his eyes he would see the *John James* diving into the Petey, over and over.

The skin would be getting solid already. Might as well have a look.

Each sector of Overworld had its own jurisdiction, but the corridors between were ruled by the Protocols, so Gun was careful to wear the polarized sandals. Most of the doors were sealed, either by the nanobots or by the Protocols. Overworld and the Tangle had arrived at an uneasy but stable accommodation. The Tangle bled off small amounts of water and oxygen, and in return the nanobots kept the entire 80-kilometer station complex maintained. As long as neither side claimed more territory—

At the end of a long corridor that was, itself, at the end of another long corridor, Gun came to a blue translucent door that was not sealed shut. It looked like the entrance to an aquariuum.

It was guarded by two sleeping Marines who stirred awake when prodded, glanced at the green braid pinned to Gun's quilted longjohns, and waved him through.

The door slid open, and Gun was in Heaven.

FOUR

Earth has no sorrow that heaven cannot heal.
—Sir Thomas More

Heaven was an almost spherical, egg-shaped chamber two hundred meters long, a hundred fifty across. It was said to have been at one time the largest pressurized open space in outer space—and probably still was, although no one knew or remembered or could guess what was beyond the sealed doors, in the Tangle.

Like the inside of a small world, with a mottled blue sky lighted by translucent panels, Heaven gave the illusion of completeness, a result of the shape, the color, and the constant soothing light. Was it the womb or the egg we remember in our DNA, Gun wondered? Whatever it was, it made Heaven feel more like an everywhere than an anywhere. It was a universe and like most universes, it was oddly, unexpectedly comforting.

When Overworld had been a theme park, back before the Three, Heaven had been its most popular attraction: a place for people to experience zero/g, with the safety of an enclosed space and the convenience of an atmosphere. Heaven was for flying. Its atmosphere of peace and comfort was an unexpected benefit.

As always, on just entering, Gun felt like a kid, even though he had never actually visited Heaven as a kid. Who could afford Overworld? It had never been for the likes of Gun; he had learned about it in an old *National Geographic* ("Wonders of Overworld, Disney's New Theme Park in Space," NG:518:65:0) long after it had closed.

Except for a ten-meter cargo door that opened directly into high vac, there was only one entrance. All the others had been sealed off by, or against, the Tangle. Spiralling around the blue inner surface was a railed static walkway; Gun didn't mind using it, since he was hoping the exercise would help make him sleepy. Besides, it was against the law to float in Heaven when it was occupied.

And Heaven was occupied.

Drifting at the center was a huge dark cloud, of gray streaked with rose. It was hard to tell its size, since it was folded in on itself many times, and was still vague around the edges; but it was already much reduced in size from the eight-hundred-kilometer-long shadow that the Sierra teams had gathered into the hold of the *Penn State*. The skin of the Petey shrank as it gained substance and solidity. It was at present halfway between existence and nonexistence, and it looked like a thunderstorm, rolling and boiling silently and far away (even though it was less than a hundred meters away), now as faint as a cloud, now dark, now light. It crackled occasionally, still losing its charge and its color.

The air in Heaven had a faint smell of ozone.

". . . a week, maybe two," Gun heard a voice say. It sounded close at hand, but acoustics in the egg-shaped space were funny, he knew.

"That's all?"

"It varies. When it is first killed it's as insubstantial as smoke. It cures here, in atmosphere; it begins to exist."

"Begins . . . ?"

". . . shadow, cast on this universe by another . . ."

"Folklore . . ."

". . . say that all physics is folklore!"

Laughter.

". . . first Peteys in almost two years. May be the last for all we . . ."

". . . new Protocols expected any day . . ."

". . . why prices are getting so . . ."

The voices were fading; Gun searched the blue arc on all sides but he saw no one else in the gallery, though much was hidden behind the dark, rose-streaked cloud. The Petey still had most of its color and much of its cloudiness. As it cured, it would become thinner and more solid, until it was a two-dimensional, rose-streaked shadow, the most valuable substance on Earth.

". . . turned on its back . . ."

". . . couldn't have been an accident . . ."

They were talking about Shorty! And Hadj.

". . . and it was gone . . ."

The voices were getting louder.

". . . say they want to stop the hunts so they can let the currency float."

"—legalize the banned organizations. The Friends and the Fundamentals . . ."

Couldn't have been an accident? What else could it have been? The voices died just as Gun saw two women and a man emerge from behind the gray and rose cloud high "above." He could see by their gold braid that they were mostly Sierras. They were spiralling around heaven, like ants crawling across the sky, their voices faded in and out.

". . . Ranger held for questioning, because . . ."

". . . nothing the Fundamentals would like better . . ."

Held for questioning? Gun turned and started back around, toward the entrance. The voices were louder as if walking by his side.

". . . no one wears it any more anyway . . ."

". . . Petey? How would I know, dear? No one undresses for me. . . ."

"You'd be surprised to see who's wearing what these days. So to speak."

The voices were close, almost in Gun's ear, but he still couldn't see anyone. Just the roiling mass of the Petey skin, close at hand, getting darker, thinner. When one side was solid, it would have only one.

". . . rumors are just to keep the prices high . . ."

Gun wondered how small the Petey skin would get. His share depended on the price, which depended on the Barcelona market that had established the Petey skins as a second currency in the world, a new standard to replace easily synthesized gold.

"Isn't there some way to force it? To make it darken, the way they force apples or tomatoes . . . ?"

"The whole value of the Petey is that it's natural. . . ."

"That's a laugh, to call something natural that's not even from this universe. . . ."

"That's only a theory. Natural has several meanings. . . ."

"Naturally. . . ."

The voices faded again just as Gun was surprised to see the speakers almost on him. The path was converging on itself. The group, which Gun had thought was a woman and two men, was in fact just a woman and a man. The woman was smoking one of the new fog Marlboros that precipitated inside the lung and were never exhaled. They were the only kind permitted off-planet. The man and woman both were wearing blue and gold. Gun knew enough not to nod, and they both looked right through him.

The third person—not a person, really—was a gen, one of the biorecorders that had been created before the Three. Gun rarely saw them up close, since they never hung out with Rangers. Though they had no sex, they were all called "shes." This one looked almost pretty in her short, sleek black skirt and sleek black tee shirt, cut off to show she had no navel. Of course, they all looked the same. No one even knew for sure how many there were.

Gun admired the way she slid along on the static strip; even with her awkwardness she was better than most people, who were clumsy in zero/g.

The Sierras had stopped talking while Gun was passing them. They looked right through him. The gen, on the other hand, fixed her black eyes on Gun. Her gaze unnerved him; it was as if she wanted to tell him something. But that was absurd, Gun knew ("Biogens: Roving Witness to Our Heritage" NG:537:94:3). Gens never told anyone anything; they only asked questions.

The gen tapped her thin wrist as she passed and Gun looked back at the analog over the door—and realized he had lost track of the time. That was the problem with Heaven.

The shuttle was already loading to leave.

FIVE

What heart would have thought you?
—Francis Thompson

Ding ding. Watch the closing doors.

Too late! The *Lion King*, the tube train to Olduvai Station, Overworld's only working shuttle port, was pulling out. Gun sighed as the door slide shut in his face. Even if he caught the next train in a half an hour, he would be twenty minutes late for shuttle departure.

Damn! Dejectedly, Gun made his way back through the empty halls of Cinderella, to Sleepy. Hadj's hammock was gone, and so was the package, wrapped in brown paper and tied with string. Hadj, at least, must have made the train, which meant he would make the shuttle.

Damn! Gun should have paid attention to the time. Now he was stuck on Overworld an extra day at least. Maybe two or three. He went back out into the hall. Maybe a movie after all; anything that would put him to sleep.

He was halfway to the Glass Slipper when he heard a whisper behind him.

"Ranger?"

He turned. There was no one there.

He headed down the hallway again.

"Ranger?"

It was a gen. Perhaps even the same gen he had seen in Heaven. Could there be more than one on Overworld?

She tapped her wrist again, then pushed off and floated around a corner. Was Gun supposed to follow?

He did. He couldn't think of anything else to do.

Around the corner there was a Minnie and a Mickey, facing each other across the narrow hall. The Mickey's door was still swinging.

The gen was inside, up on the ceiling by a vent grill. The grill was protected by a yellow OFF-PROTOCOL ribbon, which the gen ignored. Gun watched her pull it aside and pull herself *through* the grill. Apparently it was just a projection.

Was Gun supposed to follow? He did.

His first few nights on Overworld, as a Cadet, Gun had been awakened by a strange sound—a distant, persistent *snik-snak*, heard through the walls. It was the sound of the Tangle, he was told, leaking back through the vents.

Unlike the train tubes, which followed the long curves of Overworld, the vents wound their way through the Tangle itself. Their entrances and exits still conformed to the old Disney-Windows maps, but their internal geometries were no longer accessible or even discoverable. Not that anyone tried. The vents worked, that was enough; they were kept functioning by the maintenance nanobots. They were essential to what was still habitable of Overworld, and apparently essential to the Tangle as well.

The vents even had their own legend—the Lost Cadet. Late for a class, he had taken a short cut through the vents and arrived an hour before he had left, or years later, or never, depending on which version of the legend you heard. The *snik-snak* was his fingernails scratching at the walls.

Now Gun was the Lost Cadet—crouched in one of Overworld's forbidden, off-limits air vents. The vent curved off in two directions, both "down." One way was darkness; the other way, he could see the gen. She was carrying something in her arms.

Gun's first impulse was to run, to go back the way he had come. He tried to ease back through the grate, but it resisted his foot and then his hand. It was a one way—holo from one side and steel (or plasteel) from the other.

Gun was stuck. He had no choice but to finish what he had started. To follow the gen.

The vent tunnel was about three and a half feet in diameter; just large enough to float through, arms extended. Gun kicked with his feet and tried not to think about moving his arms; when he did, he felt the cold touch of claustrophobia. He couldn't hear the *snik-snak*, just the cold hum of Overworld's machinery.

There was long curve ahead. Gun could see the light at the far end, at the same time he could see the curve in the light. The vent was picking up some of the uneuclidean geometry of the Tangle. Gun knew better than to look too hard and try and figure it out. Instead, he just followed the gen.

What did they wear under their short, sleek black skirts? What was under their tee shirts? The *National Geographic*, usually so candid, had been unspecific ("An Orbiting Oral History Project Carries on a Beloved Teacher's Dream" NG:517:98:5).

Push, coast, push, coast—barely touching the sides, his hands held out in front of him to ease him off the walls on the long turns. The vents had their own smell—the sharp chemical smell of Overworld mixed with the smokey electrical stink that leaked in from the Tangle. Then, after a while, Gun noticed a sound. The hums and whirrs of the Overworld were underlain by a distant crackling, almost but not quite not heard.

He stopped and put his ear against the wall. There it was. A soft *snik-snak,* a low insect clackering below the hum of Overworld's machinery. It was a dreadful yet somehow hopeful sound. They were building things. Building themselves, building a world there on the other side of the walls.

Gun caught up with the gen at a wide spot in the vent tunnel; a triangular chamber with a lit grill on the floor. The gen was stopped, and Gun saw now what she had been carrying. It was the package, wrapped in brown paper and tied with string, that had been on Hadj's hammock.

She handed it to him. It was soft and kind of squishy.

The grille underfoot was shimmering, and Gun knew that if he didn't pass through it now, it would block him.

He pushed off the wall with one hand, and floated "down" through the grill. Down the hall he could hear the murmur of Rangers loading, and the hiss of an airlock. "Last call, Orlando shuttle," said a robot voice.

Gun looked at the analog over the door.

He had done a "lost cadet." He had arrived before he had left.

SIX

What large, dark hands are those at the window grasping in the golden light?

—D. H. Lawrence

The Rangers sat in two short rows on molded seats. There was one empty: Hadj hadn't made it after all. Gun found himself sitting beside an optimized dwarf named Big Carl. Regular persons™ did well in high vac. They found the coffin suits almost spacious, and their short limbs maneuvered them well. Not to mention the savings to Disney-Windows in trucking them up and down from orbit. It was rumored that they had their own separate lottery; otherwise, how could they have been over half of the Ranger roster, while less than one percent of the population?

Gun and Big Carl had never been friends. In fact Gun had never been friends with any of the Rangers except Hadj.

"What's in the package" Big Carl asked.

"Don't know," Gun said.

"Look's like Shorty's handwriting."

"I don't know," Gun said.

"Whatever it is, it's soft," said Big Carl. "Squishy."

Gun put the package under his seat. He closed his eyes and pretended to sleep.

Reentry was terrifying, like all landings.

The shuttle was an ancient, smelly, worn-out and used-up ship that didn't have a name. Shuttles didn't have names; it was considered bad luck.

The whole ship shook and howled. The closest thing the Rangers had to a window was a bad seam in the forward airlock door; as they dove deeper into the protesting atmosphere Gun watched it turn cherry red, then orange, then white. There was a sharp smell of rubber burning, like insulation off a wire.

The noise eased off into a whine. Then a rush, like hot wind.

Gun woke up. His pretense of sleep had turned into the real thing, or at least a dream. In the dream Hadj and Shorty had turned their backs and were walking away. Gun had tried to follow but his feet wouldn't do right.

He felt immensely, terribly lonely. "Did you ever have trouble getting your mail?" he asked Big Carl.

"What kind of trouble?"

Gun told him about the cop that had shown up on his screen.

"Could this be an alimony or support hold?" Big Carl asked.

"I've never been married," Gun said.

"Anybody political in the family?"

"I guess," Gun said. "A cousin."

"A Friend?"

Gun wished he had never opened the subject. He nodded gloomily.

"Still in prison?" Big Carl asked, still smiling; still shouting.

Gun nodded gloomily.

"Ah so!" said Big Carl as the shuttle touched down on the ten-mile section of I-4 it used as a runway. "Dum, De Dum Dum."

SEVEN

And a quiet sleep and a sweet dream when the long trick's over.

—John Masefield

As soon as the shuttle touched down and the Rangers locked out, they were arrested.

"Welcome back, welcome back," the deputies muttered as they went down the line, snapping on the plastic cuffs. The Rangers were ferried, legs still weak from almost a year off-world, on an electric baggage train across the tarmac, through the side entrance, past the dry pool, into the soaring central courtyard of the Outer Orlando Palm Court Ramada Reception Center.

The Outer Orlando Sheriff was waiting for them in an enclosed court overlooked by the cell tiers. It was as if he were campaigning: he shook everybody's hand as he personally took off the cuffs. The internment, which under the interim Protocols made the engagement with the Petey legal, and legitimized the ownership of the skin, was a plum for the Sheriff. "There's free coffee," he said. "If you have any property, check it with my sister." He gestured toward a young woman with red knuckles wearing white coveralls instead of a uniform.

Gun realized he had left Shorty's package on the shuttle. Just as well, he thought. No one would ever know.

The coffee was the only thing that was free. The Sheriff owned all the machines that stood in ranks around the lobby, plus the two pay terminals where detainees, inmates, convicts and ordinaries were waiting in long lines.

Gun changed the last of his paper money to coins—illegal in space because they were too heavy—and bought a sandwich from one machine and a newspaper from another. Newspapers and sandwiches were free at Overworld, but they had both been stale for the past two months. And the catered stuff was never as good as the stuff you bought out of machines anyway.

Gun saved his last two tens for the pay terminal, to check his mail again and pick up his space pay, but the lines were too long. He decided to use the shower instead. It was a major Earth pleasure. He undressed and stepped in; he put his head under and let the water fall over his hair, weighty, unhindered; and let his hair fall into his eyes, and let the water drip down, off his nose. There were certain things about Earth that Gun liked, and water falling was one of them. Gravity straightened water out, like a comb. Sometimes he wondered why gravity wasn't strong enough to comb out the rest of the Universe, which was all in whorls and tangles.

He dried off with a towel and put his uniform back on, then found a place on one of the palm-stained sofas, away from the other Rangers. He was sick of them. He just wanted to get out of jail and get to the Dogg. But there was no sense hurrying it; the internment would last well into the afternoon.

Gun leaned back on the couch and looked up at the other prisoners, the "ordinaries," whose per diems were paid by anti-crime or victim organizations, looking down from the tiers surrounding the courtyard. The Palm Court Ramada had once been a hotel. It was a prison whose bars were gravity, and in space you lose your faith in gravity. It was hard for Gun to believe that if the ordinaries above stepped over the rail they would fall. But the ordinaries obviously believed it. They squabbled among themselves or stared down dumbly; occasionally one would wave.

Someone called out from six floors up; someone answered back from two floors below. The ceaseless, drab life of prison motored on, like a primitive animal incapable of fine motion, or memory, or dreams, but very much alive. Hungry, sad, never happy; never still.

"Are you Joe?"

Gun looked up. It was the Outer Sheriff's sister.

"You left this on the baggage train." She handed him the package wrapped in brown paper and tied with string.

"It's not really mine," Gun said hopefully. "I'm not Joe." But she had already turned on her heel and gone.

Making sure no one was watching, Gun stuck the package under the sofa.

On first return to Earth after months in zero/g, the gravity doesn't get to you. The body compensates; the legs feel almost springy, having stored up energy they didn't have to use for months. Then the weariness hits all at once.

"Hey," said a small, deep voice. "Loan me a couple of tens."

It was Big Carl.

"I'm saving them for the pay terminal. To check my mail."

"So? Look at the line."

"Oh, all right," said Gun. He could log on later, at the Littlest or the Dogg. He gave Big Carl his last two coins. They were dragging him down anyway. The gravity here in Orlando felt like vines, pulling at every part of his body. He was glad to empty his pockets.

The bursar from Disney-Windows had arrived: he was coming through the revolving barred door with his folding table under one arm and his scuffed pay-out case under the other.

Gun smiled. He would be out of jail soon. He closed his eyes. He could almost see Tiffany. Almost was as close, he knew, as he would ever get.

"Call for you," said a small, pipey voice.

Gun sat up. Had he fallen asleep? An older man in the green and yellow coveralls of an ordinary was leaning over him; Gun recognized him as one of the trustys who had helped serve coffee.

"Phone call?" Gun looked back toward the line of Rangers at the pay terminal.

"Not exactly," the old man said, dropping his voice to a whisper. "It's through commissary."

"I don't get commissary," Gun said. "I don't need commissary. I'm just a day prisoner here. A Ranger."

"I can see by your uniform that you're a Ranger!" the old man said. "I'm not stupid." He handed Gun a scratched, bent plastic card with a big "C" on it. "You're taking half my turn."

"I don't want half your turn."

"Just take it!" the old man hissed. He took Gun's arm and with surprising strength, pulled him to his feet. "Somebody's asking for you. Over here."

There is nothing so weak as a Ranger in his first few hours on planet. Gun let himself be steered to a box the size of a twin coffin, with a sliding drawer, slid out.

"Get in."

Gun looked around for a guard.

"Don't worry about the guards; they're brain dead. You're not allergic to Vitazine™ are you?"

"No, of course not. I have an account at the Dogg."

"Then get in. Lay down. Press GIRL."

Gun lay down. He was tired of arguing. The commissary was a few hours fishing, an afternoon with a pretty girl in lingerie, a fast ride in an electric car, compressed by Vitazine™ into a ten minute weekly rec period (the minimum required under the interim Protocols) that simmed out into a couple of hours subjective time. Prison R&R.

The drawer stank of sweat and stale air. Gun closed his eyes as it groaned shut. The sweet stench of Vitazine™ filled his nose. Without opening his eyes he saw the menu. It was short and sweet:

GIRL
FISHING
CARS
EXIT

With an imaginary finger Gun pressed GIRL, and he was sitting in a windowless room on a wooden bench. A girl was sitting next to him, wearing an oversized white tee shirt that read:

PROPERTY
OUTER ORLANDO
RECEPTION
CNETER

She was blurry around the edges, and Gun couldn't tell if she was wearing anything under her tee shirt or not. Her skin flickered and her eyes were a shocking blue.

"You're Ryder?"

Gun imagined nodding.

"You can really nod," she said. "Muscle feedback is set up here. Crude but it works."

Gunther nodded. "You can talk?"

"I'm not supposed to but this is prison. I try to help these guys get along."

"Who are you?"

"Commissary Taffeta. I have a message from your friend."

"Hadj? Turkish looking guy?"

"How would I know? I'm the visual. He's upstairs on Murder One, got here yesterday."

"Is he a Ranger?"

She disappeared for a moment. When she came back she was clearer. Gun could see that she was wearing white cotton panties under the tee shirt.

"That's it, a Ranger," she said. "Somebody loaned him his commissary time."

"Hadj, is that you? What's going on? I thought you were still on Overworld!"

She flickered again. "He says they brought him down on the shuttle. In handcuffs in first class with the Sierras. He has a nice laugh. Wants to know, did you bring the package?"

"Package? Wrapped in paper, tied with string? Tell him I, uh . . ."

"Wait a minute, he's getting cut off," she said. She flickered again. "Says you know what to do with it."

"He says what?"

"He's not speaking very clearly. These new guys don't know how to work commissary. The old timers use me to communicate from one tier to another. I don't mind."

"What's your name?" Gun asked.

"I told you. Commissary Taffeta."

"And I'm supposed to do what?"

"Whatever he said. He's gone. He just borrowed a couple of minutes. Something about a package."

"What am I supposed to do with it?"

But the girl was gone. The bench was empty. Gun was looking at the MENU:

GIRL
FISHING
CARS
EXIT

He pressed GIRL but nothing happened.

He pressed CARS but nothing happened.

He pressed EXIT and he was sitting up as the drawer groaned open.

"You weren't supposed to use my whole time," the trusty complained.

"Sorry," said Gun. "Guess I'm a little slow." He got out of the drawer and looked for the package where he had left it under the sofa. It was gone.

"Disney-Windows," the bursar cried. As the Rangers lined up to get their bail and pay there was an immediate rise in the level of noise. All the ordinaries, even the condemned on the upper tiers waved and seemed glad to see them go; it added something to their long days, and prisoners are generous about the freedom of others. They wish their fate on no one.

Gun got in line behind Big Carl.

"Those bastards," Big Carl was saying to the Ranger in front of him, who was holding a newspaper. It was *The Outer Orlando Register*, and it read:

NEW PROTOCOLS EXPECTED ANY DAY
Smoke Rises over 1600 Pa.

Below the headline was a photo of white robed figures in ranks holding sticks aloft, like flagpoles without flags.

"What bastards?" asked Gun.

"The Fundamentals," Big Carl said. "They're all stirred up. I overheard the Deputies talking it. They're chasing anybody in a uniform."

"With sticks?" asked another of the Rangers, from the front of the line. "The thing I hate is the sticks."

"They can't use the sticks anymore," said yet another Ranger.

"If there's a new Protocol they'll bring back the sticks."

"The thing I hate is the sticks!"

"Next!" It was finally Gun's turn.

The Rangers got their share certificates and their dailies as they were being bailed out. It made use of the stop at the Reception Center; it was the kind of consideration that made Disney-Windows a good company to work for.

Gun stood in front of the bursar at his folding card table, wondering how such a table could stand in such a storm of gravity. The gravity was pulling at him like a wind, and he could barely keep his eyes open. He looked over the bursar, toward the back wall; toward the city that would have been visible on the horizon, over a few miles of scrub and asphalt and stucco ruins, if the lower floors of the reception center had windows. The only windows were on the upper tiers, Murder One and Two. Gun knew that from there the Dogg would be clearly visible. Soon he would be at the Dogg, in the gentler pull of imagination and desire. . . .

"Wake up, Ranger, and sign here."

Sleeping again! Gun wondered if he had been dreaming of Tiffany. It was possible, since he couldn't remember. The idea appealed to him—that they met somewhere beyond even memory.

For his signature Gun got a gray and rose sheet, rolled up like a diploma. He didn't have to unroll it. It wouldn't be good for another two weeks, or maybe even three, when the cured and graded skin was put on the exchange in Barcelona.

But there was no deposit receipt for the money that had been automatically sent home to K-T and deposited into his account at the Dogg. "What about my dailies?" Gun asked.

The bursar checked his screen, which was invisible to Gun. He tapped it with a pencil. "Ryder?"

"Right."

The bursar leaned across the card table and unsnapped Gun's green braid.

"Hey!" said Gun. He reached for the braid, but the bursar snatched it out of the way.

The bursar called the deputy over. "This guy's getting all excited," he said.

"Excited?" Gun asked, getting more excited.

"I have to hold his braid since he's on Hold," the bursar said, tapping the screen with the pencil.

"Hold?" asked Gun. "Let me see!"

"Excuse me?" said the deputy. He slapped his palm with his stunclub. "You're still in jail."

"No, he's not," said the Outer Sheriff. "I don't want him. He's not even on the list. Give him his bail receipt."

"I'm not going anywhere without my braid," said Gun—and immediately regretted it.

"Excuse me?" said the Outer Sheriff.

"Nothing," muttered Gun.

"Ryder, you coming?" called out Big Carl. "You're holding everybody up. We've got a ride to the 'rail."

"How much do they owe you in dailies?" the Outer Sheriff asked.

Gun closed his eyes and tried adding it up. The allowances were deducted from his Ranger dailies, leaving barely enough for coffee and a donut. Gun's *real* money would be the shares from the Petey skin, and it wouldn't be good for weeks—if the market held.

"I don't know," he said.

"We're out here," said Big Carl.

"I'll sort it out later," said Gun. He stepped forward and the Outer Sheriff waved him on, toward the revolving door.

"Courtesy bail," explained the Outer Sheriff. "Disney-Windows didn't bail you out because I never arrested you. At least officially."

"What about my braid?"

"Jeest!" The Outer Sheriff's hand went to his waist, where a gun might have once ridden. "Ask Disney-Windows about that!"

Gun decided to shut up. He would get a new braid at the Dogg anyway, when his uniform was cleaned. He started out the revolving door after the other Rangers, but he felt a hand on his shoulder.

"Joe!" He knew without turning around that it was the Outer Sheriff's red-knuckled sister.

She stood a half a head taller than Gun. She had a rash on the bottom of her chin.

"You forgot your property," she said. She handed him the package, wrapped in brown paper, tied with string.

Even after only a few hours inside, even without your dailies or your mail or your braid, getting out of prison is a liberating event, almost like the release from gravity when a ship first throttles down and slides into zero/g.

Gun stepped out of the barred revolving door of the Outer Orlando Reception Center, feeling light on his feet. It was odd, looking at the sky from underneath. Storm clouds were brewing to the east, and fires were burning on the horizon to the north and west. Orlando Proper was still invisible, hidden behind a low wall of pine and palm.

The other Rangers were on the monorail that was pulling off into the pines. Gun wasn't sorry to see them go. His uniform would get him on the next one, unless someone was checking for braid, which was unlikely. He allowed himself to relax and take a deep breath. The air smelled like fire and rain and roots and leaves. Like home.

It felt good to be alone.

The train pulled in, empty.

The door "pinged" shut and Gun had a wide seat all to himself. As the 'rail pulled out of the station he leaned back, enjoying the sunlight through the dirty glass.

Even the air smelled good. There are no good smells in space; the only smells are bad smells.

Gun sat up suddenly, awakened by a wild screeching. The car was slowing for a station. Behind, in the distance, he could still see the gantries and towers of the spaceport. Below, scrub covered an abandoned suburb either shelled during the Three or torn apart by scavengers after. Alligators sunned on the black asphalt streets and on the doorsteps of the ruined houses.

The 'rail stopped and three men in off-white robes got on; two of them held a stained banner that read MURDER MOST FOUL! The third held a sign that read, STOP THE SLAUTER. Spelling was not one of the things the Fundamentals considered fundamental.

Gun closed his eyes again; it was best to ignore them. He closed his eyes and thought of Tiffany; or thought of thinking of her. It was almost as much fun. He wondered what she looked like. He wondered if, this time, she would take him to her Upper Room. . . .

The monorail slowed for a bad stretch where the superconductors had failed, and the wheels screeched along track; a flock of ducks flew up and around like a reversed snowstorm. Not that Gun had ever seen a snowstorm. But he had seen them in *National Geographic*. It used to snow as far south as K-T. It had snowed a lot in Wyoming, when there had been a Wyoming ("Where Spaces Are Still Wide Open" NG:523:09:4). Dry, dusty, blowing, fence-drifting snow. Cowboy snow.

Gun set the package on the seat beside him and unrolled his Petey Certificate. It gave him a sense of accomplishment just to look at it. Under the soaring triad (a duller rose than in real life: but what hue printed on paper could compete with that scream of colors?) in quaint serif numbers was his cut: .00132 of .0048 of .007 of 15/16. The last figure meant that 1/16 of every skin went to finance Petey research and conservation (a joke, according not just to Hadj, but to all the Rangers); the .007 was the *Penn State* crew share, and the .0048 was the Ranger share of the crew's total. The .00132 was Gun's share of the Ranger's share. It had gone up from the .00118 he had gotten on his first full braid Voyage last year.

Even with the most pessimistic projections of the price of the Petey skin, Gun knew it should come out to somewhere between eighteen and thirty thousand dollars. Not bad for a three day voyage. Of course the three days had followed a 266 day rotation on Overworld.

It was all future money, not available until certification, still several weeks away. In the meantime there was his Ranger scale, his dailies, plus the space bonus for the three days in high vac. One third of this went to K-T, automatically, to buy medlotto tickets and treatments for Gunther's father, who had begun to succumb to the Darkening two years before. Another third went to the Dogg. The remaining third was Gun's pocket money, which he could access from any pay terminal as soon as . . .

Ding.

"Orlando Proper, watch the closing doors. . . ."

At the Orlando Proper terminal, Gun had to pick his way between and over sleepers wrapped in damp, smelly blankets; people who were unable to come into the city Proper, and yet who were unable to leave it, perhaps tied by benefits, or history, or even that most tenuous and yet tenacious of human ties, sentiment.

It made Gun tired to just think about it. The gravity hung off his limbs like vines as he stepped over a janitor that had died, its blinking light (MORT! MORT!) giving an eerie glow to the dusty floor. Just as he was about to enter the tunnel to the street, he was stopped by a cop.

"May I have your hand, sir?"

Gun turned, surprised, and looked down. He had never been stopped by a cop while he was in uniform. Perhaps it was the missing braid.

"Your hand, sir."

Gun covered the cop's dome with his palm.

"Please follow me, sir," the cop said.

"Where? What for?"

"Please follow me, sir."

Gun had no choice; refusal to obey even a dysfunctional cop had disagreeable consequences. In fact, the dysfunctional ones were often the worst, since even their supposedly noninjurious warning beatings sometimes turned fatal.

Gun followed as the cop wound back across the lobby station floor, its path a clear track, almost shiny from the wheels, through the litter on the floor.

It stopped at a little table marked LOST & FOUND.

"You left this package on the 'rail, sir."

EIGHT

An altogether new way of seeing things.
—Robert Louis Stevenson

The Littlest was on the way, or almost on the way, to the Dogg. Of course, almost everything in Orlando was almost on the way to the Dogg, which was near the heart of Proper and a fixture of the once-world-famous skyline.

The wide streets were almost empty. Palmettos waved in the breeze that always circled the dome, clockwise in the summer, counterclockwise in winter.

The monkeys made sorrowful noises overhead as Gun wound his way between the low buildings. He could hear chanting and shouts in the distance. A bottle crashed onto the pavement somewhere.

Gun ducked back into the alley as tens, then twenties, then hundreds of demonstrators danced their way around a corner and down the street toward the station.

"Stop the Slaughter," they chanted. Their signs read STOP THE SLAUTER. They carried spooky looking Petey balloons, which looked more like rose and purple eggplants, some of them as big as ten feet around. Others carried icons of extinct or mythical Earth species: elephant, whale, dino, rhino, their elaborate fanciful forms childlike next to the extreme simplicity of the Petey.

They all carried sticks.

It was an illegal demonstration right here in Orlando Proper. Or was it illegal? A cop was motoring quietly along behind the demonstration. As soon as he saw the familiar floppy hound's ear in the distance (the other, sticking-up one had been shot off in the Three), Gun felt his steps quicken in spite of the still-unfamiliar and always-unwelcome tug of full/g. Soon he would be in the comfortable one-third/g of the Dogg.

He also felt a familiar lightening, an upward striving, in his heart. Soon he would be with Tiffany. Perhaps she would lead him to the Upper Room—if not this time, then the next.

But first, he had to keep the promise he had not, so far, been able to break.

The Littlest Mermaid was a long, low building—fairly long and very low—green with kudzu vines. The front of the bar had small windows in the nipples, eyes and armpits, while the back was lit through opaque scales of green glass. Gun had to duck his head to enter the door between the navel and the lower belly scales. It was like being in a play house. Gun knew, because he had been in Iris's once.

The bar was almost empty. The light inside was green, from the translucent scales. There were no tables. There was a pay terminal in the back, by the game machines. A regular person™ was rapping on the screen with a coin.

Tap tap tap.

Gun knelt at the bar. The bartender was wiping glasses with a moby and watching an execution on TV. He didn't look like a regular person™, but he didn't seem to be kneeling either. Then Gun looked behind the bar and saw that he was standing in a trench.

"You must be Joe," Gun said.

The bartender looked down at the JOE embroidered on his shirt, then looked back up with exaggerated surprise. "So I am. What can I do for you, Ranger?"

Gun set the package wrapped in brown paper and tied with string onto the bar, but before he could explain what it was, Joe—the bartender—waved his hand as if to make it go away.

"Not authorized to take packages," he said. "This is not a UPS bar."

"This isn't a send, it's a delivery," said Gun. "It's for a customer, or rather from a customer. See, here on the brown wrapping paper, under the string."

"Says 'Joe' all right," said Joe. "But doesn't say who it's from or who it's for."

"His name's Shorty. He's the Ranger, that is, the Sierra that was killed in the big accident on the Petey range a few days ago."

"Never heard of it. Or him."

"It was his last wish," said Gun. "It's for his—mother." He was surprised to find little tears springing to his eyes.

"His mother?" Joe took the package and placed it on the shelf in front of the mirror, between two bottles, a Jim Beam and a Gentleman Jack. "Well, OK," he muttered.

Gun smiled. Mission Accomplished. "One other thing. Can I get some change to access your pay terminal?"

"You can once I sell you a beer," Joe said. "What'll you have?"

"Strawberry Heineken," said Gun. "But the problem is . . ."

"No problem." Joe reached down into a cooler, opened a bottle, and set it on the bar. The bottle was normal, not small. Regular persons™ liked that, Gun had noticed. He supposed it made everything seem like a bargain.

"That'll be twenty," Joe said.

"That's the problem," Gun said. "I can't pay you until I get some cash out of your pay terminal."

"Terminal's occupied," Joe said. He nodded toward the *tap-tap* in the back. "But that's no problem." He reached across the bar and pulling the rolled-up Petey certificate out of Gun's pocket.

"Hey!" said Gun.

Joe laid the certificate on the bar and cut off a corner with a thumbnail.

"Hey!" said Gun, again.

Joe rolled the Petey certificate up and slipped it back into Gun's pocket. Then he opened the cash register and put the corner into the drawer. He spun a twenty across the bar. "You even get change," he said. "Enough to access the Dogg."

Gun was surprised to find himself blushing. "How'd you know that's where I'm heading?"

"The look," Joe said. "You get to know the look."

When Gun first became a Ranger, he used to think about Gordon a lot, and he liked to think that Gordon would like the Dogg. Gordon was always quoting Thoreau. Or was it Walden? It was hard to keep those old guys straight, but it didn't matter: the important point was that Gordon loved all those classical guys who were into Simplicity, and not just Thoreau and Walden. All of them, Dylan and Remus and Rodale too.

The Dogg was all about simplicity. It was a simulated simplicity, of course. A virtual, a sim-simplicity. But that made it even simpler. In the Dogg, you didn't need clothing, and furniture was provided. With Tiffany you didn't need friends. You didn't need food or drink or a bathroom for that matter. No toil, no trouble, and certainly no envy (Gordon would especially like that, Gun thought: the Friends were totally against competition) since you were the main, if not the only, person in the world. The Dogg was, like "Pirates," a perfect world. Of course it was only temporary, but a week of sim-state in the Dogg could seem as long as a nine month tour on Overworld.

The exterior of the Dogg, the part between the paws that fronted on Sewanee Street, had lost none of its grandeur since Gun's last visit. More rust had run down over the windows, but that only made them shine more golden in the afternoon sun; sort of like hair. One ear was missing and had been since the Three. The Dogg had been a motel just before the war, according to Hadj. What a motel was, Gun didn't exactly know. He suspected, though, that it had something to do with the heart. Like the Dogg.

The lobby of the Dogg was deserted, and windy, as usual; Proper's giant buildings with their graceful animal forms generated their own air currents. Little windstorms of dust and wrappers danced across the floor. The real clerk was busy with either paperwork or a crossword, so Gun went straight to the wheel of suites. He was a regular and didn't need to check in. He could check his mail in Tiffany's rooms. It would be a READ ONLY, since he would be in sim-state, but so what? He didn't plan to answer anybody anyway. And it would be pleasant to read his mail with Tiffany lounging beside him in the half dark. It would make even one of Gordon's lectures go down.

Gun dropped his twenty into the access slot. By the time the wheel stopped and a suite groaned open, he was already undressed and in his robe. He laid his uniform and boots at the head of the suite and lay down beside them.

The lid closed as the suite slid into the darkness. The last thing Gun smelled was the sweet odor of the Vitazine™ hissing in.

NINE

Her eyes were fair, and very fair . . .
—William Wordsworth

It was like waking from a dream. Gun was standing in a deep-paneled parlor, where the light hung like crystal dust in the air. He was barefoot. He hadn't remembered that. He hadn't remembered anything.

There was a long damask couch in the corner embroidered with cut flowers. Roses? He could see the suggestion of a window out of the corner of his eye, but when he turned to look for it, it was gone. No matter. It took things time. The objects in the room, only half-seen, were dark, comforting, maroon.

There was a slight smell of flowers, but it was not fresh. Nothing was fresh. Everything was musty; it was a comforting, familiar smell. There was a low table with a brass top, with unfamiliar objects on it. Gun picked one up and looked at it, then put it down without discovering, or wondering, what it was.

It wasn't what he was looking for anyway. He wasn't looking for anything. He knew it took things time.

He looked back toward the couch, and there she was, wearing

a long silk robe in a deep purple and maroon plaid, with a soft French terry lining, shawl collar and cuffs; tassel belt, patch pockets. The robe was open at the top, and Gun could almost see Tiffany's maroon full coverage bra with scalloped underwire cups and lace trimmed straps; back close. He knew he would have to go higher to see her lace trimmed matching maroon panties. Had he always started this low? No matter. It was perfect already. Her bare feet were buried in the pile rug. Her toenails like her lips were ruby, ruby red, and she seemed to be smiling.

At him. Of course.

"Tiffany," he said.

She seemed about to blink.

"Tiffany at last!" he said. He knew it took things a while to get up to speed. Especially speech. She raised one hand off her lap in a suggestion of a gesture. Was she wearing a ring? It was green, no, gold.

"My dear Tiffany," he said. He was never at a loss, here, for something to say.

She was standing now, and there was the door, and he walked through it into another room where Tiffany was wearing a sand-washed silk chemise in mallard blue with dyed-to-match embroidery on black net along the neckline and deep cut, cross-laced back; princess seams. It was so short that he could almost see the sandwashed silk panties cut high on the sides underneath. But not quite. He would have to go higher. But what was the hurry? Gun walked across the bare wood floor toward the window. Walking was so easy here in the Dogg; the gravity was less intense, somewhere between one-half and one-third/g. He felt as if he were floating again.

"It's been a long time," Gun said; and he knew as he said it that it was true. Tiffany smiled as if pleased by his eloquence. It was no big deal, Gun knew. Eloquence, even poetry, came with the territory here in the Dogg.

Outside the window he could see each individual blade of grass. Had he always started so low?

Not that he was complaining. The light in the room was like moonlight. Or like what moonlight would like to be like. There was another door, arched and accented with rose wallpaper. Gun walked through it into a pearl-lit greenhouse filled with tropical plants, like a little India, where Tiffany was wearing a stretch panné velvet bodysuit with a low sweetheart neckline and long empire sleeves, cut high on the sides and full in the back, with snaps underneath.

Little pearl snaps underneath!

"May I call you Tiffany?" Gun asked, even though he knew he could. He could call her anything he wanted to. She existed only for him. Through the greenhouse glass he could see the trunks of trees. He yearned to go higher but he forced himself to slow down, *slow down*. Girls liked to go slow. He picked a little leaf off a plant and it grew back slowly. He picked it off again. It grew back again, even more slowly.

"You're as beautiful as ever," Gun said. The nice thing about being in the Dogg with Tiffany was that he was never tongue tied; he could always think of something to say, something appropriate, something that sounded right.

"You're so nice to come home to," Gun said, the poetry flowing as naturally (or so it seemed) as song. Song! But he yearned to go higher. Across the room there was a wide door surrounded with scrolled white woodwork. Gun walked through it and immediately saw that he was much higher.

Through French windows at the far end of the room he could

see treetops, and Tiffany was wearing a front-close scalloped lace demi bra with lace-accented, wide-set straps and stretch satin full cut panties with lace side inserts, all in pink. Azalea pink. But there was a phone on the wall.

It was ringing.

Gun knew better than to answer it, but Tiffany picked it up and handed it to him. As soon as he put the receiver to his ear he heard a flat tone and the room was gone. Tiffany was gone. Gun was flat on his back in the now-open suite, looking up at the dusty, chipped, stained ceiling of the lobby.

"Tiffany?" He tried to remember what she had been wearing, what she looked like; but she was gone.

The subtle stink of Vitazine™ was in his nose. The light, even through the translucent roof panels set in the long neck of the Dogg, was harsh, too bright.

Gun pulled on his boots and clomped across the floor to the desk wearing just his robe, without his uniform.

"Excuse me?" he said.

"Oh, it's you," the real clerk said without looking up from his crossword puzzle.

"Something booted me out," said Gun. "I just got here."

"That was me," said the clerk. "You've been here two days. That's all you were paid up for."

"I'm on direct payment," said Gun.

"You *were* on direct payment." The clerk hit a key and his face changed colors with the screen, replacing the crossword with a scroll of colorful number cells. "Your regular payments stopped three months ago, in July."

"I don't get it."

"Money," said the clerk. "Is that so complicated? You owe rent."

"It's a mix up," said Gun. "Let me just explain to Tiffany that . . ."

"Tiffany won't want to hear about your troubles unless you're paid up," said the clerk. He shrugged and hit a key. The colorful number cells were replaced by a black and white crossword puzzle. "I suggest you retrieve your uniform before the suite closes, and tell your troubles straight to Disney-Windows."

TEN

Destiny often helps the undoomed man.
—Beowulf

The Ranger," said Joe. "Back from the Dogg already? It's only been a few days."

"I had a little problem," said Gun. Then he decided not to lie; not to Joe. "A big problem."

"Sorry to hear that," said Joe. The Littlest was almost empty except for a couple of regular persons™ at the bar and one at the pay terminal at the bottom of the tail, tapping on the glass with a coin.

Joe was wiping glasses with a "moby" which flickered as it passed in and out of existence, taking the dirt with it. He pointed with the swab to the package, wrapped in brown paper and tied with string, wedged between the bottles behind the bar.

"Your pal's mother never came by," he said.

Gun shrugged; it was no longer his problem. He pulled out his Petey certificate and unrolled it on the bar. "You know the little thing you did with the corner?"

"Sure." Joe did it again. Then again.

"Hey! How come you cut two corners?"

"Geometry," said Joe, as he rang up the two triangles. "Every time you cut a corner, you create two more corners, but they are worth only half as much. Get it?"

"Not exactly," said Gun. "Maybe I better drink a beer while I'm waiting to access the pay terminal."

"Sure thing," said Joe, sliding him a Strawberry Heineken.

Gun rolled up the Petey certificate and stuck it back into his pocket. "So every corner is worth twenty bucks?"

"Or half. Or half that," Joe said. "And so on, at least till the price is announced. Could be worth less, then; could be more. There's a rumor that when the new Protocols are announced, they are going to ban the hunts altogether. That would send the price through the ceiling."

"They've been saying that for years," said Gun. "I'll be at 'Pirates' anyway after one more hunt. I won't want for anything."

" 'Pirates of the Universe' ? Congratulations," said Joe. "This is your lucky day. Looks like the terminal's free."

The tapping had stopped.

"Guy fell asleep."

The back of the bar was sea green; it was like being under water. Not that Gun had ever been under water, but the light looked familiar ("Watery World of the Reef Dwellers" NG:534:93:1). The monitor on the terminal flickered stupidly, expectantly, like a dog wagging its tail. Not that Gun had ever owned a dog, but he knew about them ("A Border Collie's Day" NG:495:84:7).

He dropped in a ten.

"Welcome," the machine said, and the display repeated:

WELCOME

Gun breathed a sigh of relief. So far so good. All he had to do was find his dailies and withdraw enough to square up his rent at the Dogg. He would sort out the rest of it—the missing mail, the Administrative Hold—later, after he had spent some time with Tiffany.

The familiar bank icon appeared. Gun pressed it, and the pig turned readily toward him. But why was the pig not smiling?

A HELP insert informed Gun that the frown meant that there had been only withdrawals since he had last checked in, before the hunt. That would have been the regular Dogg payments, plus the money that was sent automatically to K-T for his father's medlotto tickets.

But why no deposits? Gun pressed BALANCE, and the machine asked for his palm print.

He pressed his hand against the screen, then drew it back in alarm when he saw a figure he had seen only once before, on the screen at Overworld. It was the cop with his arms folded.

Gun clicked on the cop's snout.

"ADMINISTRATIVE HOLD," the cop said.

There was a drill Gun had learned in Ranger school, a first reaction to emergencies. It was especially for zero/g and high vac, but it was supposed to work in any environment where panic had to be avoided. Gun had never used it in full/g. He fixed his eyes on something stable—in this case, Joe, behind the bar (in space, it had usually been a star)—and took three deep breaths, then three more.

Better.

Gun went back to the keyboard and backed out to the MAIN MENU. This time, instead of the pig, he pressed the mailbox.

The mailbox came up, same as last time. The number on the side said there were still three items in the box. Same as last time.

Gun pressed on the door, to open it, and the mailbox disappeared.

The cop appeared.

"ADMINISTRATIVE HOLD," said the cop. Was it Gun's imagination, or did he look meaner than before, as if he were running out of patience?

"Shit," said Gun. He took three more deep breaths and walked back to the bar. The gravity felt like somebody had turned it up. He took another long pull from the Heineken; the last.

"You okay?" Joe asked.

Gun nodded. "Yes. I mean, no. I mean, how about another beer?"

Gun caught the Strawberry Heineken Joe slid him and looked up at the TV over the bar. "What're you watching?"

"Reruns," said Joe. "An afternoon fryer."

It was "The Chair." On the screen, a man was being strapped into a wooden chair. The condemned was about thirty, with a nervous, philosophical expression. He had one minute for his talk. The applause was perfunctory, spotty. He seemed disappointed.

The victim's family was introduced. They were the ones who would pull the switch. The condemned's family stayed in the background, looking appropriately troubled even though they would receive the promotional fees.

There was a sharp crackling sound, then a crackle of applause. Gun had already looked away. He had never liked daytime TV.

"You got a problem," said Joe.

Gun looked up, surprised. "What do you mean, a problem?"

"I saw the whole thing." Joe pointed toward the pay terminal in the tail of the bar.

Gun decided not to lie; not to Joe. "You're right, I got a problem."

"Only one thing you can do."

"Oh, yeah? What's that?"

Joe pointed to the front window of the bar. He was pointing *through* it, through the smeared glass and scratchy vinyl, through a half mile of hazy air over dry sand and scrub pine, toward a giant kneeling figure on the horizon.

"You're going to have to see the Girl."

ELEVEN

And again she lashed her team and again the stallions flew.

—Homer

Designed in the great days of Disney-Windows, before the Three, Orlando Proper's tallest building was made in the shape of a 14-story girl, sitting on her knees, listening to a seashell. The shell and one pigtail had been blown away by a missile, but the listening girl was still intact. The administrative offices, not of course open to the public, were in the slightly tilted listening head. The hearing and review offices were somewhere near the breasts. Gun was hoping he wouldn't have to go further than reception, down between the knees.

Between the Girl and the Dogg, it was raining. It was always raining somewhere under the dome. Gun sidewalked to within a few blocks of the Girl's big knees, where the street ended in a low wall of trash and scrub. From here it was overland. The dome near the missile hit had never been repaired, so the girl was surrounded on three sides by a jungle of scrub and scald kudzu.

A covered walkway led into the palmettos. Gun took it wearily, holding to the railing, stopping every few feet to rest. But even when you were holding on, gravity never let up. It blew straight down the world like an invisible wind. How did children manage? Gun wondered. He couldn't remember. How had man's ancestors managed? Gravity in the trees would have been a remorseless enemy, and sometimes friend; but in the open savannah it must have been a constant drag, like a wounded child or an infirm parent, old and crippled and fat, slowing everything down ("Lucy's First Steps" NG:521:98:2).

Rallying what seemed the last of his strength, Gun climbed the plywood ramp at the Girl's left knee; he didn't feel like attacking the stairs. The ramp was steep, and just when Gun was wondering how someone in a wheelchair could actually negotiate it, a legless man with a child pushing his chair appeared at the bottom. The man honked a horn and four boys appeared as if by magic from the scrub that surrounded the building. From his position halfway up the ramp, Gun could glimpse their camp through the oversized leaves: Navajo blankets and comic books, stacks of cans and bottles; an old woman (a mother? a hostage?) bent over a smoky fire.

With a "whoop" the boys pushed the man in the wheelchair past Gun, up the ramp. Then they ran back down, the lead boy waving a bill, whooping, shaking the ramp with flatfooted booming steps, while the younger boys followed.

The ramp led to a terrace centering on a revolving door, which was being entered by a short line of people, mostly in uniform, but a few in colorful business-alls. Gun walked on ahead of the wheelchair man and got in line. He didn't want to seem rude, but he was in a hurry. The more the full/g got to him, the more he needed his quiet time with Tiffany in the cool darkness of the Dogg.

The revolving door operated like a turnstile; the glass took the palmprint, while a slot to the right took an access coin. With each access, the door turned a quarter turn, emitting a puff of smoky air; and each person or pair of persons slid through.

Two men went through, together. They moved slowly, both wearing heavy penalty shoes.

A woman with a child went through.

Though he didn't want to admit it, even to himself, Gun was beginning to fear the worst. The glitches were too consistent. What if they weren't glitches at all? What if . . . ?

"Your turn, Ranger," said the wheelchair man from behind.

Gun stepped up to the door and dropped in the last of the coins Joe had given him. He put his palm against the glass and pushed.

Nothing.

Just as he had feared.

He looked for a scanner and saw one taped to the sill above the revolving door. Was it reading that he wore no braid?

"Excuse me."

As Gun stepped aside, he saw that the "child" pushing the man's chair was not a child at all, but a doggit™, one of those new dogs that walked upright. Cute from a distance, up close they looked kind of mean. This one was dressed in a filthy Buster Brown suit.

"I can help," said the wheelchair man. "Grab the back of my chair, Ranger."

At first Gun thought that "Ranger" was the doggit™'s name, but then he remembered ("Man's Best Friend Gets Even Better" NG:564:56:9) that the same genetic twist that had them walking upright had them all answering to the same name. Gun grabbed the back of the chair, and the man pulled a towel from underneath him, folded it, put it on his lap, and patted it. "Come up, Napoleon. Up here!"

The doggit™ climbed wearily onto his lap. Gun could see that the crotch of its Buster Brown suit was damp.

The wheelchair man pressed his palm against the glass and the door rotated enough to accommodate the wheelchair and Gun pushing it.

"Wheelchair accessible," said the man. "Protocol stuff."

Gun pushed the wheelchair man into a large, dark, smoky hall with an arched ceiling, shaped (though it was hard to tell from the inside) like two knees.

"Thanks," Gun said.

"Think nothing of it," said the wheelchair man, pointing one finger at his temple. "I was a Ranger once myself."

"You were?" He looked too old to Gun.

"I wasn't always wearing a handicapped uniform. I helped build 'Pirates of the Universe.' "

"You did?"

The wheelchair man patted his two stumps, one after the other, in rotation. "I'd be there now if I hadn't lost these. No disabilities allowed there, of course. Are you from 'Pirates'?"

"Not yet, but I will be," said Gun. "One more Petey hunt and I'm in."

"Not without braid, you won't be. But I guess that's why you're here. Push me on in. Down, Napoleon! It's cooler away from the door."

It was cooler deep inside the Girl, but still warm. The lobby was permeated by low sounds, as indistinct and commingled as smells: coughs, shouts, sobs, and somewhere in the distance, an indoor siren. A dark crowd in drab uniforms milled under neon displays: PAY TERMINAL RECEPTION, PERSONAL CONTINGENCY, DISPENSARY, COMMISSARY CLOSED . . .

"You look confused," said the wheelchair man.

"I was just wondering which line to get in," Gun said.

"Depends, doesn't it? Depends on whether you're here for status or money problems. Of course in the end they all come down to money problems, and all money problems are status problems in the long run. So the question is, what kind of money: present money, past money or future money?"

"Past money, I guess, since I already made it," Gun said. "Or maybe future money, since Disney-Windows owes me."

"Disney-Windows owes everybody money," the wheelchair man said. "That's their secret. See the long line there, all the people with blankets and food? That's RECEPTION. It'll take you a day and a night to get to the head of it. It's quicker to go to PAY TERMINAL. There you can get a clerk for only $25 a minute, but the clock starts when you get into the line and you have to pay up front. Now I ask you, how many people come to the Girl with money, at least hard money?"

"Not many?" Gun guessed.

"Damn right. Now see that line over there? Napoleon, I'm going to slap you silly!"

Gun looked down and saw the doggit™ urinating against the wheel of the chair. The urine flooded the hub and dripped off the spokes like liquid gold.

"That line is PERSONAL CONTINGENCY. There you can get a clerk, but you don't have to pay up front. They take their fee out on a contingency basis, later on, after. But they'll only take your case if they owe you money."

"That sounds like me," Gun said. "Which line you getting in?"

"Me? I'm just here to hang out. They used to have air conditioning. At least you're not going to get beaned by a bottle monkey. You retired?"

"I don't think so," Gun said. "I hope not."

"Next," said a voice from somewhere overhead.

Gun woke up. He had been dreaming of his first girl friend, Donna. She wasn't copy-protected like Tiffany.

The line moved up another step. It seemed to Gun that a couple of hours, at least, had passed, but it was hard to tell. He didn't mind the standing in line. Standing wasn't as hard as walking in gravity; you just locked your knees. And if space prepared you for anything, it was waiting. Space itself was a kind of waiting. Emptiness waiting for the universe to finish existing and get back to basics. Knowing all it had to do was wait . . .

"What time do you have?" the woman in front of Gun asked. Gun pointed to the clock on the wall. "That doesn't tell me anything," she said. "It's analog."

Gun told her the time.

"What's P.M.? Are you getting smart with me?"

An hour later, as he got closer to the counter, Gun was disappointed to see one of the clerks flicker. "I thought these were real clerks," he complained to the woman who had asked him the time.

"They *are* real clerks," the woman said, in a whisper. "They're projected from upstairs somewhere. They're not going to come down here." She waved a hand indicating the dark, giant lobby filled with people standing or sitting on packages. In the distance, a man was vomiting into the space between a Marlboro machine and the wall. "Last month a guy tried to set himself on fire with a Marlboro lighter. Or set somebody on fire with a lighter. Anyway, you know what I'm saying. I wouldn't come down here if I was them. Know what I'm saying?"

"I guess," Gun said. He looked around the room. The wheelchair man and the doggit™ sat in the corner by the Coke machine. Everytime Gun looked in their direction the man waved, and Gun waved back. It was something to do. The doggit™ was fishing under the Coke machine for bugs to eat. Gun tried to remember if real dogs ate bugs. Of course, doggits™ were real, too.

Everything was real. That was the motto of the Academy: *Todas est Veritas*.

"Next."

The woman who had asked the time went toward the left window, and Gun was next in line. The girls in all three windows looked suspiciously alike; and even more suspiciously, like the building itself. Or was it just the pigtails?

"Next," the overhead voice said.

"Put your hand ON THE GLASS." said the girl.

Gun pressed his hand against the dirty glass.

"I'm not getting ANYTHING. What's your name?"

"Ryder, Gunther."

She typed something in. There was no sound of keys, because the actual keyboard was on another floor.

"You were A RANGER?" Her voice went up and down in volume as she brightened and dimmed.

"I *am* a Ranger."

"It SAYS HERE that you WERE a Ranger cause you're on

HOLD." She gestured toward the screen facing her. Gun could see the reflection of one of the neon signs through the girl's head; otherwise, she was right there.

"What does that mean? Let me see!"

"Excuse me? Maybe you want to TRADE PLACES AND TAKE OVER my job? It also SAYS HERE THAT you are OWED some money."

Gun breathed a sigh of relief. "You bet!" he said. "I just got back from Overworld. I have space time coming—dailies—plus salary, plus points. We all share in the proceeds from the voyage. Plus my mail. But what does it mean, I'm on hold?"

"Is that any REASON TO BE RUDE?"

"Is what any reason to be rude?"

"Thank you," she said. She seemed to be confused; she spoke in fragments, and her voice went up and down. "We're just TRYING TO HELP. Can make your DAY MORE pleasant. It says here that SAYS HERE THAT says here that SAYS HERE . . ."

Gun waited while she flickered and stabilized.

"Says here that you are on ADMINISTRATIVE HOLD."

"What does that mean?"

The girl smiled. "Thank you. That's why we're here, CAN MAKE YOUR DAY MORE PLEASANT. Now, according to Disney-Windows's Employee Plan, you are entitled to a hearing before any SUSPENSION OF PAY OR PRIVILEGES. It says here that it was ALL EXPLAINED at the hearing."

"What hearing? I never had a hearing."

"The hearing is TO COME. To make your day more."

"I don't even want a hearing," Gun said. "I just want my money. I just want my job. I'm a Ranger. I'm next in line for 'Pirates of the Universe.' "

"Excuse me? If you KNOW EVERYTHING, you DON'T NEED us," the clerk said. She was smiling, though her voice sounded angry.

"Sorry," Gun said softly.

"What about your mail? Personal mail CAN LEAD TO a lot of pleasure."

"Sure, why not?"

"We are here to help IN ANY WAY we can." She hit the phantom keyboard again, shaking her head and clucking, suddenly perky. "It says here that you have THREE PIECES of mail, including a letter from a PRISON, of which one CAN BE RELEASED."

"Who are the other two from—the ones not from the prison?"

"We're not allowed to look through your mail. We only know the prison letter, because as an internee document, IT'S A NAKED FILE. The Preservation of Personal Privacy Protocol prohibits my looking through your mail."

"Can't you just tell me who they're from?"

"EXCUSE ME? Are you asking us to break the law?"

"No, no," Gun said. "Maybe I should just get my money."

The girl smiled. The girl in the next window was smiling too, smiling the same smile. The man at the next window looked angry, too. Maybe we're all holos, Gun thought, all of us on both sides of the counter. Maybe it's the Universe's way of saving on Creation . . .

"If you would like to do that, you can," the girl said.

"Do what?" Gun realized he hadn't been paying attention.

"File a REQUEST FOR AN UPSTAIRS HEARING, like I was explaining, in order to DETERMINE THE REASON or reasons for the Administrative Hold. Then you can GET YOUR MONEY."

"Money," Gun said. "Yes, let's do that."

The girl punched some keys and studied the hidden screen. She was no longer flickering. Her hair was darker and she seemed more sure of herself. Her voice was lower and more composed, and Gun wondered if he had been switched to another clerk.

"That will be $700."

"For what?"

"The request for the upstairs hearing."

"Forget that, then. Just let me get my money."

"I don't think you understand." She was definitely a different girl. Her voice was slower, almost sweet. "You can only get the money if you have filed the request for the hearing. If it is filed with us, we can release a percentage of your pay, the percentage depending on the severity of the charges, which is unknown as yet. The service fee for the release is 25 percent of the ultimate total, not of the released. The service fee for the filing charge is $115 which will be fifty percent deferred until the total is paid, and fifty percent paid in advance. But the advance can be paid out of the money released, which is also an advance against the final determined percentage."

"So I can get the money now and use it to pay the filing fee."

"Of course."

"So let's do it. But I still don't understand how Disney-Windows can charge me money to get my own money," Gun said—foolishly, regretting it as soon as he had said it.

The girl started to flicker: and it was the other, the agitated girl again. "We are not DISNEY-WINDOWS," she said. "We are SERVICE Recovery Interstitial, a SUBSIDIARY of Disney-Windows. You can deal directly with Disney-Windows, IF YOU PLEASE." She wore lipstick; she didn't; did; didn't. "All you have to do is get in line A-22. There's NO CHARGE for their service."

She pointed across the room, to a line of small encampments. It was dinner time and a smoky haze hung over men playing cards and women cooking on small indoor stoves. Two children were either playing with a rat or torturing it to death.

"Just give me the money," Gun said. "I'll stay here in this line."

"Excuse me? You mean the advance." She was composed again, with the darker, straighter hair. "And you have to buy a hearing application ticket first."

"It's a lottery?"

"Of course. How many chances do you want?"

"Just one."

"One won't do anything. How about six?"

"Six, then."

She hit the key six times, then looked up with a smile. "You'll get a white ticket if you win a hearing."

"And if I don't?"

"You can still get your advance."

Finally, Gun thought. "How much do I get?"

"Let me check." The girl, or almost girl, studied the screen. "We can release $27443, of which we would take a contingency fee of one third, leaving you $18412."

$18,000. That would be enough to get him back into the Dogg. He could wait for his hearing there, in Tiffany's cool dark rooms.

". . . minus our filing fee, minus the one-time consultation fee of $12155, minus the interest paid in advance . . ."

"Interest?"

"The money is a loan against your salary," the girl said. "It is not your actual salary. We charge only 12 percent, but Windows-Fiduciary charges us 18, of which we pass along to you directly only nine, so the total interest is 21, payable one third in advance, making a total of fees and charges of, leaving you with $7127, of which . . ."

"Never mind," Gun said. "Transfer it straight to the Dogg, account number . . ."

"Can't do that," the girl said with a smile. "It's future money, not good until your hearing."

"Oh."

"I can't release money you don't have," said the girl. She smiled. "But I can discount it. In ready cash you are worth, let's see, $40. Two twenties."

"Print it out," said Gun. For the first time since he had graduated from the Academy, he felt like crying.

The girl hit the keyboard. "Check the machine by the door. Better hurry so somebody else doesn't get it."

Gun looked toward the door. A doggit™ was urinating into the slot of a cash machine. "Thanks," he said, and turned to go.

"Wait," the girl said.

He turned back around.

"You get one piece of mail. As a courtesy. Our compliments. Free. Which one do you want?"

"I don't care. You decide," Gun said. "Not the one from the prison, though."

The girl hit PRINT and handed him a slip of paper. It read:

COME HOME.
REMEMBER YOUR PROMISE.
GORDON

TWELVE

Nothing is so astounding as the vitality of the social organism—how it persists, feeding itself, clothing itself, amusing itself, in the face of the worst calamities.

—John Reed

Like Birmingham, Atlanta and Chattanooga, Huntsville had been part of Florida, and before that, Alabama or Mississippi (Gun forgot which one); but under the Interim Protocols, the city now ruled the once-occupied rural areas, which were mostly pine woods laser fenced for genetically augmented "aug-hogs." As a subunit of Orlando, Huntsville was, therefore, still on the monorail; and Gun's transportation was free as long as he wore his uniform and none of the conductors noticed his missing braid. He slept the entire four hours.

At the border, travel became a problem. The TVA "meltdown" (so-called) was almost a half century ago, but since K-T had been even then no longer administratively part of the USA, clean-up was never considered. Under the Interim Protocols, commercial travel between the Tennessee and Ohio rivers wasn't allowed; thus, there was no scheduled passenger service across K-T.

It was a problem, but a problem Gun knew well. When he was

at Academy he had gone home twice a year. Since he had become a full braid Ranger, eligible to spend his free time at the Dogg, he had gone less often. The last time had been eighteen months ago. The only scheduled way to get from Huntsville at the northern edge of Orlando, to Evansville at the southern edge of the Jeff (the administrative region of Jefferson, once the three-state region of Ohio/Indiana/Illinois) was to go around on the French airships, using the PWP (permanent weather pattern) jet stream loop left over from the last century; but the *bateaux* were open only to Sierras and above, and used more for tour than travel, by people who didn't care where they were going or when they got there. When Gun was at Academy he had gone home twice a year on the unreliable but relatively inexpensive BMT (bootleg mass transit): windowless twelve person passenger containers with bench seats, providing a noisy but fast nine hour ride to Evansville via Nashville on the daily truck train that threaded its way up the slabs of the old interstate.

The BMT, or "smokey," was slow, and cramped and smelly; sort of like space travel.

Gun bought a BMT round trip by clipping more corners. His Petey Certificate had gone from a rectangle to an octagon, and was beginning to look like a jagged oval—a font approximation. The rig rolled out right on time.

Gun had tried calling home, to Mayors' drugstore, but it was busy as usual. The rest of the phones in Morgan's Ferry were down, as usual; K-T's phone service was all satellite, and the Three was still going on up there, since the unmanned satellites were self-sustaining and self-repairing.

There weren't any windows in the pod; it was like the shuttle in that respect. But Gun was able to find a crack—so many things in the world were cracked!—through which he could make out the passing low hills and grown-over fields that had once raised cattle and corn and tobacco, and even before that, it was said, had entertained the buffalo on their occasional eastern forays ("Shaggy Monarch of the Door Prairies" NG:545:76:2). It wasn't long before he slept; it wasn't like he hadn't made the trip before. And it helped that western K-T was such spectacularly unspectacular country, just rolling hills and scrubby trees: like a discarded sketch for a more interesting, finished land.

It was fall, and as the smokey went north the green turned to red and browns, as if the planet were growing older before Gun's very eyes. But hadn't it been fall for a long time? Gun missed most of the seasons, between Overworld and the Dogg. He fell asleep and dreamed not of Tiffany, for she was copy-protected, but of Gordon, as he knew he would. In the dream Gordon was out of prison, and Gun was in.

When he awoke it was dark, not only on the Earth but in the sky. They were under the perpetual cloud cover of the Upper Middle South, the river country that fed the storm systems of what had once been America, mixing cold water and warm air.

"Pirates of the Universe?" one of Gun's fellow travelers asked. He was a thin, dark man in business-alls, Asian or Indian in origin, soft of voice.

Gun nodded. It was the uniform. It was almost true, anyway; or it would be. Hopefully.

"I thought the whole idea of 'Pirates' is that you have everything you need, right there?"

"Going home for a visit," Gun said.

"Home? Nobody lives in K-T!" The man was almost belligerent and Gun was beginning to regret talking to him. The other passengers, barely visible in the dark container, either slept or pretended to sleep.

"On the northern edge," said Gun. "Near the Danelaw."

"Danes—" the man spat. After the Three, when America was auctioned off, Scandinavians (all called, for convenience, Danes) had bought up the cheap cities around edges of the free-enterprise zones. Many of the former Americans were jealous.

Gun closed his eyes and pretended to sleep. Soon Gordon returned to lead him back into his dream.

There was only one stop on the Huntsville-Evansville run—Cumberland Crossing wood station on the near (northern) side of a long, patched-together bridge, on a limestone bluff overlooking the gathered waters of the Cumberland, the Green, the Red, the Barren and the Tennessee rivers. The passengers got out and stretched while the smokey's crew took on water and firewood.

Nashville was a glow off to the west, where no one lived anymore. In the winter, the glow made an interesting display when it met the Northern Lights, which had been extending their reach south for more than a century and sometimes played above the tops of the clouds. To the north and east were low clouds and below them, lower hills.

Gun heard a hiss; or was it a kind of singing? At the edge of the lot, where the locals were selling bread and fish, he saw a "Big Softee," one of the K-T limbless variants, in a grocery cart under a blanket. Its mother (either real or functional) was lifting the blanket for short, ten dollar viewings. Gun had the feeling that the softee looking out with its single big eye was as disgusted as the travelers looking in.

But the sightseeing time was short; the big charcoal steam turbine's whine mixed with the howl of gears as it wound up into the low knobs of the western K-T coal fields. Back in the cramped pod, Gun tried to find sleep and dreams again. He was sitting by a crack, but there was nothing outside but low smoking hills where the abandoned and exposed coal seams had ignited; smoke mingling with the hiss of steam from the dripping rocks, seeping in from the little rivers. The land was steep to the east, and he assumed they were passing Madisonville. There would be people back in the hills and the river bottoms; either they had never left or they had sneaked back in, some to mine the escarpment for trash, some just to loot their own abandoned homes. Generations had stayed. There was said to be a softee in every third home.

Then even these ghosts were gone. Skirting the silvery sea of the Green River, the highway crossed like a low-flying bird between dark hills with "rockcastles" showing like bones through old clothes. It was afternoon when they reached the Ohio at Henderson. Gun would have to cross the river, then re-cross it again to get home to Morgan's Ferry, since there was no transport up the river on the K-T side. He hoped to get a ride in Evansville.

There was a three-hour wait at the bridge, while a pontoon was being replaced. The air smelled like dead fish and mud. While he watched the sun go down behind striped banks of clouds, Gun wondered what Gordon could have meant by his message. "Remember your promise."

Since Gordon had been in prison, Gun had made several promises. One was to send money home. That was the only one he had kept. Or maybe he hadn't. If his rent at the Dogg wasn't paid, maybe his father's medlotto allowance hadn't been paid either. But how would Gordon know? And how had he sent a message from *outside* the prison—had he been transferred?

Gun hated thinking about Gordon because it led to thinking about home. About Donna, waiting for him. About Hump, more and more distracted with the Darkening. About Iris, never going out of the house. The only one Gun missed was Glenn, and Glenn didn't miss anyone: that was the only good thing you could say about his condition.

A woman with dreadlocks and a luminous catfish colored face cooked fish-ke-bob over a driftwood fire in an empty Cloverine drum. A doggit™ fetched wood for her, a task to which it was not well suited since it had "arms" but no hands. The wood that was small enough to carry in its mouth burned up quickly.

The river seethed by, cold and fast, cloaked in its icy fog. It looked like a river of cloud, not water; cloud from some Northern sky, giving up the ghost. . . .

Gun spread out his paper; it was long enough to allow him to lie on his back with his knees in the air. He didn't intend to go to sleep, just look at the sky, but sleep was hanging off him like kudzu. He knew he was sleeping when he found himself back in the Dogg. Alone, of course. Tiffany was copy protected; she could appear in neither dreams nor memories. The rooms were pleasant, though, even empty. The gravity was gentler, one-third. . . .

Whaaaamp! The truck's horn blew. There was a chill in the air as the truck train steamed up and rolled onto the creaking, water slopped bridge. Gun climbed inside and gave up trying to sleep and stared through the crack at the trash-littered, icy water, as thin and featureless as Time.

Soon he would be home.

* * *

Evansville was, like many of the small cities in the Jeff, a shell in a shell in a shell. Perched on a long turn of the Ohio, still intact on its northern bank (although the southern bank was flooded) was the shell of a nineteenth-century midwest river town, overgrown by ailanthus and locust and stained by muddy water; north and west of this was the shell of a twentieth-century rust belt factory town, declining since mid-century; and surrounding all this was a soft encircling shell of drive-ins and shopping centers which had closed down one by one in the dawn of the new century with the Depletion.

All of the old folks and many of the younger ones still remembered the old days, the "car days," when entire countries, indeed half the world, ran on oil pumped out of the ground, almost for free. It was shipped in boats so big they took a hundred miles to turn around, from Arabia and Alaska and the North Sea, to Japan and California and the USA.

The Depletion hit first in the offshore oil reserves, with a mutation of one of the oil-eating bacteria that had been engineered to clean up oil spills. Scientists had never agreed which one had mutated, or how it had happened, because it kept changing, and by the time they had identified and isolated it, it was several hundred generations into its destiny. It was a joyously energetic long polymer chain that digested oil and turned it into sugar and water, giving it more energy and adaptive ability than any other life form known.

For a few hundred thousand short generations the oil eater sat on the top branch of the evolutionary tree. Its appetites, like its energies and its capacities for change, were prodigious. It was, in a sense, only the latest in a long line of creatures, machines, and civilizations that had lived out their brief but flashy life spans fueled by oil; and like the civilization it replaced, it didn't last long. Less than ten years after its birth, it had spread through every crack and cranny of the earth's crust, finding and devouring every last remnant of oil. Having exterminated its host, it died. When it was gone, the only oil left was in tanks and drums and cans, each now as precious as gold.

Evansville had, in fact, died several years before the Depletion. Less than a city but more than a town, it was like a corpse in which a host of various bugs and small animals lived. One of these, connected with the Jeff's still-considerable highway system, was the Cloverine reshipment warehouse, where Gun headed when he got off the ferry. The salve that cured either everything or nothing (depending on who you asked, and when you asked them), Cloverine was shipped in drums all over the former USA plus Canada, Mexico, Quebec and California. An old friend from Morgan's Ferry worked at Cloverine, and Gun figured when the shift changed he could find a ride up the river.

"Gunther? Are you looking for me?"

Gun was.

"Whit" Whitmer was still skinny and bone white, as if the years since high school had boiled something out of him. His hair was thin and his eyes were too bright, darting away from Gun's face as if it were a sun. "Donna know you're coming?" he said.

"Unexpected trip," Gun said. "I'm looking for a ride home."

"Home?"

"As far as Tell City, I mean."

Whitmer couldn't seem to keep his eyes on Gun's face; they kept reaching toward the gloomy corners of the warehouse, and Gun realized he was looking at a man who was in the first stages of the Darkening.

"You came to the right place," Whitmer said.

* * *

Whitmer's smokey was adapted from a '49 International pickup. It had been fitted with two facing benches in the back. The other passengers sat silent and grim, not joking and laughing like people with tickets usually did. They were the unlucky ones, the ones who had to live in Tell City; the day laborers, who didn't know from one morning to the next whether or not they had a Cloverine job.

There was a soak box behind the cab, and when the benches were full Whitmer pulled out an armload of oil-soaked lath and shoved it into the tin firebox of the stove. He lit the fire, and ran forward and opened the hood. Gun could hear the *whooosh!* as the truck was primed with a squirt of precious NearGas. Then Whitmer jumped into the cab and hit the starter. As soon as the cylinders began to hit on the oil-rich smoke, he threw the truck into gear and started off without waiting for a warmup or wasting any precious fuel.

The truck wheezed and chuffed out onto the road, jouncing through the rich deep Indiana mud, the engine hitting only two or sometimes three out of every four licks. At the first stop Whitmer climbed back into the bed from the cab, stoked the fire, and went from person to person collecting the fare. Gun unrolled his Petey certificate and held it out to be clipped. The corners were getting more and more rounded. It was becoming a circle.

The truck followed old Jeff 39, up a high bluff overlooking the river. The icy Ohio made its own morning fog, but already it was clear and Gun could see all the way across to the silvery shallows of the K-T "shore"—even though there wasn't much dry land until twenty miles inland.

The Jeff side was high and clear; the road ran along the top of a bluff, long sections of it paved. The hillsides were planted in wet-pine. Over here there were no caves, and therefore, no "wing meat."

Tell City was made of brick—a single wide brick street between ancient, two-story red brick buildings. Gun was fascinated, as always, by the careful, intricate, repetitive lines of the mortar joints, imagining the men who had built it, working for days doing the same thing over and over. It seemed an extravagant and wonderful way to raise structures out of the Earth.

He found Glenn at the landing, pulling lath out of the soak box. Glenn looked up and saw Gun boarding the *John Hunt Morgan* and smiled without surprise, even though he hadn't seen his cousin in almost two years.

"Hello, Glenn," Gun said. "Hello, Gun," he prompted.

"Hello, Gun," Glenn repeated, with his perfect smile. He had the perfect handsomeness of a movie star of the last century, but his was a still picture. He wore a uniform especially made for him by Iris, his sister, with unauthorized braid and stiff epaulettes. There was no uniform for ferry captains.

Gun had learned long ago, on his first trips home from Academy, not to shake hands with Glenn; it confused him. Instead he clapped his cousin on the shoulder. "Good to see you," he said.

"See you!" said Glenn. Whatever he had, it wasn't the Darkening. It was more like a lightening. It left him anything but gloomy, and it never got worse. His brain moved slowly, but it seemed in perfect time with the slow sweep of the twelve-mile-wide river and the ferry stitching back and forth, back and forth.

Gun helped turn the launch around and chock down the wagons on the boat. The passengers came on last, putting their coins or bullets (good for currency in K-T) into the hat nailed to the rail. Glenn cast off and they spun out into the cold current, the ancient 350 chuffing at a labored 1850-2000 rpm. It sounded a little off to Gun; there was a whistling sound. The passengers clustered near the front rail, spitting into the water.

Glenn drove with the choke, while Gun stood at the bow with a long pole to ward off logs and debris. The river was clear and after a while he turned his pole over to one of the passengers and joined his cousin at the wheel. "What's that whistling? A valve?" he asked.

"Valve," Glenn said, pointed toward the hood.

"Sounds like a burned valve to me," Gun said.

Glenn grinned. "Burned valve."

"Need to take it to Maceo," Gun suggested.

Glenn made a sour face, then nodded happily. "Maceo!"

It was a little over an hour ride across, from Tell City to Morgan's Ferry on the K-T shore. The water was cold and swift and milky white. The warming that had raised the oceans had cooled the midcontinent, here where the meltwater came down still cold from the pack ice that choked Hudson's Bay.

"I should have worn my winter uniform," Gun said. It was a joke. There were no winters in Orlando, and no winter uniforms. But Glenn didn't get it. Gun hadn't expected him to. Glenn never got it. "Uniform," was all he said, approvingly.

"Yep. Petey Ranger, Glenn."

"Peteys."

Gun nodded and smiled. It was, all in all, as satisfactory a conversation as he'd had since returning to the planet.

The boat scraped ashore and the passengers drifted off to find their own boats, hidden among the trees or the half-drowned buildings. Gun walked up the asphalt street, past the plate-glass front of Mayors' drugstore. Donna was inside in her white blouse and black skirt, almost a uniform, waiting on the passengers who had just gotten off the ferry.

Gun would have stopped in but she looked busy.

Gun would have waved but she looked busy.

He hurried on up the street. The one house, three trailer Ryder complex up on the hillside gleamed in the late afternoon sun, welcoming him home.

THIRTEEN

Home—the nursery of the infinite.
—William Ellery Channing

Academy only lasts one year, like high school, but it's a long year, especially if it's your first away from your home not to mention off the surface of your planet. Or any planet. Halfway through his Academy year Gun had a nightmare—one of those dreams you dream you have dreamt before, and dream you will dream again, and thus remember as a recurring dream even though you may have had it only once. In the dream he heard a whispering and when he put his ear to the wall to listen, instead of the *snik-snak* of the Tangle he heard his name, called home from the Academy on a black ticket. ("Death in the Family," free round trip anywhere in the late contiguous USA—which did not include K-T, but which did in the dream; and besides, it was a simple enough matter to make the final leg across the river from Tell City, since in the dream, as in the real world, his family owned the ferry.) It was his mother in the dream. His mother was dying, again, but this time he knew her and she knew him. In fact, she was asking for him—by name! Then there he was, downtown in Morgan's Ferry (in the dream, the town still had a downtown), and he ran home along the path that led up from the street, past the old house foundations, through the rotting leaves that whispered when he kicked them away, just like the whispers behind the walls of Overworld; just like leaves in real life. And all the time, Gun was aware that it was a dream. He tried to get into the house but the front door, the one that faced the street, was locked. He turned the knob but it spun in his hand the way a palm-sensitive knob will spin for the wrong hand, over and over, never catching on anything, like a planet spinning on its historyless axis.

Gun remembered the dream but he remembered more the waking up, in the dark, smelly, weightless dorm, hearing the faint snores of the other Cadets (it was a large class, the last full Academy class), hearing the *snik-snak* of the Tangle seeping through the sealed-off vents, and realizing, somehow, that that house in his dream represented his childhood, rendered inaccessible. Over. Never to be entered again. Gone.

That was on Overworld, almost five years ago. And now it was happening on Earth, in Morgan's Ferry, for real. The knob was spinning, useless, in his hand. Gun remembered the dream, suddenly, for the first time in five years; it rose in his consciousness like bile in his throat, sharp and painful.

He forced the dream aside and tried the door again.

The knob spun in his hand. The lock had been replaced and didn't know his touch.

A horn honked down at the river. He looked down the hill, through the going-leafless trees, to the muddy street where a pile of stone and timber at a drowned intersection served as a wharf for the ferry to Tell City. The *John Hunt Morgan* was leaving for its last trip of the day. Glenn, tiny, the homemade braid on his hat gleaming, was steering the boat through the sunroof of the Pontiac that served as pilot house and engine room.

Why was the lock changed? First the terminal access, then the money, then the mail. What was going on? Gun was beginning to worry. His peaceful, carefully constructed world, consisting of three independent parts—Overworld, the Dogg and K-T—was coming unraveled. Gun didn't want to try the knob again; it was too much like tempting fate.

He rapped on the door, but as soon as he heard the sound of his knuckles on the warped tin, he knew it was pointless; no one would hear him. No one ever went to the front of the house.

"Hello?" he called out, tapping on the door frame with one fingernail. "Welcome home," he said, more softly, to himself.

He stepped down off the porch. The front door opened to the town, or what had once been the town. The back door opened onto the rocks of the hillside, which led to the Yard, the source of the Ryder family wealth. The only connection between the front and back was the three-trailer-long house itself and the steep side yard, a commotion of dry leaves.

Gun felt strange as he kicked his way through the leaves around toward the back. What if someone took him for a burglar? But that was absurd. Burglars didn't wear uniforms, even uniforms without braid. And there was nobody to see him anyway. All the other houses on Water Street were empty and had been for years.

The Ryder compound was built on a hillside, so that the front of the "T" that extended toward the street was high off the ground. As he passed the parlor on his way back to the kitchen door (where he hoped he could get in) Gun had to stand on his tiptoes to look in the window. The front parlor was dark. As a child he had played there on rainy days when he wanted to be alone. He was relieved to see that nothing in the parlor, at least, had changed. There was the old string rug his mother and her sister had made. There on the sideboard, standing in ranks like toy soldiers, were the plastic framed photos of Hump and Ham as high school twins, Sunday school twins, football playing twins, deer hunting twins with a buck (probably one of the last from this part of the country); Hump and Ham at four, at eight, eleven, eighteen; Hump and Ham as grooms marrying their sister wives, fresh and pretty from Bowling Green (the one with the red hair Gun's unremembered mother); and finally Hump and Ham as brother widowers, prosperous owners of a ferry and a junkyard, the region's largest oil reserve.

Stepping over a fallen limb, Gun walked up the hill toward the back door, past the parlor's second window. He could see in the second window without tiptoeing. There was the other end of the string rug; there was the piano (his Bowling Green grandmother's, he was told) with a picture of Iris at age nine winning a spelling prize, a prize she would keep on receiving for eternity, or until the picture faded, whichever came first; there were Glenn and Gun as babies, dressed to look like twins though they were only cousins born in the same week, with (Hump once said) only one brain between them. There was Iris in a high school band uniform, already getting fat; Iris with the boys, already looking grown at twelve. Then Iris with Glenn and Gun, drooling orphans whose mothers had both been killed in the same car wreck. It was one of the last of K-T's car wrecks, during the Depletion. There was Iris in a cap and gown for her HS graduation. There was Glenn at the boat, already smiling his impenetrable, world-proof smile, embarking on the lifelong voyage that would take him nowhere. There was Gun with his first BB gun. There was Gun with his first girlfriend, Donna, already wearing her black and white Mayors' almost-uniform; and Gun in his first Ranger uniform, a green and gray dress affair, missing only (for he was still a Cadet) the braid.

It was all there, through the glass. A world fixed in time like ice, unchanging, behind a locked door. The past.

Gun was past the window, heading around the black, windowless end of the house, when he realized what was wrong. He backed up. There were no pictures of Gordon. What about the shots of him and Iris as kids, cowboy and cowgirl? What about the hunting shots; or the joke shot at the Yard, of Gordon, the eldest son, in dark glasses pretending to drive the Mustang convertible? Or Gordon in his freshman uniform at Harvard Terre Haute, or the shots of him, home on vacation, with Ham and Hump? He had been the family's pride and joy, but now the pictures were gone. There weren't even spaces on top of the piano or sideboard to show where they had been.

There had of course been no pictures of Gordon's ten years underground with the Friends. But what about the jail shots after his surrender (or, as he called it, his capture); or the pictures taken during the visit Gun and Iris had made together to the prison: the three of them in front of the Tetons, obviously a wall mural, clothed in snow?

Gun heard a metal door slam. He heard a buzzing sound, a rude snort, and almost by instinct he pulled back around the side of the house, out of sight. Then he heard a sound from the kitchen, that womanly kitchen sound of wood on pottery and the soft clink of glass that sounds almost alien to one who has been in space a long time, where there are no kitchen sounds.

He stuck his head around the corner of the house.

He climbed the stairs to the back door.

Iris, who had served Gun both as mother and big sister,

though she was neither, was standing at the table making biscuits, her red hair faded with gray, broad in the shoulders and broad in the beam, wearing old loafers and unfamiliar un-piped uniform pants that were vaguely, disturbingly familiar. Iris in a uniform? Standing beside her on a chair was what, at first, for a wild moment, Gun thought was a child.

It was a doggit™ in a white dinner jacket and stained white pants. Why people put pants on them, Gun didn't know; they couldn't keep from staining them, or didn't bother to, or even want to, being dogs. Of course, the pants were in some obscure but essential way part of the whole idea of getting a dog to walk upright.

How long had it been? Less than two years. But Iris looked ten years older, at least from behind. She stirred the dough wearily. If Gun was twenty-six, then she was almost forty, the same age as Gordon, and showing it.

The doggit™ stood back out of the way and Gun reached to open the door, and found that the lock on the back door, too, had been changed. The knob spun in his hand.

It was almost as if he had cried out. Iris looked up and stared at Gun with what seemed, at first, horror. Then alarm; then surprise. Everything but simple pleasure.

She opened the door from the inside and took a step toward Gun but it was the doggit™ she hugged, scooping him up off the floor and holding him to her breast, pee-stained pants and all.

"Well, Napoleon, look who's here!" she said. Napoleon didn't, of course, answer. "Gunther Ryder, where'd you come from? I didn't see you coming down the path!"

"I went to the front door but I couldn't get in. And now the back door is—"

"The front door! Nobody ever goes to the front door. But you know that. And now here you are. In your uniform." She touched him for the first time, on the wrist. "Where's your braid?"

"Getting it cleaned," Gun lied as he shrugged past her and stepped through the door.

Shutting the back door behind her with one foot, Iris set down Napoleon and hugged Gun briefly, not using her hands; holding him, it occurred to Gun, like a doggit™ holds firewood. There was a buzzing, a sound like a motor from the front of the house. Gun was about to ask what it was when Iris cut him off with a question of her own:

"What took you so long?"

"Took me so long?" Gun stepped back; all this hugging embarrassed him anyway. "I just got off rotation. I mean, I just got back on planet."

"I wouldn't know anything about that," Iris said, picking up her dough again and pounding it on the table. "All I know is, why didn't you answer my message? You and Gordon both promised you would take care of your father's medlotto tickets, and we haven't gotten a payment since Gordon's escape."

"Gordon's *what?*"

Iris reached over with one foot and shut the door. "Don't act like you don't know," she said in a fierce whisper. "There have been people poking around here ever since Gordon escaped, claiming they have papers on the farm, the house, the ferry. Repossession papers. I guess you don't know anything about that either, especially since . . ."

"Gordon escaped?" It didn't seem a good time to mention that he had gotten a message from Gordon.

"Don't raise your voice," Iris said, lowering her voice. "There are people sleeping. Of course Gordon escaped. You don't read your mail? Upstate is making proceedings after our property. That's why they had the locks changed. We're only here temporarily until the appeal. And what's worse—"

"How could Gordon escape? What about the implant?"

"Not so loud. *You* tell *me*." The buzzing in the front of the house got louder, and was joined by a whining at the back door. Iris opened the door and the doggit™ came in carrying a load of small wood, dropping it stick by stick as it crossed the linoleum floor toward the wood box by the stove.

"He helps me and I help him," Iris said, picking up the dropped sticks. "Glenn has a bunch of them. They help with the boat, I guess. But this one was afraid of the water. Weren't you, Napoleon?"

"How could Gordon have escaped?" Gun asked again. "He was carrying an implant."

"*You* tell *me*. He didn't write to ask for our permission, you can bet. I wouldn't have even known about it except that Donna read me the papers from Upstate. They were all in Latin. Law papers. Have you seen Donna?"

"Sort of."

"Well, I had her send you two messages, one from Hump about the law papers and one from me about the medlotto tickets. Don't you ever read your mail? Where are you living now, anyway?"

"When I'm on planet—here and there," Gun said. He was beginning to regret coming home already. "Where is Hump? Where is Ham. And what's that buzzing noise; is it coming from your room?"

"Hump's up at the Yard. Why don't you go up and see him and your dad. Bring them back for supper. Their days are getting longer and longer."

She shooed him out the door with her broom. The doggit™, Napoleon, sitting at the top of the steps, watched him go with neither regard nor disdain nor interest nor affection.

Nor anything at all.

FOURTEEN

Earth is the cradle of the mind.
—Konstantin Tsiolkovsky

The Ryder home backed up to a low ridge that was covered with hickory and ash, and honeycombed, like all of Morgan's Ferry and the surrounding island-hills, with shallow caves that used to be dry and dead, but were now dripping with moisture and filled with sounds and smells. It was said that the caves connected every spot in Morgan's Ferry, but Gun knew better. He and Whitmer had explored them all. They connected a lot, but they didn't connect everything.

At the bottom of the kitchen stairs, a path led up into the woods and then between the big rocks that crowned the ridge. From the top, Gun could see the whole town of Morgan's Ferry, pearlescent in the gray light of the permanent underclouds that followed the river. There was the half-flooded old shopping center, with the pier for the *John Hunt Morgan;* there was the wharf where even this late in the day, island farmers were unloading flatboats for tomorrow's first ferry; there was the light array of the Video Cat; and there was Mayors' drugstore.

One family, the Mayors, ran the business of the town. Another family, the Ryders, connected the town to the world via the ferry. The rest of the people of this northern edge of K-T were unlisted and unlicensed, unpropertied and unsung, hidden out in the low rocky island hills raising goats or tobacco on land that didn't officially exist anymore, since the flood. No one knew how many people lived in K-T these days, anyway, because the Interim Protocols that had created the no-trade and nuclear waste zones prohibited census tallies.

Gordon escaped? As he walked up the hill, Gun wondered: *where, when?* Where had the letter come from? And what was the promise he was supposed to remember?

Gordon had been a prisoner for the past ten years, and underground for the ten before that. Gun hardly knew him; only that his absence had always dominated the Ryder family.

When Gordon was underground, his organization, the Friends, had paid a stipend to the family. When he was captured, the stipend had been cut off. Gordon had used Gun's one prison visit to convince him to send a stipend to their father out of his Ranger salary. It had gone for medlotto tickets, which provided a chance for treatment and a certainty of funeral expenses.

Now that stipend, too, had apparently been cut off. Gun wondered if the Administrative Hold was a result of Gordon's escape. Maybe there was a clause in his contract about family and prison. He wished now that he had read it. What was it Big Carl had said about politicals in the family?

Dum de dum dum.

Gun trudged on up the hill. The gravity was bad enough, and the mud added insult to injury. And now, adding to the burden was worry. Would he ever make it to "Pirates of the Universe?"

Would he ever see Tiffany again? All Gun wanted was to get away from all of it—the problems, the promises, the memories, the gravity, the mud. The family. He tried to imagine Tiffany but all he got was a soft indentation on a sofa, heart-shaped where she sat waiting for him.

Gun felt a sudden loneliness, so intense and so unexpected that it made him stumble in the muddy path. On Overworld or on the *Penn State* he occasionally had that lonely, stumbling feeling; but there, in zero/g, he just let it pass over him. Here it almost made him fall.

He squeezed his eyes shut until he could imagine the stars, like sparks from a struck universe. They were lonely too, but a different kind of lonely. He wished he had never come home to Morgan's Ferry.

But here he was. Standing between the stones that crowned the low ridge like the logic of an argument showing through the words. He opened his eyes and started down the back side of the ridge. Going downhill, gravity actually helped.

On the far side of the ridge, in a long field that sloped down to a line of trees standing in unnamed water, was the Yard—the three acres of bumper-to-bumper chevrolets that constituted the Ryder patrimony.

From the top of the path, Gun could see the whole field of Buicks, Nissans, Cavaliers, Toyotas and Fords, each variety sitting in rows like steel and glass corn, faded but still colorful. If Gun squinted, the Yard looked like a crazy quilt, one of the threadbare pieced tops his mother had brought in her hope chest from Bowling Green so many years ago.

Weeds grew between the chevrolets, but no trees; Ham and Hump kept the woody brush down. Switching over from row to row, Gun got to within a few car-lengths of his father and uncle without being spotted. Hump was sitting on a tire next to the front end of a tangerine-colored Pontiac chevrolet on blocks, handing tools to his twin brother hidden underneath.

Gun stepped on a stick and Hump looked around. "Well, look who's here," he said.

Hump at least smiled at Gun and held out his hand—but he made no move to get up. He was a little man who wore a suit jacket over coveralls. He was almost bald. Gun stooped to shake hands with his uncle, as small as a troll and weighted down by the tools that filled the pockets of his jacket.

There was a clink underneath the chevrolet; a grunt, a groan. Gun's father.

"Hello, Ham. It's me, Gunther. Home."

There was another grunt and groan from underneath.

"Well as long as you're here, sit down a spell," said Hump. "What happened to your Ranger braid?"

"I don't travel with it," Gun lied. Lies had always come more easily to him than the truth anyway. And with his family, he didn't have to bother keeping his story straight; no one remembered what anyone ever said.

Hump opened his pouch of Red Man and took a delicate little twist and stuck it between his cheek and his gum. He didn't offer any to Gun. It wasn't really Red Man. Hump kept the pouch for old times sake and filled it with a neighbor's product, a sorghum-sweetened twist of the dark, sour local bootleg leaf known as Green River.

Gun sat down on the fender of the Pontiac, gently, so that it wouldn't sink on its springs.

"So I guess you finally got my message," Hump said. "I sent it to your compartment in Orlando and to that space ship both."

"I've had trouble getting my mail."

"You don't know what trouble is," said Hump.

"Seven eighths," said Ham.

They both looked down. A hand holding a small combination wrench stuck out from under the chevrolet.

Hump found a wrench in the breast pocket of his suit and traded it for the one in the hand. The hand disappeared.

"Trouble? You mean the escape?" Gun asked.

"You don't have to whisper, boy. The whole world knows all about it. Gordon never worried about what people thought anyway, now did he?"

"No, sir."

"Now Gordon's got us in a whole pack of trouble, with all those law papers we signed. That's why we need you here, better late than never, I guess. Your father can't sign anything. And I can't sign for him, since you're twenty-one."

"Twenty-six," said Gun. "What law papers?"

"Three-eighths open, and a visegrip." The hand appeared from under the car.

"Those Upstate papers," Hump said, clinking the wrenches into the oil-stained palm. "Remember? Papers so that Gordon would go to prison instead of the afternoon execution shows."

"So now Upstate holds papers on the Yard," Gun said.

"Papers!" said Hump scornfully. "Now, you think I've got papers on all five hundred and eighteen of these chevrolets?"

"Three-eighths open and a visegrip," Ham said again.

"Nobody does," Hump said, as he switched the small wrench in Ham's hand for a much larger one. "Nobody ever did. Well, maybe they did once. But they replaced all the paper records with electronic records, and all those were wiped out in one afternoon in the Three." He looked up toward the blank bottoms of the clouds. "It was that orbital war, the one they say is still going on up there."

The clouds returned his stare.

"Yes sir," Gun said. It didn't seem a good time to mention that he had gotten a message from Gordon.

"Well, the thing about papers is," said Hump, "you can't unsign papers. You have to sign *more* papers to undo the papers you've already signed."

"Yes, sir."

"Well, there you have it. Now that he's escaped Upstate gets the Yard and the ferry, not to mention the house, in thirty days—twenty days—unless . . ."

A small, square plastic tub was being pushed out from underneath the car. A grizzled head stuck out from underneath the Buick, sliding out on a piece of cardboard. An ancient red, white and blue "gimme" hat was perched on top of white hair that stuck out on all sides, as if electrified.

Ham crawled out from under the car, pulling his cardboard after him.

"Hello, Ham," said Gun, again.

The old man nodded. His bright blue eyes—bluer than ever—darted around the junkyard, looking for darkness. He found it and trotted off, across the hill. Hump followed, clinking with tools. Eager to help, as when he was a boy, Gun pulled the plastic tub, which was on a rope, over the short nubby grass to the next chevrolet Ham had chosen, a Plymouth station wagon.

"Three-quarters," said a voice from underneath, and Hump leaned down to switch wrenches in the hand that appeared. All the chevrolets in the Yard were on blocks, a foot and a half off the ground.

"Unless what?" Gun asked.

"Unless we sign their new certificate."

"A new certificate?"

"Then they won't take the Yard," said Hump.

They moved on to the next chevrolet, and the next, their little train sliding across the hillside under the pearl gray sky. Each chevrolet held a little oil. It was Hump's version of Zeno's paradox, that the amount of leftover oil in a chevrolet was infinitely divisible, and it had worked for years. The Yard yielded a gallon a day of the black sludge that kept the ferry running. By keeping the amount harvested always the same, Hump kept alive the illusion that the supply was inexhaustible.

Every twenty minutes Ham crawled out from under the chevrolet, gave his son a pat on the shoulder, and crawled back under the next one. Gun had done this routine many times. The work was like sympathetic magic: the brothers never removed all the oil, and somehow there was always a little left. There was the oil pan, and then the sludge on the rocker arms, and then what could be wiped out of the pumps, and then the black goo that could be scooped from the front wheel bearings; and then a rich, smelly 90W hypoid from the third member (or the transaxle, in the rare front-wheel-drive cars that had stick shift); and then there was always the hard grease that could be scooped out of the housings of the rear wheel bearings; not to mention the thin, maple-leaf red hydraulic oil that was drained from the transmissions, front and rear, then squeezed from the little cork clutches; or the thick paste that lay in the ball joints or between the rack and pinion; or the clear fluid that rode in the power steering housing. There was even a little oil in the steering housing itself, and often along the door hinges. There was always just a little more.

The carbon-seeking bacteria that had sought out and found every last bit of oil under the earth's surface had died in the air, before it could get to the oil left over in the cars; and sensing that this might be the case, the two brothers had bought out and traded out all their neighbors as the rivers rose. They had gathered to the stony bosom of their hillside junkyard all the wrecks that could be salvaged for a hundred miles around, and even pulled a few from the water.

It was non-renewable resource, of course; it had been all along, even when it rode in the cracks and crannies of the earth. But Ham and Hump always seemed to be able to find just a little more. It was gathered every day, slowly, patiently, drip by drip, and scraped out with popsicle sticks. A gallon a day: this was the amount of oil which, stripped and fortified with sorghum alcohol, and burned with green wood and small coal, and converted into wet smoke, would run a 350 for three trips across the Ohio and back, with a little left over.

Only the labor changed, never the harvest. The oil that used to take an hour to gather, then two, then half a day, now took all day. What had once been drained into pans was now scraped with sharp sticks from crevices. In the old days, the brothers had guarded the yard with guns; then later with dogs. Now the oil that was left took too much labor to be worth stealing. But it was still there. The Yard was like a toothpaste tube; there was always a little left.

Ham got under an International pickup. Gun knelt down and saw him worrying a last tablespoon of mud-thick, molasses-dark substance from a long-neglected steering box worm gear.

Ham handed the spoon out to Hump, who scraped it into the plastic tub. "Time to go home," he said. He pointed to the stained inside of the little plastic tub that held their harvest. It was up to the line.

Ham crawled out from under the International. He seemed pleased, his eyes lingering on the rich dark surface of the oil. It was darkness that he loved.

Gun stretched. He was hungry. He was tired. Maybe it wasn't so bad to be home after all. Over the flooded trees down the hill to the west, the sun was sinking and small dark clouds scudded along the bottoms of the pearl-gray overcast sky. Days ended dramatically down here on the planet.

"What kind of new certificate do they want you to sign?" Gun asked.

"They want *you* to sign it," said Hump. "I've already signed it."

The three started up the hill toward the dark edge of the woods. Ham seemed disappointed when they reached the edge; the woods were never as dark as they seemed from outside. His eyes started again looking for darkness, which was not, here under the leafless trees, hard to find.

"What kind of certificate is it?" Gun asked.

"They call it a Death Certificate," Hump said, following Ham, who was looking up as if with relief toward the rapidly darkening sky.

FIFTEEN

We all hate home.
—Philip Larkin

There was an empty chair at the supper table. At first, Gun assumed it was set aside for Gordon. It seemed a nice touch, but uncharacteristic of his family. Were the Ryders getting sentimental?

Gun looked around the table while Hump said the blessing and saw that only Glenn's eyes were closed, screwed shut tightly, as if with delight; as if in a game. Iris was staring over Gun's shoulder, toward the doorway; and Ham's eyes, which never closed because of the disease, and wouldn't until death, were looking frantically around the room for a dark corner, finally resting on the dark mound of deep fat fried wing meat heaped on the platter in the center of the table.

The buzzing noise from the hallway had stopped.

". . . and the kingdom and the power and the glory, forever, amen," said Hump.

"Amen," said Glenn.

"Let's eat," said Iris, nodding toward the doorway, from which came a deep grumbly sound; almost a laugh.

Gun turned and saw, then, who the extra chair was for; saw, finally, the source of the buzzing noises he had heard earlier. A fat, blue uniformed figure filled the doorway; then moved, somewhat improbably, into the room and halfway around the table, making the aluminum floor creak under it, and lowered its bulk into the empty chair.

"Round Man!" said Gun.

"I wish he wouldn't always come late," said Hump.

"Late," said Glenn.

"He can't help it," said Iris. "You know he's not allowed, as a Resistance officer, to participate in the prayer."

Round Man reached for the wing meat platter even before his massive rear end had touched his seat. Peering out through folds of chin and cheek was a face that had once been the face of a handsome young man and now was protected by fat from aging as if by a pink helmet.

"What's he doing here?" Gun asked. Although he already knew.

"He's been here since Gordon escaped," Iris said. She seemed glad to have him back. He had been her boyfriend in high school, before he had drawn the ticket that had sent him to the Resistance Academy in Indianapolis. The Resistance ("Resistance to Crime is Surrender to Duty"), was a uniformed lottery job, like Rangering.

Gun hadn't liked him then. Especially after he had caught him in bed with Iris. He liked him even less now.

"The Resistance doesn't have any authority over here" said Gun. "He should be in Tell City where he belongs."

"Pass the gravy," said Round Man.

"Gravy," said Glenn.

"Since we signed those papers, Gordon's is a civil case, not a criminal case," Hump said. "And the Resistance has a contract with Upstate."

"That's why the locks were changed," Iris said. "Round Man's holding the house in escrow until we sign. We have thirty days."

"Twenty two," said Hump. "It was sixty when I wrote to you, Gunther."

"Pass the biscuits," said Round Man.

"I think he looks nice in his uniform," said Iris. "It's nice to have two men in uniform at the table."

"Uniform," said Glenn.

"Yours isn't a real uniform Glenn," said Iris. "Not that it isn't nice."

"All you got to do, boy, is sign that certificate," said Hump. "If you don't, Upstate gets the house in twenty two days. Plus the yard. Plus the ferry. How's Glenn going to make a living?"

"Certificate," said Glenn.

"You mean the Death Certificate," said Gun.

"You don't have to say it like that," said Iris.

"Pass the butter," said Round Man.

"How else is there to say it?" asked Gun.

"You two quit arguing," said Hump.

"Wish somebody would pass the wing meat before it cools off and flies away again," said Round Man.

"Is that all he does, is ask for food?" asked Gun, passing the plate.

"He's not allowed to talk about the case," said Iris.

"I can't believe it," Gun said. "We're feeding the man who's trying to kill Gordon."

"Gordon," said Glenn.

"Nobody wants to kill Gordon," said Iris. "Besides, he lets us in and out. Pass the wing meat please."

"You mean the bats," Gun said, passing the platter.

"You don't have to talk like that!" Iris said.

"You're the one who told Glenn he didn't have a real uniform," said Gun.

"He doesn't," said Round Man.

"You stay the hell out of it!" said Gun.

"Hell," said Glenn.

"Watch your language at the dinner table," said Hump. "All of you. Pass the wing meat."

"Bats," muttered Gun.

A flickering of lights greeted this announcement. The electric would be going off in an hour or so. It was bled through a cable from Tell City across the river, and resold by the hour to two or three houses by Mayors' drugstore. But when the store closed at nine, it went off.

Gun wiped his mouth and stood up. "I'm going for a walk."

"You're going to see Donna?" Iris asked.

"I'm just going for a walk," Gun said.

"She may not want to see you. Whitmer proposed to her again last week."

"I'm just going for a walk," Gun insisted.

The hill sloped up sharply from the back of the house so that by the time he had taken ten steps—twelve—through the whispery leaves, Gun had to look down to see in the window. He could see Iris doing the dishes while the doggit™ stood beside her (on the stool) watching with its idiot concentration. Since it had no hands, Iris had to both rinse and dry. Glenn was lighting Ham's Marlboro for him since Ham couldn't tolerate looking at the flame. Another, smaller window gave off light in dim waves of blue and rose, and Gun knew that Hump was watching the TV that was kept on more for light and activity than for information or entertainment. The jagged spikes on the screen sometimes resolved into people with guns, people going through revolving hotel doors, or even more poignantly, given the fact that most of the people in the world hadn't seen an actual functioning chevrolet for almost a generation and a half, people getting in and out of cars. The endless reruns beamed down from satellite had been patched together by the satellite defense systems into a seamless screen, a crazy quilt of old shows interrupting one another in random patterns meant to confuse and disorient enemy communications. The Three was long over but the defense systems persisted, a centerless "net" that had so far resisted all efforts to dismantle it. From somewhere in orbit, old "lucies" and "cheers," "cosbies" and "roseannes" rained down over the planet, switching from one to another in mid-stream. Except in areas where cables had been reinstalled, the screen had made telecommunications erratic at best, and impossible most of the time.

It made TV strange and strangely interesting. It meant that the phone muttered but never rang. Picking it up, you were more likely to get Ricki Lake or David Letterman than a caller, since the orbital net's offense/defense had long ago saturated what was left of the old optic cable net; and there were no callers left anyway.

There were, of course, no stars visible from the ridgetop. Not with the underclouds that followed the river like a high fog.

Nights in Morgan's Ferry were tedious affairs. Gun often thought that they were what had prepared him for life in space, and Gordon for life in prison.

Gun couldn't get used to the idea of Gordon free. He seemed to belong in prison, chained to a picnic table in a visiting area. He couldn't imagine him walking down a street or sitting in a stuffed chair. And now he had escaped—to what? To where? And why? Especially since the Friends were defunct.

In the old days, Iris claimed, you could see all the way across the river to Tell City, in the Jeff, and all the way up to the stars, in their unranked spray across the universe; but now the fog so dimmed the world that it gave out by mid-river, even when there was a moon, and in mid-sky even without one.

In the old days, Iris said, the town had stayed lighted at night. There had even been a gas station. Now there was only the red and blue lights of the Video Cat, doubled by their reflection. And the lights of Mayors', where Donna was closing up.

According to the clock on the old city hall, which was the only part of the building that showed above the water, it was 8:55. The clock hadn't worked in half a century, maybe even a century, but Gun knew it wasn't far off, for through Mayor's plate glass window he could see Donna closing drawers, putting merchandise away, wiping counters. She had had this job since she was fourteen, almost ten years ago.

In the old days, when she and Gun had gone steady, he had waited for her here in the shadows. In the old days, before he got his ticket, she would cup one hand over her brow and look through the glass before turning out the light, to see if he was waiting for her in the shadows.

Then, in the old days, after locking the door, she would turn and head up Water Street, instead of down, toward home.

Tonight she backed out the door and locked it, then pulled her scarf around her even though there was no wind, and no chill. She started up Water Street without looking back.

Gun followed.

In the old days, when they were going steady, before Gun had drawn his Academy ticket, Donna would turn off at the top of the hill and take to a short path down to the near edge of the Yard, where the Ryder's family's chevrolets were parked in rows, all facing off the edge of the bluff, like buffalo being stampeded over a cliff ("Hunters of the Plains" NG:542:46:5).

Tonight, as in the old days, she stopped, and stood waiting by the orange and white '56 Oldsmobile that had been "their" chevrolet. It was several seconds before Gun realized she was waiting for him to open the door. Girls shouldn't open car doors, she had once said. She had read it somewhere; she had even showed it to Gun in a magazine.

He stepped out of the shadows and opened the door.

The interior of the chevrolet smelled of rain, and fog, and chrome. Donna lit a Marlboro while Gun slid in and closed the door behind him. It made that *click*, and once again he was home.

"Well, look who's home," she said, blowing smoke out the chevrolet window, into the dark, wide world.

"How'd you know it was me?"

"Word gets around. You know what they say: God made the country, man made the city . . ."

"And the devil made the small town," Gun said. "Right. I hear Whitmer proposed to you again."

"He does every week or so. I don't pay attention."

"Maybe you should. He has a Cloverine ticket."

"He has the Darkening, too. Or maybe you didn't notice."

"I notice. I notice everything."

Gun put his arm across the top of the seat. His hand fell to her shoulder. She let it rest there. "Tell me about 'Pirates of the Universe,' " she said.

"You want to look at some pictures?" Gun asked.

"Maybe. But that's all. Promise?"

"Promise."

Donna handed him her marlboro to hold while she untucked her blouse in front, in back, then reached up behind her back to unbutton her bra.

Gun handed her back her marlboro, then reached under the seat until he felt the familiar fat spine and slick stock.

He put the magazine on her lap. She opened it to "Pirates of the Universe: Disney-Windows's New Heaven on Earth, for Theme Park Living."

"Let's look inside the houses," said Gun.

"You wish," said Donna.

"We looked inside the houses last time," said Gun.

"And that was after you were here for a two weeks."

"One week," said Gun.

Instead of answering, Donna handed him her marlboro. Then she reached up under her blouse, and with that combination of dexterity and magic that had always amazed, and delighted, and excited Gun, pulled her bra out through the armhole.

She put it into the glove compartment. It closed with the

same smooth, satisfying *click* as the door, only smaller.

Gun pretended to be studying the pages. "Each house has its own yard," he said.

"We'll start with the yards, then," she said.

SIXTEEN

Not as she is but as she fills his dreams.
—Dante Gabriel Rossetti

Gun woke late. He could tell by the slant of light through the trees that it was fall, and by the noises in the kitchen that breakfast was over, and by the weight pulling at his flesh as if to pull it off his bones that he was on-planet. Home on Earth. So why was he smiling?

Then he remembered.

"Stay out of that!" Gun heard Iris say in the kitchen. He could tell by her high-pitched tone of voice that she was talking to the doggit™, Napoleon. Gun tried to remember what the real Napoleon was famous for. All he could remember from high school was the famous pictures of her being burned at the stake.

Gun was back in the room he had shared with Glenn for so many years. Because it had been decorated by their mothers, while they were pregnant, the room had never been changed. The great whale and airplane and Petey pictures were still pinned to the wall; the faded drapes still hung with their cowboy images that had been cut and sewn by one of the mothers fully thirty years before. The mothers had also picked out the wicker toy chest; the little paperboard desk, now too warped to write on; the wastepaper basket with its dinosaur and Petey design.

The door was open and Gun could hear snoring down the hall, from Iris's bedroom. Hump slept in the other main bedroom, at the other end of the hall. Ham, who sought smaller and smaller spaces as the Darkening progressed, slept in a narrow closet under the house. Glenn slept on the *John Hunt* and only came home for meals.

Gun could still taste lipstick. Lipstick and Marlboros. When he closed his eyes he could see Donna's fingers, turning the glossy pages on her perfect lap, while his own fingers unbuttoned her white blouse, page by page. Being home wasn't so bad. He could even see spending the next few months here. He would get over Tiffany. How hard could it be, getting over somebody you couldn't remember?

First, though, he would have to sign. That was clear. Gun could see now that Gordon's escape was a problem. It threatened more than just the Ryder family fortune, the Yard and the ferry. It threatened his future at "Pirates." The escape was probably what had put him on Administrative Hold. If he didn't get off Hold, he wouldn't be on the list for the next hunt. And if he didn't make the next hunt, he wouldn't be eligible to move to the theme park. All Donna's waiting would have been for nothing. He had promised her, when he had drawn his Academy ticket, that he would make it to "Pirates" someday and that he would take her with him. He had promised her again last night. It was one promise he would be glad to keep.

If he signed, maybe he wouldn't even need the hearing.

Stepping out into the hallway, Gun saw Round Man's Resistance uniform piled on a chair. He was surprised to see a .22

revolver on top of the pile of braid and leather and canvas. Resistance officers were not allowed to carry guns in K-T. Listening to make sure Round Man was still snoring, Gun picked it up and sneaked a look in the chamber. It was loaded. Gun shook out the shells, and then, reconsidering, put two back.

He slipped the other four .22 shells into his pocket.

"Well?" asked Iris when he entered the kitchen.

Gun felt his glow from the night before dissolve. "Well what?"

"Well, what about the medlotto tickets?" Iris was ironing, and the doggit™ was sitting at the table, eating cereal from a large bowl with a strap-on spoon. "You promised you would buy one every month."

"I have to wait till I get paid," Gun said.

"I thought it was automatic. That was the idea. Do you want some breakfast?"

The doggit™ was slurping the last of his cereal from the bowl, the strap-on spoon forgotten.

"I'm really not hungry."

"Suit yourself. Well, what about the other thing?"

"Other thing?"

"You know. The law paper."

"You mean the Death Certificate."

"I wish you wouldn't say it like that." Iris stood on a chair and pulled a cylinder of paper from the space between the wall and the owl clock. "Hump left it here for you," she said, as she unrolled it on the table. It looked like a Petey certificate except that none of the corners were cut, and the picture in the middle was of a hanged man.

Gun winced when he read the words across the top:

"Certificarum de Mortuarum."

Under that, in a simpler script, on two lines,

"Gordon Ballantine Ryder,
501— ."

"They leave the last date blank," Iris said. "The networks fill it in."

Under Gordon's name were four signatures: Ham's scrawl, Iris's neat "Iris Ryder," Hump's block printed "HUMP" and Glenn's "X X."

There was a spot for Gun's.

"What are you waiting for?" Iris asked. She handed him a pen.

Gun signed it: "Gunther Ryder, D-W Ranger."

She rolled it back up. "Now get going."

"Going?"

"Glenn's waiting for you down at the ferry," Iris said. "He says you promised to take him to Maceo to get a valve fixed."

"He does? I did?"

"He says you did. You know he's afraid of the softees."

Mayors was already open. Gun stopped by on his way to the ferry landing, intending just to say hello. But Donna had a customer. She was waiting on an old man who pulled a load of wingy, leathery nuggets about the size of potatoes in a small wheeled wagon. Mayors' factored in wing meat. They had been picked asleep and would be packed in night moss to ship north for the New Englanders who liked to boil them alive. The old man was trading them for medlotto tickets.

While the greasy-faced old man was unloading his wagon into

the cooler, Gun asked, "What about Ham's medlotto tickets. How far is he behind?"

"Three months," said Donna.

Gun spread his Petey certificate on the counter. "Will this cover it?"

Gun thought he would have to explain what the certificate was worth, and how Joe had cut the corners; but Donna acted as if she knew exactly what to do. She opened the medlotto drawer and took out a tiny pair of scissors and cut off two corners.

"Hey," Gun said.

"Hey nothing," Donna said. "You're still short. Got any change?"

Gun set a .22 shell on the counter.

"Now you're high," Donna said. She reached up on the shelf and pulled down a carton of Marlboros. "Take these to Glenn. Then it'll be about even."

"Glenn doesn't smoke," Gun said.

"Somebody does. He's been buying a carton a week. Maybe he's trading them in Owensboro."

"Will I see you tonight?"

"Better get going!" said the old man. "Glenn's been waiting down there at the pier for you for twenty minutes."

"I don't see why not," said Donna.

"Here to keep my promise," said Gun stepping onto the steel deck of the *John Hunt Morgan*.

"Promise" said Glenn, smiling. It was one of the special words that made him happy. He had tacked a sign onto the sassafras railing at the landing. It read:

NO NOON FERRY
AFTERNOON FERRY late

They rode down the center of the river, between the little islands of fog. Downstream, the current was fast; the engine ran just fast enough for steering. The leaking valve sounded worse at idle, hissing like a kid sucking a bad tooth.

Glenn opened the throttle a little, to keep the back end from coming around. Gun leaned against the Pontiac cab, next to the Chinese-made 7.62mm "bear" gun the Interim Protocols required on Ohio River crossings, even though no bears had ridden the icebergs down from Hudson's Bay since Gun was a child. The icebergs themselves had thinned out; it was rare that one made it past Cincinnati. On the far shore the Jeff was all pines, planted in rows. On the near shore, yellowed sycamores, long dead but preserved against rot by the icy water, marched by like pale soldiers with their hands in the air, surrendering.

Owensboro was eight miles down the river. It took the *John Hunt Morgan* less than an hour. The smudge on the horizon resolved as they drew nearer into a bare mud bank of yellow clay, covered with old tires, odd trash, steel springs and wood scraps. Glenn got more and more nervous as they approached. A few people, mostly local islanders, picked their way through while others, the Danes, watched, keeping track of what they found on clipboards. They were white as ghosts but many of the islanders were black or brown. African origin. Everything here was for sale and nothing was free, not even the landing. A Dane made a mark on his clipboard as soon as the *John Hunt*'s blunt nose struck the clay. The Dane showed Gun the marks, and Gun gave him the Petey certificate to clip. He was prepared to show him where to cut it, but the Dane already knew. He cut eight corners. The certificate was getting smaller and more circular every day.

No one lived in Owensboro, according to the agreement struck decades ago when the edges of the Danelaw had been peeled away and sold off. The town shut down every night. That appealed to Gun. Owensboro was like Overworld, an artificial place; an island in an island universe.

Gun left Glenn with the *John Hunt* and climbed the muddy stair to hunt for Maceo's mother in the square. It didn't take long to find her. She sat in her throne-shaped chair under the faded plywood "Big Softee" sign. Maceo lurked under a blanket nearby.

"Cash only," the mother said, when Gun showed her his certificate.

He gave her one of the three .22 shells he had left. She pretended to be offended by his offer, but Gun held his ground; he knew that she would make plenty off the crowd that gathered to watch. All Gun had to do was provide the engine—and of course, the new valve.

While the mother rolled Maceo, still hidden under his filthy blanket, out of the ornately carved shed where she kept him, Gun set out around the square to obtain the valve. He recognized none of the merchants; they had all turned over since he had come here as a boy, tagging behind Hump and Ham. The fourth table he stopped at had a coffee can blossoming with valves like steel tulips.

Gun was able to buy a knife-edged antique 350 exhaust valve for another .22 shell. He didn't even try the Petey certificate.

A small crowd had already gathered at the boat by the time he got back to the waterfront. The mother had brought them along, singing out "See the Big Softee!" as she wheeled him down to the waterfront. She made a good portion of her money from spectators, and from the hawkers who catered to them. It was always amazing to Gun, the types who enjoyed seeing Maceo at work.

Glenn was not among them. Already he was hiding his face and peering through his fingers as Gun gave the valve to the mother, and helped her maneuver her son's chair onto the low steel deck of the *John Hunt Morgan*.

Glenn went to the back of the boat, far from the engine.

The spectators squatted in the mud bank or on chairs, rented from vendors who followed Maceo and the mother from place to place.

The mother made a spinning motion with her ancient crab-like hand, indicating that Gun and Glenn were to start the engine. That was easy enough to do: it was still warm from the journey, and the charcoal fire that fed it was still smoldering. The 350 had no carburetor; the charcoal smoke was fed directly into the manifold through a narrow stovepipe with a butterfly damper for a throttle. Glenn hit the starter switch from the Pontiac wheelhouse, while Gun opened the damper and primed the pipe with a small squirt of expensive NearGas.

Whump.

Whump.

Thum thum whum whum. And the engine was running, stumbling a little, hissing a lot.

The mother wheeled Maceo closer to the block and positioned his "hand" over the hole at the top of the manifold. It made a sucking sound through his "fingers." She moved them for him, testing the vacuum, searching—Gun assumed—in the noise for the bank, the cylinder, the valve that would have to be replaced.

The crowd was quiet. Mud was sucking at boots and bare feet as the engine sucked the air out of this universe and into the tiny, fiery one inside.

The mother was singing as she drew her son's hand across the venturi. Then she let go and drew her own hand across the front of her wrinkled, wattled neck. Gun made the same sign to Glenn, who shut the engine off.

The mother pulled the chair back. She pulled the blanket off her "Big Softee" and the crowd let loose a low sigh of wonder and horror mixed, even though most of them had seen Maceo many times before. Gun looked toward Glenn but he was ducked down in the wheelhouse.

Either the old lady was stronger than she looked, or Maceo lighter: for she was able to lift him in her arms and set him beside the engine, so that he was leaning against the block. Boneless, he fell over in a heap. The mother straightened him as if he were a rag doll.

Then she turned toward Gun. She took the valve that he was holding out toward her and polished it on the filthy hem of her wool dress. Already bright, it brightened more.

She handed it to Maceo. His "fingers" moved for the first time independently, curling around the stem. Mud sucked shoes and toes as the crowd shifted—"Aaaahhhh"—from foot to foot. This was the part they liked.

The mother leaned back, watching. Gun pulled the stovepipe off the manifold, exposing the hole where a two-barrel carburetor had once sat. Maceo's "hand" and then a lot more of him disappeared into the manifold. To the "shoulder" and beyond . . .

The mother's face twisted in a grimace as if she were doing it all by remote control. The crowd was hushed except for the far off sound of an old person crying. For some reason Gun had never been able to figure out, watching Maceo made old people cry. Mud sucked shoes as people strained to watch Maceo's dark, vinyl- and canvas-clad bulk roll first this way and then that over the engine block. It was as if he were wrestling it.

There was another sucking sound. Someone was weeping. It was the mother, looking up toward the pearl-colored, low-riding K-T sky.

Maceo seemed smaller, perhaps because so much of him was twisted inside the 350. Were those feet, kicking at the air, under his vinyl and canvas dress? If so, he was less limbless than most softees.

There was a shudder and a click. Was it a sound the valve made, slipping under its springs and keepers? Or was it a sound Maceo made, or his mother, as part of the show?

The mother pulled and Maceo came out, dark and slick, oozing and oily, and when she let go he fell back and rolled sideways off the engine block onto the patterned steel deck of the *John Hunt Morgan*. The deck rang when he fell. The crowd gasped, laughed, all but cheered.

Gun stepped forward to help but the mother pushed him away, shaking her head. By herself she pushed, pulled, persuaded, eased and squeezed her "Big Softee" back into his chair.

She rolled the wheelchair, with her son in it, off the boat. The crowd drifted away while the boat stayed put, as if it were the land that were in motion. Glenn raised his head from the back. He opened his eyes.

"It's over," said Gun. "Let's go."

"Go," said Glenn. It was one of the special words that made him smile.

Soon the boat was chugging contentedly through a willow-grown channel. Owensboro was receding behind.

The procedure had worked. The engine neither chuffed nor did it whistle. Glenn was at the wheel, steering between the clouds that floated downstream (they might hide snags) and smiling once again, and Gun wondered: why was Glenn so afraid of Maceo?

Was it because he had no face?

SEVENTEEN

And in hir houre he walketh forth a pas.
—Geoffrey Chaucer

The way back to Morgan's Ferry led not up the center of the river, against the swift current, but through the long, sycamore-marked lanes of the flooded highway. It was a road on the water. It was a slower trip. Glenn followed it upstream, until he reached the long turn lined with dead cedars that marked the end of the yellow clay low country and the beginning of the rocky highlands now known as the island hills. From here it was a short turn around the bluffs to Morgan's Ferry; but Glenn turned inland instead, between low cliffs.

"Don't you have the afternoon run to make?" Gun asked.

Glenn, grinning, didn't answer.

Ahead, Gun recognized the low, cut-back cliff that led to Morgan's Cave, where he and Whitmer had spent so much time as boys. There was a doggit™; no, two, standing in the mud at the top of the bank. They were wearing sailor suits, stained with mud.

Glenn cut the engine back.

"Why are we landing here?" Gun asked. Instead of answering, Glenn was grinding the gearbox, snagging the little two-bladed prop into reverse. Gun threw the painter to the bank and one of the doggits™, the smaller, caught it in its mouth and snubbed it to a tree by tottering around the trunk on two feet. Doggits™ are funny, Gun thought. They hate to go on all fours, and won't unless they absolutely have to.

The other doggit™ just watched.

Gun turned and looked toward Glenn, who was, unaccountably, beaming as the boat nudged into the soft clay bank. It was too slick and steep to climb. One of the doggits™, the larger, was holding a long stick in its mouth. Gun grabbed the stick, and the two doggits™ together pulled him up the bank.

Gun heard the gearbox rattle again, and saw the *John Hunt* already backing away. Glenn tossed a brown and blue box underhand and Gun caught it. The Marlboros.

The doggits™ had already started up the slope toward the cave. Hesitating for only a moment, Gun followed. He was later to remember that he was already beginning to suspect what he was going to find.

Morgan's Cave was not really a cave but what was called locally a "rockhouse," a broad opening under a cliff like a giant yawning mouth, sloping up in sand and dust to the back, where it met the stone slabs of the ceiling. Morgan's Cave was unusual because high in the back, behind a fallen slab, was an entrance to a real cave that had been blasted out by guano miners in the 1840s. The cave had also been used by Confederate guerrillas as a base to raid across the river into Indiana back during the war called the Civil War.

Gun followed the doggits™ up the sand slope. Gun's feet

slipped backward two steps for every three: a familiar feeling to him from space where there was no such thing as firm footing. The doggits™ had dropped to all fours.

They stopped at a pile of wood behind a fallen slab—twisted, broken firewood in clumsy, three foot lengths. They stood up on their hind legs again and held out their arms toward Gun.

Gun piled their "arms" with wood, then picked up a load for himself. They went down, and in, and Gun followed.

Inside the entrance, the cave pitched downward sharply. To the right was a sand slope; to the left, a creaking stair. Just as Gun and Whitmer had done when they were boys, the doggits™ stayed to the middle where the sand met the steps.

At the bottom two upright wooden beams defined where a door once had been. Beyond was darkness; and through the darkness, after a few blind terrifying yards, another door.

Gun followed through the door. Beyond was a dim light and the far off sound of falling water.

Letting his feet find the way, Gun followed the doggits™ down a long passage, past a deep hole to his right. He and Whitmer had called it the Bottomless Pit. Once Gun had shined a five-cell flashlight down it and seen the beam eaten by darkness.

The tunnel narrowed after the Bottomless Pit, and Gun began to feel the claustrophobia he had felt here years before. The terror was familiar, almost comforting; like the return of an old friend. It was the mirror image of the terror he felt in space when he saw the Universe falling away in every direction. Here it was the same Universe closing in. There, the earth was a stone in a universe of hole; here his world was hole, in a universe of stone.

It was ten years since Gun had been here with Whitmer, ten or even twelve, but Gun still knew every turn in the tunnel;

every low spot in the ceiling. The doggits™ knew it too.

No one knew whether "Grant's Tomb" at the end of the passage was natural or blasted out of the stone. Whitmer had thought it was natural; Gun always thought it was created, or at least enhanced. Just as the Bottomless Pit had no bottom, Grant's Tomb room had no top. A small fire burned in the center of the twenty foot diameter chamber, and crouched in front of it was a hooded figure in a dark Arabic djellabah like Hadj had worn under his space suit. Gun knew who it was even before he saw the pale blue eyes and the short blond hair already going gray; even before he stepped into the skinny outstretched arms.

"Gordon!"

Gun had only hugged his brother once before, on his prison visit. He stepped back. Gordon looked old, even older than Iris, though they had been born, like Gun and Glenn, only hours apart. Gordon's hair was thin and he looked out-of-focus, like a holo-clerk. Then Gun saw that it was because he was shivering.

"Why are you shivering?"

Gordon held out both hands toward the tiny fire, and smiled across the flames at Gun, a smile that was more of a grimace because his teeth were chattering. "Because I'm cold," Gordon said. "That's what the package is for. To get warm. Did you bring it?"

"That package was for you? It said it was for a bar in Orlando . . ."

"That was a diversion," Gordon said. "Don't you read your mail?"

"I don't even get my mail!" Gun said angrily. "I'm on Administrative Hold. I may lose my Ranger status. I can't get my mail or my money. The family is about to lose the Yard. Ham's not getting his medlotto tickets. I may lose my chance to get into 'Pirates'—"

"All because of me," Gordon said. "And yet you came. I'm honored. More than that, I'm touched. Forget the package. It's no big deal."

Gun remembered the certificate he had signed that morning. He felt ashamed. "At least you're free," he said. "How did you get rid of the implant? You still have your hand."

"Upstate quit putting the implant in the hand," Gordon said. "They lost the orbital that tracked it. Plus, it was too easy to cut off. Though it never seemed so easy to me. Remember your visit?"

Every Upstate prisoner got one visit. Gun remembered the visiting room. At the next table on either side was a handless man, a recaptured escapee who had used a chainsaw or a knife to get rid of the "handcuff" or electronic locator surgically implanted in his wrist bone.

"Now they use a heartcuff," Gordon said. "They put the locater in the wall of the heart. The ventricle, I think. It's a thermodefibrillator, a mechanically powered heat exchange unit. With every beat of my heart, my chest cavity gets a little colder and a little colder and a little colder. Watch this!"

He blew a white cloud into the room.

"I thought that was the Marlboro," Gun said.

Gordon shook his head. "I do smoke a lot, though. It's the only thing that warms me up. The only thing that can stop the freezing is a transmitter inside the prison. It sends out a signal that neutralizes the heat pump; shuts it down by cutting one number out of the sequence. So they don't have to find me; with the heartcuff, they count on me finding them. Or freezing to death."

"They can't track you? Then why do you stay in the cave?"

"Security," said Gordon. "I don't feel right out there in the open. Plus, there are freelancers around. Bounty hunters. I think there's one in Morgan's Ferry. He could pick up my signal if weather conditions were right and he got lucky."

"Round Man," said Gun.

Gordon nodded.

"What about food?"

"I don't need food," said Gordon. "We're all on slow release at Upstate. They give you a tablet every eighteen months. Cuts down on the pleasure you can find in prison, and saves them on food and toilet paper. They've got the staff cut to almost nothing."

Gun looked around the chamber for the doggits™. They had left. "Glenn'll wonder what happened to me," he said, standing up.

"Glenn knows," Gordon said. "He's making the afternoon Tell City run. He'll come back and pick you up when it's finished. It was my idea that he combine the visit with the trip to Maceo. Kill two birds with one stone, and give the *John Hunt* an excuse for being down this way. You know how he hates the softees."

"So who helped you escape?" Gun asked. "The Friends?"

"Not the Friends, but a friend," Gordon said. "A new friend. A girl friend. You're my prisoner here till Glenn gets back. Sit down, relax, and I'll tell you the whole story."

"You work on your dreams in prison," Gordon said. "It's like you have come to inhabit a dream, and in dreams there is incredible freedom, even in a dream with stone walls and steel bars. There is a freedom that has to do with what we are in the universe, a kind of unique tissue that dreams.

"We only get commissary at Upstate once a month. But ten years is a long time. A few years ago, I got friendly with the girl in commissary and she started showing up in my dreams."

Taffeta? Gun wondered.

"Commissary Taffeta. She would come and visit me in my dreams. At first we would just talk. Sometimes she would take me places. Not the real world, you understand. But the half-world, the VR world she inhabits. She could leak back and forth between VR and dreams, certain dreams. Like I say, we lifers work on our dreams. They become *places* that can be *inhabited. . . .*"

Gordon wasn't shivering anymore. His own voice seemed to warm him. He was smoking a Marlboro, dragging the smoke down deep into his lungs; it came out, mixed with the fog and the words, and drifted away toward the darkness, like voice made visible.

"Night," Gordon was saying. "That's when we work on our dreams. When we dream the world shrinks to the size of a coffin, or a cell, or a bed, or a body; and at the same time expands to take in the whole universe. It's a kind of breathing, from small to large, from in to out. It's the in-between sizes, ordinary prison life, that are hard to take. Anyway . . . One night, not so very long ago, come to think of it, there I am, letting my spirit ride that wave that runs along the front of a dream, when a sound brought me back into my cell, into my self.

"It was the sound of the door at the end of my cell block, opening. Since it was too late for that particular door to be opening, I figured it was C-T coming to visit me in my dream. . . ."

"C-T?"

"That's what I call her. Sometimes in the dreams she would

come through doors. Dream doors. But the doors at Upstate are loud. An old prison is a regular orchestra of groans and screeches and clangs, always a little different depending on whether it is night or day, summer or winter; in the winter the notes rise a half tone and the slam becomes slightly more bell-like. . . . Am I putting you to sleep? When you and Glenn were babies, I could always put you to sleep."

I'm awake, Gun dreamed he said. "I'm awake," he said. He sat up straighter. "You heard the door."

"Yes, I heard the main tier door. It never opens after eleven o'clock count, but there it was. I was beginning to doubt that it was a dream. I pinched myself, but I can pinch myself in my dreams. I can wake up and keep dreaming; it's a trick. As I said, we work on our dreams.

"Then I heard steps, coming down the tier. It was sounding less and less like a dream. Then there she was, in front of my cell—"

"Commissary Taffeta?" Gun said. "That's impossible. She's not real—"

"Not her. A gen."

Gun felt a sudden chill. Somehow the gen seemed familiar.

"She was wearing a guard's uniform and opening my cell door."

"A guard's uniform?"

"They use women at Upstate. But you could tell it was a gen by the little black eyes, the sleek black hair. . . ."

Gordon leaned over to light another marlboro from his little cord.

"That's when I decided it was a dream, after all. C-T had told me she had been linking with the gens through the VR net. I figured she had a hand, so to speak, in this. And as I said, she and I are very tight. I trust her."

"But she's not real!" Gun protested.

"C-T? What do I care? As I told you, in prison we honor our dreams. I pulled on my jacket and went with the gen. I followed her through eleven doors, through the prison, and we never ran into another soul. We used the side doors and access doors through the shops, the kitchens, avoiding the core of the prison, where the night administration tends to cluster."

"I thought you said it was a dream."

"A complicated dream. A dream with keys. I was beginning to relax into it. One dream we share in prison—we old-timers—is the dream we call the Dream of Doors, of slipping through doors, one after the other; of watching them slide open in front of you, like clouds falling away in front of an airship. It's the dream that replaces the dream of flying, and it's a sign you've been down so long—ten years or more—that the prison has penetrated to the bottom levels of your consciousness. It's the old con's badge of pride, in a way; the pride of despair. So I figured I was having a complicated version of the old con's deepest dream. You still with me?"

I'm awake, Gun dreamed he said. "I'm awake."

"Well, hang in there, for we are approaching the outer wall. You can almost tell by the sound. Upstate is an old prison, two centuries at least, and made of brick and stone, and noisy. The doors are loud like cathedral bells. Each opens with a scream and shuts with a boom, and each one seemed it must awaken the entire prison and set off every alarm. Yet it didn't. That's how I knew it was a dream. We went through classrooms, and infirmaries, and libraries, all unused, or hardly used—in the old days, right after the turn of the century, Upstate held ten thousand men. The last room I remember was filled with coils of cable and some snow tires left over from the last century when there had been trucks. And snow . . ."

Gordon was seized with another storm of shivering. Gun looked around the chamber for help. The doggits™ were back. They lay with their snouts on their paws, looking mournfully, peacefully into the fire. They looked like dogs.

The shivering continued. Gun got up and threw a log onto the fire. He pulled the blanket more closely around Gordon's shoulders. Nothing helped.

The little stack of Marlboros was diminished by half but still considerable. Gun selected one, lit it with a brand from the fire, and put it between Gordon's lips. The shivering slowed, then ceased.

"Thanks," said Gordon. "They warm the lungs, which are close to the heart. Guess I'll warm up when my heart stops beating. Where was I?"

"The wall."

"Oh, yes. The wall. Of course, you don't perceive it as The Wall, not unless you're in the yard. It's just another inside wall, of plaster over stone. We stepped over the piles of cable and tires and there it was."

"The wall," Gun prodded. He was remembering that Gordon sometimes needed to be poled through his stories like a john boat through a shallow slough.

"The door, actually. It was a little arched steel door, locked with a padlock. Padlocks are unusual in prison. The gen started going through her key ring. I was in no hurry. I figured this would be the end of the Dream of Doors."

A cough. But without the shakes this time. Another Marlboro was lighted off the last.

"Her smallest key was the one that opened the padlock. The door groaned and screamed when it was opened. It was rusty; it was as if it had never been opened before. She stepped back and motioned that I was to go through. I knelt down and looked out. There was a wide lawn, and on the far end of it, a dark line of trees. There was the moon, making long shadows across the grass. In prison we are familiar with the moon, that captive chained to earth, but I hadn't seen grass in moonlight in so long that it seemed like another, an unearthly substance."

"So you went through," poled Gun.

"Not yet. I was afraid. This may sound strange—stupid—but this was the first time I realized that it was not a dream but an escape. 'Where am I going?' I asked. 'Who is doing this?' Of course she didn't answer. They can only ask questions. . . ."

"What did you do?" Gun prodded.

"I didn't do anything. She, on the other hand, handed me a card and took my arm—her little grip is like steel—and pushed me through the door. I fell onto my knees and I heard the door clang shut behind me."

"A card?"

"I'll get to that. Meanwhile, there I was. It was all I could do to keep from banging on the door and begging her to let me back in. But somehow I knew better. I stood upright in the moonlight. It's cold, not like sunlight. But you know about moonlight. I've never been in space, like you, and stepped off into the void, but I think I know what it feels like, now."

"What kind of card?" Gun asked again.

"A Petey card. I'm getting to that. But first, there was the moonlight. It was as light as day. It flattened me back against the wall. I was afraid to run. . . ."

Gordon fell into another fit of shivering. Gun, experienced this time, lit a Marlboro and stuck it directly between his lips, bypassing the trembling fingers.

"I was afraid to run, so I walked. I figured if they wanted to shoot me, OK. Have at it. I was sure at any moment I was going to feel a bullet slicing in between my shoulder blades. I was waiting for it to take my breath away. I walked across the grass, toward the trees."

"And you made it," Gun prompted. Poled.

"As you see. But first, I stopped and turned to look behind me. I had never seen the guard towers and the prison from the outside. The guard towers were dark. Empty. That's why I hadn't been shot, I guess. The prison looked like an empty tomb. I slipped into the trees and there was a sort of path, and there I was. In the darkness."

"Free," said Gun, who felt, himself, free. He stood up and stretched.

"Not exactly free." Gordon shivered again. "Let's say I had new worries. For one, there was the heartcuff. How long before I would start to feel it? For another, who had sent the gen? If it was C-T, OK. But if it was the Friends, I was worried about a setup. I knew there had been new splits in the organization.

"It was dark in the woods, but ahead I saw what looked like a river of light but which turned out to be a road with the moonlight on it. I stood on the road and looked at the card the gen gave me. I have it here."

Gordon reached into a pile behind him in the darkness and handed Gun a card. It was a Petey card from the "Pirates of the

Universe" series, which Gun had collected in his childhood. It was one of a set of three. Put together, they showed a light storm passing from left to right, upper to lower, across a Triad. It had tooth marks in one corner.

"The left hand card," Gun said. "What's with the tooth marks?"

"The doggits™," Gordon said. "They bite everything."

"I see it but I don't get it," said Gun.

Gordon shrugged. "I didn't either. Then I heard a truck coming and I hid in the bushes. When he stopped, I figured I was caught. But it was a Cloverine truck. The driver leaned out the window and showed me—"

"A 'Pirates of the Universe' card."

"The right hand card. How'd you guess?" Gordon started coughing again. He was shivering so hard that the blanket fell from his shoulders. Gun put it back and lit another Marlboro from the butt Gordon had dropped. The doggits™ looked on mournfully.

"Thanks," Gordon said. "And that's the whole story. It wasn't that hard to get here from Evansville."

"That's not the whole story!" said Gun. "Who sent the gen? What's in the package?"

"Don't know. C-T told me you were bringing the package in a dream. Turns out she's the one who sent the gen. They're working together on something."

"On what?"

"It's not too clear," said Gordon. "In the dreams when I can talk to C-T it all makes sense, but when I'm awake I can't get the details straight."

"You still dream, then. You and her."

"Oh, yes. And I know from the dreams that the package has something to do with the heartcuff. With the freezing. Doesn't matter anymore."

"I know where it is," Gun said. "It's at a bar in Orlando. I left it there to be picked up. Maybe it hasn't been picked up yet."

Gordon shivered. "It's too late," he said. "I have another week, at most, before the wall of my heart freezes and shatters."

"I could go back and get it," Gun said.

Gordon just shivered.

"I could get back down there in a day or two," Gun said.

"I don't want to put you to any trouble," Gordon said. A horn honked outside. The doggits™ scrambled to their feet. "There's Glenn. You'd better go."

He stood up and Gun stepped over the fire to hug him. It was like hugging an icicle.

"And Gunther . . ."

"What?"

Gordon sat back down and lit another Marlboro from his "cordwood" stack. "Sign it," he said.

"Sign what?"

"You know what. The Death Certificate. It's no big deal. I'll freeze before they catch up with me anyway, and this way the family won't lose the Yard."

"You're not going to freeze," said Gun. "I'm not going to let you freeze."

EIGHTEEN

Time is the image of eternity.
—Plato

Just like Gordon, Gun thought, as he rode the rattling Smokey down through the tangled little hills south of Evansville. *He will never ask you to do anything. He would rather force you to volunteer.*

Gun was usually glad to be leaving Morgan's Ferry and heading back to Orlando, but this time was different. He could tell by the moonlight spilling through the crack in the container that it was after nine in Morgan's Ferry. He would be walking up the hill with Donna; opening the door of their Oldsmobile chevrolet. She would be unhooking her bra; opening the glove compartment. The air would be filled with little *clicks*, the rustle of glossy pages, the whisper of cloth. Gun was almost glad he had been evicted from the Dogg. He liked having Donna on his mind: her memory was as indelible as Tiffany's was irretrievable.

He didn't want to go back to Orlando but what choice did he have? He had already signed his brother's death warrant. He couldn't watch him freeze to death. Whatever was in the package, he would get it back to K-T and Morgan's Cave.

Gun had told Donna and the family the same story—that his hearing at the Girl had come up. He couldn't tell the truth even if he had wanted to. He never wanted to anyway.

Donna had said she understood but Gun could tell she didn't. He could tell by the way she turned on her heel and walked away to look for a customer to wait on.

No matter. He would be back in three days: a day and a half down and a day and a half back. Gordon would have his heart-warmer, whatever it was. Gun would be in K-T with Donna until the next Petey hunt, which would be his last. Donna would believe him then.

She would believe him for sure when he took her with him to "Pirates of the Universe" to live happily ever after.

Happily ever after!

"Wake up," said the driver, sticking his head back into the box. "Cumberland Crossing. Twenty minutes."

"Demonstrations?" Gun asked at the Orlando Proper monorail terminal. The attendant shrugged as he pulled back the OFF-PROTOCOL tape that blocked the door. A cop scurried down the street, nosing into the trash. They never knew what they were looking for until they found it. A body, a weapon. To cops, such things were like food.

"Just a cautionary," said the attendant. "There are Fundamentals out there but they haven't been bothering anybody. They're expecting new Protocols."

"Fundamentals with sticks?"

"Oh, yes, sticks."

But what choice did Gun have? Walking swiftly, but warily, he set out on his mission of mercy.

* * *

At first Gun thought the Littlest was closed: the scale-like windows at the rear were boarded up. But the door was open and the lights were on. He ducked and went in and knelt at the bar. There were a couple of regular persons™ scattered at tables and video games.

But where was Joe?

"I'm Jo," the bartender said. "What'll you have?" She was wiping glasses with a flickering moby on a stick.

"Strawberry Heineken. The other Joe was a guy," Gun said. He looked for the package on the shelf. It was gone.

"That's his tough luck," said Jo.

"I left a package here with him. Do you know if it was picked up, or did he take it with him?"

"You'll have to ask him," Jo said. "He'll be back tomorrow."

"Tomorrow?" Gun had been on the road for eighteen hours. He had been hoping to get the package and get right back onto the 'rail and sleep till Huntsville at least.

"Tomorrow," said Jo. "They just call me to fill in nights. We're open twenty four hours, you know."

Gun went over his choices. It didn't take long: he didn't have many. He could spend the night at the Littlest or under a bench at the monorail station. "I'll have another Strawberry Heineken," he said, unrolling his Petey certificate.

"Not much left of this," Jo said. She clipped twelve corners and handed Gun two tens. "Each corner is worth less, you know," she said.

"Thanks," Gun said. "I already know that." He took a swig of beer and silently cursed his fate. If he weren't on Hold, he would be staying at the Dogg, in perfect, one-third/g luxury. Instead, he was stuck in this crummy bar.

There was nothing on TV but a fryer, a rerun. But the pay terminal in back was free. Gun decided to check his mail. It would be something to read; plus it would tell him if the signing the Death Certificate had done any good.

He bought another beer to take to the back. He dropped the ten into the pay terminal and pressed his palm against the glass. Instead of the mailbox, the pig came up. And it was smiling! Did that mean he was off Hold? Did that mean he was paid up at the Dogg?

There was only one way to find out.

NINETEEN

"Honey, I'm home."
—Trad.

It was like waking from a dream. The drawer slid in, the Vitazine™ hissed, Gun's eyes opened and there she was, standing by a window overlooking a tangle of rooftops and trees, wearing a cotton blend lace trimmed demibra with wide-set adjustable straps, and a matching high cut bikini with lace insets, front and back, all in periwinkle blue. She was smiling almost directly at Gun and he couldn't help smiling back.

He was afraid he would be tongue-tied, starting so high (panties and bra!), but his fears were groundless. "Tiffany," he said, with the easy eloquence that flowed so naturally in the Dogg. He felt articulate, accomplished, smooth. There was a dark carpet and across it a door and through it another room with tall windows overlooking treetops and rain-slick streets where carriages glided under gas lights. So high! And Tiffany, of course, "dear Tiffany," standing at a small three-sided table of polished wood in a smooth seamless stretch floral jacquard bra with full cups and underwire shaping, and a tanga bikini with a wide waistband in blush peach, accented with tiny bows.

Gun joined her. It was great to be back. "Great to be back," he said. It was always right there on the tip of his tongue, the perfect phrase.

Through the glass the trees were blossoming; no, waving in the wind.

"You look so nice," he said. Was that a smile? Gun saw a doorway across the room, and he waited as long as he could before ducking his head to enter it, and he was in a library with dark wood shelves. Tiffany was leafing through a volume bound in rich morocco leather, wearing a pearl white scalloped lace minibra with point d'esprit sides and back, bow detail and wide-set lace straps, and a matching French style high cut bikini detailed in front with fleur-de-lis of see-through lace.

"Read any good books lately?" Gun asked. He could see that all the books had the same title, even though he couldn't tell what it was.

It was something. "It's really something isn't it," Gun said, and he almost thought he almost saw in her answering smile a hint of sadness. Had she missed him? But how could she? She wasn't here unless he was here. Did that mean that, as far as she knew, he was always here? But Gun knew better than to think too hard here in the Dogg, so he ducked through the door between the bookshelves, and found himself in a wide, sunny room filled with fresh flowers.

Tiffany was holding a bouquet of white and yellow daisies, wearing a black satin bra with sheer scalloped lace cups and faux pearl detail, lace trimmed straps, and a stretch satin black string bikini trimmed with sheer scalloped lace in front.

"Flowers," he said, and it was like philosophy, it rang like a bell, vibrating with truth. In the Dogg it was always possible to find the perfect phrase.

He looked for a window, to see how high they were, but there were none. He stepped through a lovely arched doorway into the next room, where Tiffany stood brushing her hair, wearing a shimmery stretch snow white push up bra edged with lace and a white satin thong bikini.

There was a window behind her, and Gun saw trees and fields far below. How far to the Upper Room? It couldn't be far, judging from Tiffany's thong bikini.

Each room promised to carry him higher, and unable to resist, Gun stepped through the low, natural wood-framed door into a room with flocked wallpaper where Tiffany sat on a love seat wearing a stretch satin strapless bodysuit with a low squared neckline shaped by an empire seam. A bodysuit? Shouldn't he be higher? He crossed to the leaded bay window behind the love seat and saw the city—it was no particular city—spread out before him with gleaming lights and a suggestion of traffic on wide boulevards.

It was beautiful but he wanted to go higher. Impatiently, he strode into another room, a sort of kitchen where Tiffany stood by a gleaming stove in a floral lace underwire bra and matching scoop front bikini with full cut back and front lace insets. He was no higher than before.

Not that she wasn't beautiful. Not that it wasn't anything short of perfect here in the Dogg, in the cool darkness and the gentle one-third/g. But Gun couldn't seem to stand still. He felt like wandering. Feeling like it and doing it must have been the same, for he found himself ducking through the doorway into the next room, and then the next.

Tiffany was always waiting. Several times he tried watching her behind him as he stepped through the door into the next room, to see if he could catch her in two places at once. It never worked, though. He always lost sight of her behind a wall or a half open door before he turned and saw her in the room ahead of him, waiting as if she had been there all along. As of course she had; in her way.

Always waiting, and always for him. Always in panties and bra (though he could never remember exactly the color or style; she was copy protected). Donna always wore white panties, never pink or black or even blue. Gun had seen them under her skirt. Funny how he could remember her when he was with Tiffany, but he couldn't remember Tiffany when he was with her. Didn't that make this the real world? And that other one, the dream?

Tiffany was gone. No, there she was, watering a plant from a crystal pitcher in a smooth fitting ivory stretch satin strapless bra, the tops of the cups delicately edged with eyelet lace, and matching lace trimmed bikini panties, cut full in the back and high on the sides. But why was she standing so still?

The water wasn't pouring.

The water wasn't not pouring either.

Gun looked for the doorway. Someone was standing in it. She was wearing an oversized men's tee shirt over full cut white cotton panties. The tee shirt was printed with big, block stenciled letters that read:

PROPERTY
OUTER
ORLANDO

RECEPTION
CNETER

Her dirty blonde hair was cut short. "Taffeta?" Gun said. He could feel his eloquence deserting him. It was an alarming feeling.

"Commissary Taffeta."

"The jail girl? My brother is looking for you. What are you doing here?"

"I was going to ask you the same thing," she said. She looked angry; it was an accusation, not a comment. Alarmingly, she stepped through the door into the room.

"I don't think you're supposed to be here," Gun said. He stepped back. He almost stepped through Tiffany, who was still watering the plant. "Tiffany!" he said.

She didn't look up. The water wouldn't fall from the pitcher; it hung in the air like a clear stalk.

"What have you done to Tiffany?" Gun asked Commissary Taffeta. "How come she can't talk?"

"She never could talk."

"But I could talk to her!"

"Talk to her, then." Commissary Taffeta went to the window and turned her back on Gun and Tiffany. She lifted her tee shirt and straightened the perfect seams of her cotton panties.

"You're not even supposed to be here!" Gun said.

"You're the one that's not supposed to be here," Commissary Taffeta said without turning around. "What about Gordon's package?"

"What about it?"

"I thought you were supposed to be picking up the package for him. At the Littlest Mermaid."

"That's tomorrow."

"That was last week."

"Tomorrow was last week?" The easy eloquence, the sophisticated wit that Gun usually felt in the Dogg was gone. Now he couldn't even keep the days straight.

"Let me show you something," Commissary Taffeta said. She walked through a white paneled door across the room, and Gun followed. He looked behind him and saw Tiffany, still standing, still pouring.

They were in a round room with a stone floor. A row of windows overlooked banks of clouds. Commissary Taffeta's tee shirt was shorter and she was wearing white cotton bikini panties accented with little white satin bows.

"Where's Tiffany?" Gun asked. "What have you done with her?"

"I don't have to do anything with her. She'll stay put," said Commissary Taffeta. "Come on, we're not there yet."

She ducked through still another door and Gun followed; he couldn't seem to help it. He was in a dome shaped room with windows only at the top. Through them Gun could see stars. In the center of the room a fat man, as large as a chevrolet, sat on a . . .

"Not here!" said Commissary Taffeta, pulling Gun back through the doorway.

"What was that?" he asked.

"Nothing." She looked scared. They were in a bare room with a painted wooden floor. Commissary Taffeta tiptoed across the floor to a window of glass so new that it still had labels stuck on it. The sky outside was blue black. "Here," she said.

Far below, Gun could see clouds with lights twinkling under them.

"Is this the Upper Room?"

"Not even close," said Commissary Taffeta. But her tee shirt was gone, replaced by an almost see-through tank top with no writing on it, and an organza trimmed white lace bikini with high cut sides and a semi-thong back.

"Commissary Taffeta," Gun said, feeling inspired.

"Save your eloquence for Tiffany," she said. "I just brought you here, this high, to give you an idea of how urgent things are. There! Look over here."

The moon rose very fast over the clouds; and behind it, three almost-ruby teardrops were barely visible in the glow from the icecaps and wavetops of light-flinging Earth.

"The Peteys! The Peteys are back?"

"They will be," said Commissary Taffeta. "We're looking from a slight future angle here."

"Maybe I've been called up," Gun said. "How long has it been?"

"Too long but not that long," Commissary Taffeta said. "But things are heating up. If you could see through the clouds, you would see the fires of the Fundamentals calling out all their forces. Disney-Windows and the Sierras are doing the same. The new Protocols are expected any day now, and there is more danger of war now than ever. That's why it's important that Gordon get the package. In case you have forgotten, he is freezing to death."

"What do you want me to do?"

"What I want you to do is pick up that phone."

It was a white enamel French eggshell standup with brass trim and a delicately painted porcelain base. Gun hadn't noticed it before. As soon as he put it to his ear and heard the flat tone, he sat up, the sharp, sweet stink of Vitazine™ in his nose. The real clerk across the lobby looked up from his crossword puzzle, surprised and perhaps disappointed.

"I thought you were going to make it all the way to the Upper Room this time," he said.

TWENTY

Well, if you want to believe that story, you can.
—Roky Erickson

The Littlest was crowded with regular persons™ standing two and three deep at the bar. They were watching the news. Crowds were gathered on hillsides in Rome, Mexico City and Singapore, waiting for the three puffs of smoke that would announce the new Protocols.

But there was nothing about the Peteys; nothing about a new triad sailing out from behind the Moon. Gun wondered if he had been fooled by Commissary Taffeta. He had seen them with his own eyes, from the window of that upper room. He remembered them clearly; he was surprised to discover that he could also remember what Commissary Taffeta had been wearing. She wasn't copy-protected; did that mean she wasn't quite real?

"What'll you have, Ranger?" Joe asked.

"You remember me!" Gun said, relieved.

"It's the uniform," Joe said. "Figured you'd have your braid back by now."

"I'm—still waiting on my hearing. I came in to pick up that package I left with you last week."

"You're just a day or so late. Somebody picked it up right after I got back from my personal day. That was day before day before yesterday. And it wasn't a regular person's™ mother, either. In fact, he was wearing a suit."

A suit!

"In fact, he left you this." Joe pulled a cardboard cutout of a kneeling girl out of the cash register.

A white ticket!

"Guess you're in luck," Joe said. "Must be the hearing you've been waiting for."

Things change so quickly these days, Gun thought. The streets were quiet, but broken sticks and occasional bloodstains showed that the Fundamentals had been demonstrating up and down the avenues. The edges of the scrub guarding the entrance to the Girl were blackened with the remains of unsuccessful fires.

The plywood ramp the wheelchair man had used was gone, burned, and Gun had to climb the steps to the deck outside the main, or lap, entrance. The climb didn't bother him, even after two days in the one-third/g of the Dogg.

The only thing bothering him was his guilt. He had let Gordon down. If he had stayed in the Littlest he would have been there when Joe returned from his personal day; he would be on his way back to K-T, with the package. He might even be with Donna.

And Gordon would be—what? Not freezing, anyway.

Gun felt bad because he had been seduced; he should have known that a night in the Dogg would turn into two or even three. On the other hand, if he had done what he was supposed to do, he wouldn't have gotten the advance view of the Peteys. Plus, he might have missed his white ticket. Today's hearing should get him his braid back. Then when the Peteys did return, he would be on the shuttle list for Overworld. Then he would make it all up to Donna. One more hunt and he would share with her the pleasures of "Pirates of the Universe."

The revolving doors were shut. The glass was smeared and hard to see through; Gun could make out vague hints of movement, smoky fires, even what looked like a large beast but might have been kids having piggyback fights.

Gun pressed his white ticket against the security sector. The door revolved and he went through. He stopped just inside, letting his eyes adjust to the darkness, his ears to the noise, his nose to the smell. There were lines snaking off in every direction, but he couldn't see where they began or ended. There must be an Information line, Gun thought. But how was he to find it?

He heard a bang behind him and turned. A doggit™ was kicking the Coke machine. Money was dropping down and filling the coin return, but the doggit's™ paw was too large to get into the slot. The beast looked familiar, but didn't they all? They looked like a brother species that had been never put into production; a cancelled animal.

"Napoleon?" Gun said. The doggit™ didn't answer but nodded half comprehendingly.

Gun scooped the money—six coins, all international, with the maple leaf, and put them into the doggit's™ stained pocket. It scurried off.

"Excuse me," said a voice. It was the wheelchair man. "I remember you," he said.

"I'm here for a hearing," Gun said.

"Lucky you. You get to go up in the elevators. Napoleon here will take you. I would take you myself but I would lose my place in line. Give him a coin for his trouble."

"I don't have a coin."

"I thought I saw you taking them out of the Coke machine earlier."

"I gave them all to him already. How about this?" Gun pulled the last of Round Man's .22 shells out of his pocket.

The wheelchair man brightened. "That's good. He collects them."

Gun followed the doggit™ back out toward the outer door, and then around all the lines, which whirled out in long intersecting arcs like the arms of colliding spiral galaxies. The bank of elevators sat in a corridor in the back. A security guard in a Resistance ("Resistance to Crime is Surrender to Duty") uniform, sat on a chair between the two elevators, reading a magazine.

"Appointment number?"

"Huh?"

"Appointment number?" the guard asked, never looking up. The corridor was dark but her magazine was lighted by a strip at the top of each page.

"Oh." Gun read the number off the back of the girl-shaped white ticket. "B-289-5V-3907-HV0497-WW44L."

"Lucky you," she said. "All the way to the top. Car on the left."

Gun stepped in. There was only one button and he pressed it. "Watch the closing door," said the elevator.

It was only as the door was closing that Gun remembered the promised reward. He found the .22 shell in the bottom of his pocket and tossed it.

The doggit™ caught it in its mouth just as the door closed.

* * *

Gun breathed a sigh of relief as the door was closed. He was on his way. But his relief was quickly replaced by apprehension. There was no feeling of movement. The guard had said he was going to the top, which he happened to know was twenty stories up ("A Twenty-Story Tribute to a Storyteller's Girlhood" NG:545:98:4), but Gun never felt the anticipated extra one-half/g.

Instead, there was an instant of almost weightlessness, then a "ding"; and the door opened on a white, brightly lighted hallway with doors on either side. At the end was a picture window, and in front of the window a receptionist.

"Watch your step," said the elevator.

Gun stepped out. The door closed behind him with another soft but somehow ominous "ding." When he looked back, Gun couldn't see where it had been in the wall. He walked down the hallway toward the receptionist, and as he drew nearer he saw that she was real—unless they were making holo-receptionists that could remain opaque in direct light.

"Can I help you?"

"I have an appointment, for today. . . ." He handed her the white girl-shaped ticket.

"Wait over there, please."

Three chairs stood in a semicircle under a big oval (eye-shaped?) window. Gun was too excited to sit. He was at least twenty stories up, probably in the very head of the girl. The window looked out on Orlando, but not on the shabby Orlando Gun knew. He would have thought the view was simulated, but he had seen it before.

It was "Pirates of the Universe."

There was the Mouse, from the front, his smile crafty but benign. There was the Duck. There were the lakes filled with water and ringed with sunlit cabins and condos; the streets, curved in a gentle grid, neither straight nor twisted but something perfectly in between. From here, the newspapers on the front lawns, the birds fluttering in the birdbaths, the kids on tricycles all looked perfect, and perfectly desirable. Each house was surrounded by maple trees (no palms, no locusts); each sidewalk led to a porch overlooked by a white door with a triangular glass window. Overhead there was no dome, for it had been replaced with real sky, and the grass was as green as clover. Children played in the streets, and dogs—not doggits™—scampered about on all fours.

Gun looked for a flicker, which might tell him it was a holo, but it was steady. It was the real thing. "Pirates of the Universe." The world-famous live-in theme park open only to Sierras (High *and* low), special lottery winners, Interim government employees and selected fully vested Disney-Windows employees.

Full braid Rangers. Like himself.

He wished Donna could see it. He knew she believed in it, but he wondered if she really believed, in her heart of hearts, that she would ever live there.

Well, she would, if he got his braid back. If he got to make this last Petey hunt. He would forget Tiffany and the Upper Room; he couldn't remember her anyway. It would be Donna and Gun, all the way, happily ever after, or at least as long as . . .

"Ryder?"

Two men were standing in an open door in the hallway behind him. They had the same features and might have been brothers except that one was more black than white and the other slightly more white than black. Both were somewhere in their thirties or forties—and both wore not uniforms but bright business-alls, and the startling haircuts favored by Disney bureaucrats. One carried a briefcase and one a notebook.

Management.

One of the men ushered Gun into a room with a small table and two straight chairs, while the other closed the door behind him. Both were smiling. Then frowning.

"What can we do for you?" asked the man by the door. He set his briefcase on the floor.

"Do for me? This is my hearing," said Gun. "Right?"

"Hearing," said the other man, who sat at the little table. He opened his notebook and looked inside. "It says you have a hearing coming up."

"Coming up? This is it. Isn't it?"

"This is your *preliminary*," said the man by the door. He crossed to the window. It was covered with plywood.

"You might call this your pre-hearing," said the man at the table, closing his notebook. He got up and stood by the door.

"Pre-hearing?" Gun said. "When do I get the Administrative Hold taken off?"

"Funny idea this Ranger has of a hearing," said the man at the window, who had been at the door.

The man at the door who had been at the table nodded. "Thinks *he* asks *us* the questions."

"Maybe it's the best way," said the man at the window, crossing to the table. He opened the notebook the other man had closed. "Ask us some more questions. Fire away."

"You don't understand—" Gun began, and the man by the door nodded.

"Now it's our understanding that's at fault!"

Gun shut up. Nobody said anything for a long time. Finally, the man at the door sighed, and said, "In the first place, Administrative Hold is a bipartite categorization, with two partially interlocked but fully independent elements."

"The external Administrative Hold status is automatic," said the man at the table. He rose and crossed to the window. "It's a civil sanction instituted automatically when one of our clients undertakes an unauthorized absence sequence from one of our subsidiaries, like Upstate."

"An escape," said the man at the door; he picked up the briefcase and carried it to the table.

"Well, I signed a paper that . . ."

"The Death Certificate," said the man at the window.

"Mortuaris Certificaris," said the man at the table. "That takes care of the external procedural sector of the Administrative Hold. It takes the lien off the family. It's civil, that's why it's in Latin."

"But not the Operational, which is internal," said the man at the plywood covered window. "The Operational Hold is Ranger stuff. That's why you lost your braid."

"So what do I have to do?" Gun asked.

"Do?" Neither man answered. Instead they both crossed to the window and began tugging at the plywood. Gun wondered if he was supposed to help them. He supposed not.

"There!" The plywood was off. Together, the two bright-suited bureaucrats set it on the floor, leaning it against the wall. Then one sat down at the table, while the other crossed the room and leaned back against the door.

Through the window, Gun could see the moon rising over the other Orlando, the shabby Orlando with the dried up lakes. Far in the distance, thunderheads were building into a storm over the Neverglades, the waterless virtual swamp that had replaced the one irrevocably damaged by farming and fire in the last century.

Or was it the century before?

"Disney-Windows has no interest in recapturing your cousin," said the man at the table. "Upstate was being shut down anyway. He did us a favor, hitting the road."

"We are, however," said the man at the door, "interested in learning the motives of those who helped him escape."

"And their identities," said the man at the table.

"And their intentions," said the man at the door.

"Which is where you come in," said the man at the table.

"Me?"

"What we want to know, is what everyone wants," the two men said together.

"The Fundamentals want something to worship," said the man at the table. He crossed to the window.

"The Friends want something to save," said the man at the door. He sat down wearily at the table.

"The High Sierras want something to hunt," said the man at the window.

"The low Sierras," said the man at the table, "want something *not* to hunt."

"We at Disney-Windows only want what's best for everyone."

"Which is by definition best for us."

"And for you."

"But . . ." Gun began.

"However," said the man at the window, crossing to the door, "a new problem has arisen, with the anticipation of the new Protocols."

"There have been splits in all these organizations," said the man at the table, rising to stand at the window.

"Factional splits and tactical realliances."

"Fundamentals with low Sierras. Friends with High Sierras."

"Even Friends with Fundamentals."

"Even low with High Sierras."

"None of this changes the basics, however," said the man at the door. "We know what everyone wants. Or we did."

"Everyone," said the man at the window, "but one."

"One?"

"We have reason to believe that there is a new faction," said the man at the window. "An unknown faction."

"An unknown grouping," said the man at the door. He sat at the table and opened the notebook. "A new faction said to be linked up with the info networks and the gens. Containing VR elements."

"Not really human at all," said the man at the window. "And therefore not really predictable."

"An ominous development," said the man at the table, closing the book. "Wouldn't you agree?" He got up and joined the other man at the window. They both stared at Gun as if seeking his approval.

Gun nodded. That seemed to satisfy them.

"We think they may try to contact you," said the man who had been at the table, "through your brother."

"The escapee."

"He was a Friend," said the other man. He picked up the briefcase and set it on the table. "A practiced and committed and accomplished subversive. If they broke him out, it must be for a reason."

"We need you to help us discover that reason," said the man still at the window. "Before it's too late."

"Which is why we are giving you this," said the man at the table. He opened the briefcase and took out a loop of green braid and slapped it down on the table.

"Go ahead," said the man at the window.

Gun picked up the loop of braid and snapped it into the appropriate clip on his uniform. He was a Ranger again. "So what do you want me to do?" he asked.

"Do?" The man at the table was making a check in the notebook.

"In case I am, you know, contacted. By this new grouping."

"Do what they want," said the man at the window.

"Do what they say," said the man at the door.

"That's it?"

"That's it," said the man at the window, crossing to the table and picking up the briefcase. "Do what they say. We don't doubt your loyalty since one more Petey hunt will secure your lifetime free membership in the world's only live-in theme park, 'Pirates of the Universe.' "

"We can't imagine you jeapordizing that," said the man at the door. He picked up the notebook from the table.

"Does this mean I get to go back to Overworld on the next rotation?"

"As soon as the Peteys are back," said the man with the briefcase. "The Fundamentals claim that there is a triad already here, lurking on the far side of the Moon."

I've seen it! thought Gun. But something told him not to say it.

"They are building fires to lure them out," said the man with the notebook, opening the door for Gun. "Superstition, probably. But just to be sure, all Rangers are on alert."

"Which means you mustn't leave Orlando," said the man with the briefcase, following Gun and the man with the notebook into the hall.

"Except for family emergencies," said the man with the notebook.

"Which reminds me . . ." said the man with the briefcase. He opened it and handed Gun a skull-shaped piece of cardboard. "This came for you just the other day."

A black ticket!

TWENTY-ONE

Thou must away, thy sand is run.
—Friedrich von Schiller

The funeral was everything Gun figured Ham had ever hoped it would be. Ham lay in his casket, eyes closed, dressed in a new suit with a string tie, his hair combed and his shoes shined while the preacher (ferried over from Tell City) droned on, and the two or three of Ham's old friends who had survived said a word or two. His brother and his children—all except, of course, for one—and his brother's children stood at the foot of the coffin accepting the handshakes and cold little kisses of the attenuated, diminished, impoverished community that had once been, that was still, Morgan's Ferry, K-T.

Hump and Iris, then Glenn, then Gun.

"A fine man," Gun heard for the fourteenth time. He nodded.

"A good soul."

"A fine neighbor."

"A good neighbor."

"Now he has at last found peace."

"Peace at last."

And so forth. A living funeral was a long and tedious affair for everyone but the deceased. Ham couldn't help but look excited, even with his eyes carefully closed.

"He was so thrilled," Iris said. "The winning ticket came in the lot you paid up before you left. So why are you looking so gloomy?" She gave him a hug. All was forgiven.

"I don't know," said Gun. He did know, but he couldn't tell anyone. How was he going to face Gordon? (If he hadn't already frozen to death?) How was he going to tell him he had failed to bring the package *again?*

"All his affairs are settled," said the preacher. "All the concerns that stuck to him, like burrs, shaken off. Behold a free man."

"He looks so refreshed."

"He looks almost young again."

On everyone's mind, if not their lips, was the question of the ferry. Without it, how could the town survive? And how could the ferry run without Ham out there every day, scrounging up the necessary fuel?

"We'll get by," Hump said.

"What folks don't know," Iris whispered to Gun, "is that the day Ham drew his funeral ticket, that was the third day in a row they didn't make it up to the line. The Yard's about finished anyway."

"Does Round Man know?"

"He don't care," Iris said. "He's like one of the family."

"You look so nice with your braid," whispered Donna's mother. "I knew they would delay the funeral until you got here. A fully uniformed family member is always appropriate, don't you think, Iris?"

Iris did.

* * *

Donna came on her lunch hour. She negotiated her way past the coffin with hardly a glance at Gun's father who lay there, breathing as shallowly as he could.

"There's a package for you at the store," she whispered to Gun.

Then she went back to work.

After the prayer and the invocation, and the eulogy, and the elegy, the preacher looked at his watch, and looked at Glenn, who was supposed to take him back to Tell City. There was still the reception at the house to go, but the preacher didn't have to bother with that.

The guests filed out to the street.

It was time to start up the hill toward the house for the reception. While the older folks looked on mournfully, the pall bearers bent down and picked up the coffin and raised it in one graceful swoop. Half of them were young, half old; three friends of Ham and Hump, each of whom had brought a son or a grandson.

The coffin led the way up the hill. Ham sat upright, looking backward, looking distinguished in his suit. The deceased wasn't, of course, supposed to sit up, even at a living funeral, but things that would have caused shocked whispers and disapproving looks a few years ago were now taken for granted. These were surely the Last Days. The sky was pearl-colored and low but above it, barely visible through the skim of clouds, great streaks of red and black smoke girdled the planet.

Iris and Hump walked right behind the coffin. Between them walked the doggit™, Napoleon.

Gun and Glenn were last of the family, right in front of the guests.

"That's the Fundamentals."

"Huh?" Gun turned to see Whitmer, catching up to walk beside him.

"The smoke," Whitmer said. "It's sucking the clouds away. The Fundamentals are burning Evansville. The smoke is punching a hole in the sky."

"Huh?"

"There's a *bateau* landing at Tell City. First one in years," Whitmer said. "I'm out of a job, but we're going to be seeing stars again."

At the house, Round Man opened the door in full Resistance ("Resistance to Crime is Surrender to Duty") uniform, his .22 stuck in his belt. He seemed to enjoy playing the host.

There were plates of wing meat, cakes, cookies, biscuits arranged in stars in crystal platters left over from weddings and funerals long ago. Ham was sitting up in his coffin, trying to get someone to light his Marlboro. Everyone was pretending not to notice.

The reception dragged on all afternoon. Gun had hoped to pull Glenn aside and ask him about Gordon, but when he looked up, Glenn was gone to run the afternoon ferry.

A glance from Iris told Gun that it was not a good time to leave. He decided to catch Glenn at the landing when he got back from Tell City, and go to Morgan's Cave from there.

It was almost dark before the guests were gone.

Hump lit a Marlboro and held it to his brother's lips. Ham sucked greedily.

"And where are you going?" Iris asked. "Is nobody going to be here for supper?" Round Man was polishing off the last of a casserole a neighbor had brought.

"Just for a walk," Gun said.

"Always for a walk."

Little black wings stuck out of Round Man's mouth like sharks' fins circling in a narrow sea. But his eyes were on Gun.

Gun had hardly dared hope, but there it was. Donna slid the package across the counter toward him.

It was wrapped in brown paper and tied with string.

"Where'd this come from?"

"Who knows. Came in with the morning stuff. Had your John Henry on it."

"John Hancock," said Gun. He found the tag. RYDER, GUNTHER was taped over JOE AT THE LITTLEST.

"Aren't you going to open it?"

"Maybe later," Gun said. "Give me a carton of Marlboros to go with it." Then he asked what he had come by to ask: "Can I come by later?"

"Don't see why not. It was a nice funeral. You should be proud. Isn't that the ferry horn honking?"

Gun helped Glenn unload the ferry from its last run, and they pushed off into the gathering afternoon. "This is it!" he told Glenn. "The package Gordon has been waiting for."

"Package," said Glenn.

The water smelled funny, like something far up north had died. A few logs twisted by in the swift current. So the whole town wouldn't see where they were going, Glenn pulled the *John Hunt Morgan* into one of the little drifting fog banks and slowed the 350 to a smoldering tick. Gun couldn't even see the back of the boat.

It was as if they were stopped. With the boat moving at the

same speed as the water and the fog, it was as though they sat on a pond. The water was still; the air was cold and still.

Out of sight of the town, Glenn swung out of the fog and followed the old flooded Highway 44 that cut through the once-hills, now-islands, to the back of the bluff that opened into Morgan's Cave.

The doggits™ weren't there to tie them to the bank. Gun had to jump carrying both the package and the marlboros; he almost lost his footing and almost dropped the package. Glenn tossed him the painter and stayed on the boat, as always. He had never liked the cave. He had never really liked the shore, Gun realized.

Gun climbed the loose sand slope, toward the cave entrance. At the back of the rockhouse, by the woodpile, there was a small fire, and Gun was surprised to find the doggits™ laying on their bellies, feeding sticks into the flames and smoking marlboros.

When they saw Gun coming they jumped to their feet.

"What is this?" Gun demanded.

There was of course no answer.

"What the hell's going on? You guys are burning up Gordon's wood and smoking his Marlboros?"

Fearing the worst, Gun hurriedly gathered up an armload of wood. He put the package on top of it and the marlboros on top of the package, then started down the sand-covered stairs into the cave. The doggits™ started to follow but he shot them a sharp look and they lay back down dejectedly by their fire.

Gun didn't need a light to negotiate the steps, the sandy passage, the rusted rails. But he wished he had one when he passed the Bottomless Pit. Far below to his right he could hear a scratching, distant din; it sounded like the *snik-snak* of the nanobots in the Tangle. There was a dim glow from Grant's Tomb ahead. Gun kept his eyes on it and let his feet find their own way in the darkness.

He wasn't surprised by what he found.

Gordon was gone.

The fire was low, but still burning. Had the doggits™ kept it going, or had Gordon only just stepped away?

And where had he gone?

Gun called out just once: "Gordon—!?!" But he didn't like the sound his voice made. Besides, it was dangerous. Suppose he and Glenn had been followed?

He threw some sticks on the fire, for light. The Marlboros Gordon had stacked were scattered; several were broken. Had the doggits™ come down to clumsily scavenge them, or had someone kicked over Gordon's little "cord"? Had he been found by a bounty hunter? The only one looking for him was Round Man, who was too lazy to leave the house. . . .

Was that a shout—or a bark? Could doggits™ even bark? Gun picked up a burning stick for a light and started out, past the Bottomless Pit, faster and faster. He was already running up the sand-covered wooden stairs when he heard the shots.

Two of them, close together.

Pop.

Pop.

The doggits™ lay on their backs, looking up. Their beady little eyes were wide open, as if they had just seen something scary. And, Gun guessed, they had. They had both been shot right in the center of the forehead. Their blood was darkening the sand.

"Stop right there," a familiar, unpleasant, unexpected voice said.

Gun stopped right there.

Round Man stepped out from behind one of the dusty moon-colored slabs that had fallen from the ceiling centuries ago. "Give me the Marlboros," he said. "Give me the package," he said.

Gun tossed them both at the fat man's feet.

"Now go back in and tell your precious brother to come out," he said. He waved the .22 at Gun as if it were a fan. "Don't think I won't shoot. I shot these little fuckers just for fun."

"Fun," said a voice from behind him. It was Glenn. He was carrying the Chinese-made 7.62.

"Drop it," said Round Man.

"Drop it," said Glenn, still smiling.

"I mean it! I'll shoot your precious cousin." Round Man stepped forward and stuck the cold little barrel of the .22 into the side of Gun's cheek.

Gun froze. He wondered if Round Man had reloaded since he had emptied the .22 of all but two shells.

He hoped like hell he hadn't.

"Precious cousin," said Glenn.

"I'm going to count to three," Round Man said. "One, two—"

Gun closed his eyes.

"One, two," said Glenn.

"Three," said Round Man.

Click.

Click! click! click!

Gun opened his eyes.

"Three," said Glenn.

BLAM! BLAM! BLAM!

Round Man was shaking the .22 like a bad flashlight when the top suddenly lifted off his head. Gun ducked but not before he got hit with the spray: warm blood and bone in his eyes, his nose. Then Round Man was just sitting down on the sand, surprisingly softly, and Glenn was jacking another shell into the chamber.

"Shit!" said Gun.

"Shit," said Glenn, frowning. It was a bad word, one of the words that made him frown.

There is something about a body in full/g that makes it heavier when it is dead—and Round Man was heavier to begin with. It took Gun and Glenn almost half an hour to drag him up the sand slope to the back of the cave, and almost as long to drag him down the stairs to the Bottomless Pit. They rolled him over the side and dropped the .22 after him. Gun waited to hear him hit; but it took too long and it was late, and there were still the doggits™ to dispose of.

The doggits™ were easier. Glenn and Gunther each took one. If Glenn was saddened by their deaths, he didn't let on. It was dark by the time they finished. It was after nine when they docked the *John Hunt Morgan* downtown. Gun left Glenn to tie up; he jumped off and ran to find Donna. He didn't want her to think he had stood her up again.

Mayors' was closed and locked. Gun checked down the hill at the house trailer Donna shared with her mother. The lights were off and Donna's mother sat alone, watching the wavering patterns on the TV. It was said that if you knew all the old shows, you could follow them running through one another, like morning glory vines in a fence.

"She went for a walk with Whitmer," the old lady said.

Whitmer?

* * *

Gun found her by the glow of her Marlboro. The light came on when he opened the door of the Oldsmobile. She was sitting in the front seat, alone.

"I thought you were going to wait for me," Gun said.

"I did. Here I am," Donna said.

Gun opened the glove compartment. He was afraid he would find Donna's bra, but it was empty, except for three old spark plugs.

"What're you looking for?" Donna taunted.

"Nothing."

"Well, you found it. I sent Whitmer on his way. He asked me to marry him again but I told him I was waiting on you."

"Did he tell you he doesn't have a job?" The fires down the Ohio in Evansville were staining the sky red.

"I told him we had a date."

"We did. We do. I got here as soon as I could," Gun said. He set the package on the seat between them. "Your hands are shaking," she said. He decided to tell her everything.

He told her about Gordon's escape, and the heartcuff making him colder all the time; he told her about Glenn and the 7.62; he told her about the package, and Round Man and the Bottomless Pit. He even told her about the two doggits™ each with a bullet hole above the eyes.

She already knew some of it. "I knew Gordon had escaped. I knew he was in Morgan's Cave. I knew Glenn was taking him Marlboros and he was smoking a lot. I even knew Round Man would catch up with him sooner or later."

"You knew all that? What *didn't* you know?"

"I didn't know doggits™ could smoke."

* * *

The clouds through the windshield were thin, like lace curtains. Gun could almost see stars through them.

"Maybe Gordon got away again," Donna said. "You said he had a friend. Your sister's going to be mad, though, when she finds out what happened to her boyfriend."

"He's not really her boyfriend," Gun said. "And she's not going to find out."

"Is that blood on the package?"

It was a dark brown spray. Gun tried to wipe it off but it was too late.

"What's in it?"

"I don't know. I never looked. Something to keep him warm."

"Let's look and see."

"I don't think we're supposed to."

"Says who?" Donna pulled the package away from Gun and peeled back one edge of the brown paper, exposing blue and gold braid.

"It's a uniform," she said. "How would this keep him warm?"

"A Sierra uniform," Gun said. He took the package from her and wrapped it back up. "It must have been Shorty's. Maybe Gordon was supposed to use it as a disguise."

"What are you going to do with it?"

"I don't know. Give it back to somebody. Take it back to the Littlest. It's off-Protocol for me to have it. It's off-Protocol for me to even look at it unless somebody's wearing it."

"They say the Protocols are about to change."

"They've been saying that for years," said Gun.

Donna lit a new Marlboro, then handed it to Gun. She reached up under her blouse and unhooked her bra, then pulled it out the armhole. She had never done it without the magazine before. The sky was still clearing to the north and west and east, swept by the suction created by the huge fires. Two, then three stars like fireflies appeared.

"Are those the same stars you see from Overworld?" Donna asked, as she unlocked the glove compartment and put her bra in with the spark plugs.

"I think so," Gun said.

"How many can you see from Overworld?"

"Hundreds," he said. "Thousands."

Donna was sitting with her knees on the seat and Gun could see her panties under her skirt, like a white road in the starlight.

"Tell me about 'Pirates of the Universe' again," she said.

"I saw it," Gun said. The magazine was forgotten under the seat as he told her about the trim lawns, the neat rows of houses he had viewed from the top of the Girl. "That's when they gave me back my braid," he said. "It was like a promise."

"What do you have to do for it?"

"Do? One more hunt," Gun said. "It could be any day now. That's why I have to head back to Orlando on the first smokey next week. What's that stuff in your hair?"

It was moonlight. The moon was rising in the hole in the sky, chasing the stars away. It was half full. And on the dark half was a light. No, three lights.

"Cities on the Moon," Donna said. "What'll they think of next."

Gun sat up straight. "Those aren't cities!" he said.

"Now you'll have your hunt," Donna said. They were sitting on the hood of the chevrolet, watching the firefly Peteys rise with the Moon.

"I'm afraid I've missed it," Gun said. "I'll never get back to Orlando in time. The Smokey is too slow and it doesn't leave until next week. The shuttle is probably already loading for Overworld. I am supposed to be on it."

"Does that mean we'll never get to live in 'Pirates of the Universe'?"

Gun was trying to think of an answer when he heard a familiar, unpleasant, unexpected voice: "What about the *bateau?*"

"Whitmer! Where'd you come from?"

"I've been looking around the Yard. I'm thinking of buying in with your uncle now that your father has passed away. There was a *bateau* landing this afternoon just outside of Tell City. Came in through the hole in the sky to take on ice. It's leaving early in the morning for Orlando, I heard them say. Riding the permanent weather pattern."

"Only Sierras and above can ride the *bateaux*," Gun said. "Hey! Where you going?"

He was talking to Donna, but she was already gone. She had opened the door and was already in the back seat, scrambling for the package wrapped in blood-spattered brown paper and tied with string.

TWENTY-TWO

What was it you wanted?
—Bob Dylan

The *bateaux* were avoiding their usual stops, which were crowded with refugees fleeing the Fundamental's fires. It was strange to see the quarter-mile-long vessel moored to the treetops of Tell City, like a dream that had refused to go away in the light.

The hole in the clouds was getting bigger. It stretched halfway across the sky.

Gun expected to be challenged on the ramp, but there was no security. He waved goodbye to Whitmer and Donna, and climbed the ramp. His feet, his head, his hands felt heavy; it was as if someone had turned the gravity up to one and a third. He had been up all night pacing the deck of the *John Hunt,* hurrying the adjustment of the fit-all Sierra uniform.

It was still a tight fit. His wrists and ankles stuck out like snags. He was carrying his Ranger uniform in a package, wrapped with brown paper and tied with string.

Gun had never seen the inside of a *bateau* before, but he had read about them ("Dowager Queens of the Air Lanes" NG:532:35:5). The elegant staterooms were all closed off, but the main salon was open. It was surrounded by windows. The furniture was covered with white sheets.

The wood floor was slippery, like a ballroom floor. Gun thought it was wrinkled until he realized that the *bateau* was lifting off. It was an incredibly gentle process for someone accustomed to the violence of chemical rockets. Gun wouldn't even have know they were rising if he hadn't seen trees through the window, dropping away.

He crossed to the window and looked down. It was like being in the Dogg, ascending to the Upper Room. Except that he was all alone.

The Bowsprit Lounge was filled with music and light: the energy and excitement of departure. It was crowded with transnationals in colorful business-alls, tourists (mostly French) and even a few Sierras in uniform like himself; well, not exactly like himself, since they were presumably real Sierras. The tables were filled. Gun found a seat at the bar.

The last few feet of the triangular, glassed-in prow were a dance floor, and a woman and two men were dancing. The *bateau* was rising swiftly, and it looked like they were dancing on the clouds. She wore a see-through blouse over a rose and charcoal bra that shimmered like an oil slick in the sun. Gun couldn't take his eyes off it. He was seeing someone actually wearing the most expensive substance in the world. He had always known that there were people rich enough to wear Petey skin ("Stellar Silk Stocking Set" NG:552:87:4) but he had never been this close to one before.

He could hear scraps of conversation:

"Fires even in Orlando."

"New Protocols expected any day now."

"Peteys so far out of season."

"Be the last hunt for sure."

"What'll it be?"

It was the bartender. Gun pulled out his Petey certificate and laid it on the bar. So many corners had been cut off that it was now only a little larger than a coin. But the rose engraving of the triad was still intact, and beautiful, and unmistakeable.

"I can't take that," said the bartender. "They're holding the market until the new Protocols come through. Could be worthless."

"Doesn't look worthless," said Gun, indicating the woman on the dance floor.

"Are you getting smart or something?"

"Can I buy you a beer?" Someone—or something—interrupted. The whisper was unmistakeable. It was a gen. She was sitting across the horseshoe-shaped bar from Gun. She got up from her stool and came around to sit beside him. She was wearing the sleek black skirt and black tee shirt gens always wore.

"Buy you a beer?" she asked again.

"I guess."

"What'll it be?" the bartender asked impatiently.

"Strawberry Heinie, I guess," Gun said.

"Do you always guess at everything?" the gen asked. It was a joke. Since he knew gens couldn't laugh, he laughed politely for them both.

"This your first *bateau* trip?"

He'd never heard of a gen making small talk; but if it was in the form of questions, why not?

"Yes," he said. "As a matter of fact, this is a trip of firsts. My first *bateau*, my first conversation with a gen." He smiled, feeling witty. The *bateau* was sort of like the Dogg, that way.

"Buy you another?"

"Sure," said Gun. "As long as you're paying." He laughed politely for them both.

"Are you worried about your brother?" she asked.

Gun almost dropped his beer. It was a good thing they can only whisper, he thought. "What brother?" he whispered back.

There was, of course, no answer. A gen couldn't answer questions. In fact, she seemed locked up. She sat motionless, waiting. Or paralyzed.

Gun was afraid the bartender would notice, so he whispered, "A little."

"Do you still want to help your brother?"

"I guess."

"Do you always guess at everything?"

"I guess; I mean, I—"

She reached up under her tee shirt and pulled out a card. "Have you ever seen one of these?" She showed him a Petey card. It was the same card Gordon had shown him. It even had the doggit™ tooth marks in the corner.

"Yes," he whispered.

"Do you want to go for a walk?"

It was cold and misty on the promenade that wrapped around the Main Salon. Through holes in the clouds far below, Gun could see the lights of fires. It looked like the end of the world.

It was getting dark. Gun wondered how fast the *bateau* was going. Riding a PWP (permanent weather pattern) airship was like drifting; every speed felt motionless. It was like the Universe itself. Who knew how fast anything was going? Plus, Gun was a little drunk. He held onto the railing. The gen stood beside him with the gentle apparent wind rippling her short, black hair. Gun wondered what she wore under her short, sleek black skirt and her short black tee shirt that didn't cover her no-navel.

He was tired. He wished he could ask her questions instead of just answering them.

"Are you cold?" she whispered.

He nodded.

He followed her into the Main Salon. She pulled back one of the white sheets, revealing a maroon sofa brocaded in cream with a delicate embroidered ruffle and empire legs, accented with scrollwork.

"Want to lie down?"

She lay down and he lay down beside her. The package with his Ranger uniform made a pillow for them both.

"Still cold?"

Gun nodded, or was it a shiver?

She wrapped the sheet tightly around them both. Her little body was cold. Her little hands were colder still. Gun could hear people coming and going but he could barely keep his eyes open. He hadn't slept in so long. Footsteps echoed on the two-mile-high hardwood floor. Her little hands were cold. Her little body was colder still.

Gun shivered and slept, shivered and slept. He woke up, or dreamed he woke up, several times. The gen was still questioning him in her dark little whisper:

"Are you still cold?"

"Do you want me to take this off?"

"Do you like this?"

"Do you want me to take this off?"

"Are you still cold?"

* * *

He was and he did and he wasn't. Then it was daylight. The *bateau* was descending through clouds; the big windows were streaming with smoke and raindrops and fog. Wrapped in the sheet, Gun was still shivering; his cold fingers touched a cold cheek: his own.

He was alone. The gen was gone.

He sat up, and stood, wrapped in the sheet. He was naked. His Sierra uniform was gone.

So it hadn't been a dream.

The pine forest just south of Orlando Proper was burning, sending a streamer of smoke across the dome from east to west, forcing the *bateau* to land at Port Orlando Proper instead of the closer East Side terminal.

That was better for Gun. Although he couldn't see the port because of the smoke; he couldn't tell if the shuttle had left or not.

It was all in the hands of Destiny; the cold little hands of Destiny. Gun put on his Ranger uniform while the *bateau* was touching down, then hid the bloodspattered brown paper and string under a sheet-covered chair. As soon as the ramp hit the tarmac, he was off—riding the first baggage train as if he had arrived on some other ship, from some other place.

The first thing he saw when they cleared the ramp area was the shuttle to Overworld, looming over the terminal buildings, still pointing skyward, leaking hydrogen steam, like a race horse ready to lunge.

He had made it.

TWENTY-THREE

Sleep; and high places; footprints in the dew.
—Rupert Brooke

The train from Olduvai to Cinderella was called the *Lion King*. It ran through the tubes that penetrated, through faux-euclidean and now-forgotten geometries devised by man but altered by the nanobots, the space between the Tangle and Overworld; it was the train that Gun had missed last time. He remembered following the gen through the vents: the long straight stretches that weren't, somehow, straight; the constant *snik-snak* leaking in from the Tangle. He remembered wondering what the gens wore under their sleek little skirts.

Now he didn't wonder anymore.

Though the tubes squeezed past and through unclaimed and untamed spaces, the *Lion King* itself was comfortable, modern, reassuring. There were no surprises. The train still stopped automatically for all the closed-down stations. The VR screens were blank but the robot voice still boomed, announcing the attractions that had closed down during the Three and never reopened:

"Baja Sea, Lhasa, Serengeti . . ."

"Mt. St. Helens. Watch for flying ash . . ."

There was of course no flying ash. No chanting monks, no leaping whales, no eagles.

And not many passengers. There were only two maintenance workers and a Medical on the tube train; no Sierras, no other Rangers. Gun was the only Ranger on the *Lion King*, just as he had been the only Ranger on the shuttle. It worried him. He was beginning to suspect that he had missed the Petey hunt after all. Maybe the *Penn State* was already out there, discharging its rails. . . .

"Last Stop. Cinderella. Thank you and watch your step in the reduced grav—"

Cinderella was closed off by a curved glass door. Gun pressed his palm to the glass and it groaned opened.

And he saw his first other Ranger.

And the other Ranger he saw was Hadj.

"I knew you would be on that shuttle, partner," Hadj said. "Come on, I'll buy you a tea. You're a sight for spare eyes."

"Sore eyes," said Gun. "I delivered the package—I think."

"What package?"

"The one you wanted me to deliver." Gun didn't want to get too specific, in case someone was eavesdropping. "The one you told me about through the commissary girl."

"Taffeta?" said Hadj, putting a coin into the machine. "That was her thing. I was just doing her a favor. She said she was doing a favor for a boyfriend. They say she has as many boyfriends as there are prisoners. Shit!"

The tea machine was broken; the flashing light said SORRY.

"They had me on murder."

"I thought it was questioning."

"It was. Then things got crazy."

"Why'd they let you out?"

"I'll show you. The charges are on Hold."

"I was on Hold myself. Now I'm off."

"I know. Come on."

"Where we going? What about the tea?"

"Heaven. Its broken. Can't you read anymore?"

"Isn't this the long way around?"

Sleepy was empty. Grumpy was empty. The Glass Slipper was almost empty. A few bored techs and partials were waiting around Gyro (the mechanical rec room) and Waldo (video toys); but there were no regular persons™; no Sierra uniforms; no Rangers.

"I wanted you to see how empty Cinderella was," Hadj said. "So you could appreciate what's going on."

"Where are all the Rangers?"

"They're on the *Penn State*."

"Then I did miss it. I missed the hunt!"

"You didn't miss it, not yet," Hadj said. "But there may not be a hunt. The *Penn State* is still tied up to Overworld. The Sierras and the Rangers are both claiming it. The Sierras are anticipating the new Protocols; they want to get out of the skin business. They want to capture a Petey. Drop in a moby and tow it into orbit. Use it as a power source."

"Like a motor, or a donkey?" Gun asked.

"More like a tidal mill. If it's true that the Peteys are actually pocket universes, then the differential along the interface would furnish unlimited energy. It might even work. Who knows? But Disney-Windows, as you know, is committed to stability. Which means keeping the world on a hard currency, low energy diet.

Which means the hunts. Which means the Rangers."

"But if this *is* the last triad . . ."

"Then the hunts are over anyway," said Hadj. "But it's not for us to decide, Gunther. We're Rangers, remember? We do what we're told."

"Then why are you here? Why aren't you with the rest of the Rangers?"

"Because I do what I'm told," said Hadj. "And the fact is, I'm on special assignment. Secret assignment. And so are you."

"Me?"

"That's why they took you off Hold. I requested you."

The door to Heaven was guarded by two sleeping Marines, who woke up briefly and let Hadj and Gun pass with a nod. The great open space was light blue, like the inside of a robin's egg. The curving catwalk was dotted here and there with figures, but none of them were talking. A strange silence reigned.

At first Gun thought Heaven was empty. But why would Hadj have brought him here?

Then he saw it.

At the center of Heaven, in the distance, was a star-shaped figure like a doll with outspread arms and legs. It wasn't spinning, so Gun had to walk halfway around the catwalk before he could make out what it was.

Who it was.

"Omigod," he said, to himself as much as to Hadj.

"Yep," said Hadj.

It was Shorty.

TWENTY-FOUR

Thy mouth was open, but thou couldst not sing.
—George Herbert

The difference between a hundred-foot-tall man and a three-foot-tall man is not very significant in a space as large as Heaven. Gun had covered another quarter of the catwalk before he realized they were not as close to Shorty—to Shorty's body—as he had thought.

"He's no longer so short," said Gun.

Shorty was almost thirty meters long. "Twenty eight point eight," specified Hadj. His eyeballs—as big as basketballs—were distended, and his cave of a mouth was wide open in a silent scream.

"He's a giant," said Gun. A giant regular person™. He hadn't exactly been a friend. But still . . . "What a way to die!"

They made a circle around the body. Shorty's quilted space suit long johns had enlarged to fit his body; so had his velcro sandals, each almost the size of a bathtub. His arms were outstretched like a Christ, in a yielding submission to what Gun knew was a horrible, if mercifully swift, death—the six to eight seconds in high vacuum that you live while your body is exploding. First the skin expands, becoming porous as its every cell explodes; then the liver and the lungs, the heart and the bowels all swell enormously, as the interstitial gasses rush out of your body, leaving a vacuum; then the eyes and brain expand, until you are a porous, frozen, spinning, swollen corpse.

But not this swollen. Shorty was almost half the size of a space yacht. And for some reason, he wasn't spinning.

"How could you have missed him during the search?" Gun asked.

"We didn't. He wasn't there. He floated up a week later, out of the vac. They found him out here bumping up against the station like he was trying to get in. I was in jail in Orlando, on the upper tiers, Murder One. They had to let me go."

"Let you go? Why?"

"You'll see why. Watch his eye."

Shorty's eye, which had been all the way to the left when they had come up on the corpse, was not pointing straight ahead. It had moved about a foot in the ten minutes they had been on the circular catwalk through Heaven. As Gun watched it moved still further. Toward him.

"Omigod," Gun said, for the second time that day.

"He's alive," said Hadj said. "He's still dying. It must be part of the Time displacement, from falling inside the Petey. The few seconds it takes to die in high vac have been stretched along the Time axis. He's not alive but he's not dead. He's a goner, but he's not gone. That's why they had to let me go."

"He's trying to scream," said Gun. "Why can't he scream?"

"He's already breathed high vac. We had a guy one time, we pulled him in the airlock still alive, but his lungs were just spongy sacs. His brain had already hemorrhaged out his ears. There's nothing we can do. Just let him scream and die. The thing is, Shorty's scream might last a month. Or a year. Or ten."

"Let's get out of here," Gun said. He was feeling sick. He didn't want to be on the catwalk when Shorty's panicked stare found him.

"They can't do anything about the *Penn State* until he dies," Hadj explained as they half-walked, half floated toward Heaven's exit. "The Sierras are using Shorty's death—his impending death—to sue the *Penn State* away from Disney-Windows. Negligence and so forth. The litigation is holding up the hunt. Plus, with Shorty in Heaven, there's no place to cure the skin. So everything's on Hold. That suits the Sierras just fine, too."

The Marines waved them through and Gun breathed a sigh of relief as the door to Heaven closed.

"Then what was Shorty doing? He's a Sierra. Was a Sierra."

"A low Sierra, as it turns out," said Hadj. "The low Sierras have secretly hooked up with the Fundamentals. All this Last Days shit. What they want to do is worship the Peteys, the way they worship everything. By setting them on fire." Hadj paused for affect. "Shorty was carrying a firebomb."

Hadj paused again. "Which was why I had to knock him down. Another few seconds and he would have set the *John James* ablaze and dove straight in."

"So you did kill him!"

"Except he's not dead. Now we have to kill him again."

"We?"

"Disney-Windows has decided to make a move before it's too late. How long are these Peteys going to hang around? If we get rid of the body, that will void the lawsuit and free up the *Penn State*. Plus it will take care of my legal problems. No body, no murder."

"We?"

"On the sly, of course. We can't let anyone know it was approved from the Girl. If we are caught, we are on our own."

"We?"

"Don't you think you owe me one?"

TWENTY-FIVE

Fear on guilt attends.
—William Havard

That night in his hammock Gun dreamed he was with a gen, sitting in a chevrolet, and she took off her sleek little black panties, and underneath there was another pair, even blacker and sleeker and smaller, and underneath them, even blacker and sleeker and smaller. . . .

Someone was rattling the door of the chevrolet and it was, unaccountably, Hadj.

"Come on!" Hadj whispered.

"Where?"

"To Heaven! Remember? You promised."

Promises, Gun thought, as he buttoned his quilted long johns. He made so many promises! He tried to remember the deal he had struck with Hadj. Was this going to secure his membership in "Pirates," or just allow the hunt that would secure it? *Do what they say!* they had said.

"Let's go!"

Hadj was already out the door and down the hall, pushing a

gym bag in front of him. Both Marines were asleep at the door to Heaven, and Hadj slipped inside. Gun was right behind him.

"See how easy?" Hadj whispered, closing the lens-like door. "Nobody expects any trouble."

The great round hall of Heaven was dim with night lights. Hadj pushed straight off and Gun followed. He had never been off the catwalk before, actually flying through Heaven. He could see why it had been the most popular attraction in Cinderella, before the Three. It was like the dream of flying come true.

Then, looming out of the darkness, the nightmare that was Shorty came true.

"Don't get too close," Hadj warned. "The Time dilation makes a field. If you slip under it, you might get caught. Once you are in it, even barely, the split second that you need to pull loose stretches out into an infinity—and so on and on forever. You're stuck. Know what I mean?"

"So how'd they get him in here?"

"They roped him and pulled him in here. Getting him out will be much easier."

Hadj took two E-suits out of the gym bag. Then a double-barrelled, rifle-gripped solid fuel thruster called a "shotgun." Then a coil of nylon rope.

The emergency suits—or E-suits—zipped straight up the front from the crotch to the neck, where the zipper went to the side, around the flexible faceplate, to the top of the head. The E-suit contained only the air trapped inside its trunk and limbs, with a tiny charcoal scrubber to keep the faceplate clear. No heat, no light, no life support. It was designed to be zipped on quickly in an emergency, and to give the wearer a few seconds—about a hundred—to patch the hole, find the airlock, or say his prayers.

Hadj and Gun zipped in, but left the faceplates open.

Hadj took the shotgun and handed Gun the rope.

"There's only twenty feet here," Gun said. "That's not enough to tie onto Shorty, much less pull him."

"The rope's for us," Hadj said. "And don't get so close to Shorty. The Time dilation field is thin, but powerful. Sticky."

Gun backed away, avoiding Shorty's basketball-sized eyes, filled with giant panic, worse than death.

Heaven's gate was not an airlock but a hinged door, thirty meters high and twenty across, opening directly into high vac. As a safety precaution, it took two to open it because unexpected or sudden decompression would blow everything in Heaven out into the void.

Which was exactly what Hadj wanted.

"You and I open the door," he said, "and hang on for dear life. Whoof! The decompression will blow Shorty out into space. Soon as he spins by, we shut the door."

"Whoa," said Gun. "And shut ourselves into an airless Heaven? These E-suits won't last long enough for a chamber that size to be recompressed. Plus, we'll be caught red handed."

"We shut the door from the *outside*," said Hadj. "That's the beauty of my plan. We cross the main arc of Overworld and reenter through the Evil Sister II airlock. I left it ajar."

"Evil Sister's a quarter mile away, all the way on the other side of Cinderella. We only have a hundred seconds!"

"Roped together, with the shotgun, we can make it! The Marines never saw us enter and we are back in our hammocks, asleep, when Shorty is missed."

It wasn't a bad plan. Hadj's plans never were.

But it didn't work. Hadj's plans never did.

Opening the door of a pressurized space directly into high vac has an explosive effect. The air and whatever is swimming in it rushes into the vacuum, smearing itself across the immense hole in the center of existence we call the Universe. It should have been easy. Shorty's body should have spun into the void like a disappearing coin flipped by a magician.

The problem was that Shorty's body wouldn't spin. Stretched on an extended Time axis, it had an unpredictable, quasi-newtonian inertia. From where Gun was hanging, at the outer edge of the opened door, it looked as if Shorty's left arm were moving backward through space while his right leg moved forward through Time, so that as his corpse whipped through the gate (for that part worked fine) his left leg snagged the rope and his right arm yanked it "down," pulling Hadj straight back into Shorty's chest.

Hadj! If Gun could have cried out, he would have. He saw Hadj trying to pull loose, but moving more and more slowly like a fly in sorghum molasses, each thrash of his arms slower than the one before, until he was wide-eyed and motionless, sailing straight past Gun.

Still not spinning.

Gun watched, horrified, as Shorty's corpse with Hadj stuck to it began to recede from Overworld, down toward the cloud-and smoke-smeared Earth that filled half the sky. Over a minute in high vac had passed, and though he wasn't yet desperate for air, Gun was cold; colder than cold. His E-suit was starting to flutter in and out as he breathed, closing around him like a shroud.

And Hadj was getting further and further away.

Gun felt the heaviness that accompanies carbon dioxide poisoning. He looked down into Heaven. It was still blue and still lit; but with its air gone, it was just a corner of high vac. The only refuge was at the Evil Sister II lock, a hundred seconds away.

Shorty was still speeding away, toward a lower orbit. But still not spinning. Above (or so it seemed to Gun) was the Earth. Blue and white. Below were the stars, millions of them, dazzling, dumb, like the eyes of beasts. In between was Overworld, soaring off in two directions, an arc like a planet's ring of shining steel and many-colored plastic, cylinders and toruses and cubes and tubes—all connected by a web of shadow that had grown in and around it and through it. The Tangle was as hard to see as the Earth was easy to look at; it grew wrinkled, coruscated, twisted like vine and smeared like lichen. . . .

Gun shook himself. The numbing cold was creeping from his toes up toward his knees. Hadj was finished. He was too, probably. He had waited too long. But Rangers don't just *die*. They die moving.

He pushed off the door, toward the smooth curve of Cinderella's main arc. He landed expertly on his feet and started pulling himself along an inspection cable, faster and faster. The Evil Sister II was below the horizon, a minute away.

An eternity.

And he wasn't going to make it. There was nothing behind him but high vac. Nothing to the right. Nothing to the left.

Then Gun saw it. Down between two cylinders, where shadow met shadow in a wrinkled darkness that repelled the eye. At first he thought it was a carbon dioxide hallucination. A blinking light—an erratic pattern—

And under it, no larger than an oil drum, no smaller than a

tire, hungry and dark as a beast's maw—something was moving in and out.

Gun pushed down toward it, letting his line drop.

Whatever it was, it was opening.

Whatever it was, it was his last and his only hope.

Whatever it was, he went through it.

TWENTY-SIX

O take my pretty apples, Mr. Dark!
—Kenneth Patchen

Whatever it was, it closed behind him. While it sealed (with a peculiar sucking sound) Gun unzipped his faceplate.

Whatever it was, he had to breathe it or die.

Whatever it was, it was breathable—smelly, dark, moist and life-giving.

He gasped once, twice; then started peeling off his E-suit so that he could get to his numb fingers and toes. He stripped all the way down to his quilted long-johns before he stopped and forced himself to take a look around.

He was in the Tangle. The idea itself was scary.

He took a deep breath, a Ranger breath, trying not to look too hard at the shapes around him. Trying not to remember the stories of the men who had seen the Tangle and gone mad.

The first thing Gun noticed (other than the fact that he could breath) was the noise. The *snik-snak* was now a buzz, a din, a constant racket.

The next thing he noticed was the cold. Everything in space

was cold but this was a different cold. This was a *living* cold; the cold of things that are born cold.

The next thing he noticed was the smell. It was electrical and biological at the same time. It was a fire smell. It made his heart pound; it made his muscles tense and his breath short. It made him want to run, and there is no way you can run in zero/g.

The next thing he noticed was that someone was watching him. Someone or something.

A gen? She was gone around the corner before he could be sure he had seen anything. But there had been something or someone there: a flash of black eyes, and black, sleek short hair.

Leaving the remains of his E-suit by the "airlock" so that he could find his way back, Gun groped his way toward the not-quite-corner. It was hard to judge distances here. Just to be safe, he looked back before he had gone more than a few steps.

The E-suit and the "airlock" were gone. The corridor branched a different way.

He turned again, and the not-corner where he had not-glimpsed the not-gen was now a long corridor. A not-corridor, curved and not-curved. Something was moving far ahead. Gun got a glimpse of black.

He had no choice but to follow.

The din got worse, and still he followed. The cold got worse, and still he followed.

He was in a panic but he was afraid to stop and examine it. He wasn't sure if he was breathing or not. He studied the back of his hand and it fluttered in the polarized light, taking up two or three positions at once.

A black eye flashed. He followed.

The din around him was almost an alarm; a sound that awakened some deep antipathy, some warning of danger coiled waiting in the genes themselves; a combination of a squealing and a scurrying. It came from the shadows.

Gun was only just beginning to notice the shadows. They were everywhere, and yet nowhere. They scurried so fast, and were so *indeterminate* in form, that Gun couldn't actually *see*, only see where they had been.

He knew what they were, though: the nanobots. They had designed themselves to turn the eye away, so that Gun didn't even notice them until he had followed the gen, assuming it was a gen, for what seemed a long time.

Time? Time here seemed like Time in the Dogg, circular instead of linear, not flowing but sitting still, like water in a pond. And Gun felt like the stone that had broken its surface; that his actions were rippling not only ahead but behind as well, changing his past as well as his future.

The bots were always just ahead or just behind; it was almost impossible to look directly at them. Only once did Gunther manage. He got a glimpse of something between cloud and swarm, something turd-sized and gray, slick as new plastic, with a blur of worrying legs which enabled it to operate in or out of gravity. The legs kept the bots nailed to whatever was around; they were surface creatures only, and Gun was glad. How terrifying would the Tangle be if he had to worry about bots squirming through the air in front of his face?

Another corner that was not a corner. Black eyes. "Where are we going?"

How foolish! To question a gen.

She was in an intersection, a junction where two—or was it three?—half-lit hallways came together. The geometry was all shifting planes and fields, and Gun forced himself to look away.

She pushed off again and Gun followed.

In, out, around. Under, through. The corridor wasn't straight, or curved; it enjoyed some proprietary geometry of its own, which gave it curves without circularity, and slopes without horizons. There seemed to be no horizons in the Tangle. Everything was always almost seen, and yet . . .

There was a turn and another turn and then another turn, but he could see them all, still behind him. The geometry of the Tangle seemed not so much non-euclidean as anti-euclidean, deliberately obfuscatory; it was a defensive geometry, designed to fractalize with difficulties in response to attempts at penetration.

There was no light, yet it wasn't quite dark. Light always seemed to be coming from somewhere that was never reached. It seemed to leak in around the off-sized intersections, each with its own size of pipe and its own, new din. And always underfoot there was scurrying, which at first unnerved Gun, until he grew accustomed to the shadowy scurrying along the walls, leaving trails of shining spit.

Snik-snak.

Snik-snak.

And it was all on fire. The fire smell of the Tangle was like the true smell of the Universe, half burned and half built. All along the walls were little clouds of creatures, forming and unforming: slickering, slobbering, sawing, healing, stripping, painting, lapping up liquids and polishing.

Snik-snak.

Snik-snak.

Light leaked down through a long grill at the top of the corridor. Behind the grill Gun could hear music, and gunshots; perhaps a movie. A laugh track? Then it was gone.

They traversed corridor after corridor, intersections coming one upon another like knots upon a string; no rooms, no chambers—just spaces half-glimpsed in passing.

The din grew lower and louder as they penetrated deeper into the Tangle. The faint, gray smell seemed almost sweet. But where was it leading? Where was she leading him?

"I have to go to the bathroom."

She stopped. After a few moments, Gun realized she was waiting. Gun pulled himself to a corner and peed into the half-darkness, onto a curved, creaking wall. Immediately a scurrying cloud appeared out of the darkness, and cleaned up the smear of urine by running back and forth across it like an eraser.

Snik-snak.

They will make it into water, Gun thought. Or into tennis shoes or rocket fuel or air or whatever it was that they needed. Or did they just dump it and steal what they needed from Overworld?

Gun let his mind go blank, following her through a long jumble of pipes so narrow that he had to stretch prone and pull himself through.

Why did he feel so at home here?

It was the gravity; there was at least one-third/g in the pipes.

The gen had stopped; beyond her was a long tubeway and at the end of it, an arch, upside down; but as she and Gun approached, their footsteps sought the sides and then the top of the tube, and the arch righted itself.

Then she was gone.

Gun was in a round chamber, shaped like a hershey's kiss or a woman's breast. It was almost euclidean. On the ceiling at the top, dim shapes floated under what seemed to be stars.

On the floor in the center was a man.

Sort of a man.

TWENTY-SEVEN

God hates those who praise themselves.
—St. Clement

I *keep it sort of euclidean in here*, a sort of voice sort of said.

The sort of man was sitting on a sofa in the center of the room. The gen was sitting on his lap.

How do you like it?

"I like it," Gun said.

He supposed he was talking to a fat man, a fatter than fat man, in an unfamiliar yellow uniform on a brocaded couch in the center of the room. Gun walked around him, enjoying the feeling of gravity. It was only about one-third/g, like the Dogg. The room might have been sort of euclidean, but only sort of, for wherever Gun moved the big man was facing him.

Sort of facing him—for he didn't have much of a face. He didn't have any eyes or mouth, only shadowy holes. His nose and the rest of his face looked normal; normal, that is, for someone at least twice the size of Round Man. He was about the size of a small chevrolet, with wispy yellow hair and a wispy yellow beard. His uniform was the same color—the color of urine on snow ("The Timberwolf Surveys His Domain" NG:453:87:9).

"I've seen you somewhere," Gun said. "I know I have."

Not likely.

"It was in the Dogg. I was with Commissary Taffeta."

You mean her.

"Where?"

Up there. I keep a little zero/g for my friends. The gen on the fat man's lap was pointing toward the ceiling of the room—a dome of segmented glass, where two figures floated like goldfish in a bowl.

One was Commissary Taffeta, wearing her Orlando tee shirt. Beside her, wearing Shorty's old Sierra uniform, was Gordon. They were floating face down, side by side. Gordon's eyes were closed.

"Gordon!" said Gun. He felt an enormous sense of relief. "Is he okay? He's alive?"

Now that's a hard one even for me, and I'm a professor. Alive? They've taken his heart out. But they're putting another one in, I think.

Gordon's tunic was half unbuttoned, and Gun could see a gray shadow on his chest. It seemed to be moving; he didn't want to look too close. *Better let him sleep.* Commissary Taffeta was holding Gordon's arm by the wrist, as if it were a stalk. Her slate-blue eyes were open but she seemed to be dozing too.

She brought him here, Gun thought.

Like I brought you here, said the fat man.

"You can read my mind?"

Of course not. You were about to ask the question. It was already formed in the prelarynx; the virtual larynx in your brain. The same way you can hear me without ears.

"I have ears," Gun said.

What I mean is, you don't hear me through your ears. You hear me through your eyes. All the ears do is wiggle little bones that excite a nerve. I excite the same nerve visually and make you hear.

"With what?"

Nothing you're conscious of. Try closing your eyes.

Gun closed his eyes. If the professor said anything, he didn't hear it. Big deal, he thought.

He opened his eyes. *It might not seem like such a big deal to you. It won me tenure.*

"Who are you?" asked Gun.

Hadn't you better ask first, what I am? For as you can see, I am not exactly a man.

"What are you, then?"

I am the George and Marge Crane Memorial Chair Endowed Professor of Virtual Linguistics at Pennsylvania State University.

"Quite a title," said Gun.

The gen on the professor's lap sat toying with the buttons on his tunic.

I have a name, too. It is Edward Labland Gabbard, Ph.D. But my friends call me God.

Apparently that was a joke. Chuckles ran under the professor's voice like a laugh track. They seemed to come from the professor himself.

"What do you want with me?"

I admire your directness, said the professor. *A rare quality here in the Tangle. I want your company, for one thing. I have been alone these many years. Gens are cute but they're not good company. They can't laugh.*

"What do you want with me?" Gun asked again.

People think they are smart, and they are indeed wonderful, but there are serious deficiencies in how they operate. Not reading, for example. It is not beyond their capacities but quite beyond their desires. They also don't like heat. So we don't know much about how the common people in Southeast Asia live, those who have remained in the flooded river valleys. We don't even know what the Dutch do in the summer.

"Is there any water here?" asked Gun. He reached behind himself as unobtrusively as possible, and ran his finger along the wall. It was damp; wet, even.

He smelled it. It smelled electrical.

And they never sleep, which means they never dream. How much can you know about people if you don't know their dreams? What in the world are you doing?

"I'm thirsty," said Gun, licking his finger.

That's disgusting.

"Maybe she could get me some water." Gun nodded toward the gen who sat silently on the professor's lap.

They don't fetch.

"That's who you are, isn't it? You are the scientist who designed the gens?"

No, not really. I was not part of the team that built the gens. I was a graduate student at Penn State, majoring in Linguistic Engineering, when I was given a part-time job with Dr. Singh's team that was putting together the gens as a history project. Biogens Historicum. They didn't come out of Engineering, you know. Singh and his "singers" (that was what they were called) were all a bunch of Humanities majors. They would get an Engineering student on loan when they had to "tweak the chips" as we called it in those days. What I did was get rid of their laugh. Didn't I, honey?

The professor was rubbing the gen's little shoulders through her tee shirt with his big, yellow-stained hands. She leaned back against his chest.

"Gens don't laugh," Gun said.

They did at first. Singh figured that if they listened too long without laughing, or at least smiling, people would stop talking. This would cut down on their information gathering. So he designed them with a polite laugh. You can imagine the problems that caused.

The gen leaned back against the professor's chest. Gun had the feeling she would have closed her eyes if she could.

Having no sense of humor, they laughed at everything. They couldn't tell the difference between sad and funny, and there was no way Singh could teach them because he didn't have a sense of humor either. It was a joke—pardon the joke. So I was hired to delete the laugh. It wasn't such a big deal. There were only forty-four gens—we called them The Four and Forty—and when you tweaked one, you had tweaked them all.

"Were?"

Several were lost in the war.

The gen on the professor's lap looked up into the shadowy ruin that was his face. Then she settled back into the hollow of his armpit.

Does that surprise you, that I am old enough to remember the Three?

Gun shrugged. Somebody that big, you didn't think about whether they were old or young.

The Three. The world war, we called it, because for the first few months it was fought, contrary to all arrangement, on the world; on the surface of the earth. Singh was killed, as were most of his "singers," during the Siege of State College. Those that weren't killed were captured and never heard from again. One hates to think of what happened to them. Humanities students tend to fight on the wrong sides in wars.

"I want to wake up my brother," said Gun. He was tired of

listening to the professor's stories. He was careful not to say it, though, even silently to himself. He didn't want to seem rude.

Better wait until you are sure they are finished. The bots are very conscientious. Look what they have done for me!

Gun couldn't tell if the professor was joking or not. His eyes and mouth were squirming masses, like ash-colored worms.

Where was I? Oh, yes. The singers. They stopped singing. I came out all right. I was Engineering, you see. I was on the right side—and later went on to become a full tenured professor, as you can see from my uniform. Oh, I know, the university has long since been destroyed, but since it was a chair with lifetime tenure I feel justified in wearing it. Wouldn't you? Are you sleepy?

Gun sat up and shook his head. "Just resting my eyes."

If you close your eyes you won't be able to hear me. I also wear the uniform because they like it. I was wearing it when they kidnapped me, wasn't I, honey? Oh, don't look so sour. They hate it when you ask them questions. The gens kidnapped me. It was just after the Three. I was up here with a Penn State team, under contract to Disney-Windows as a matter of fact (I know you are a braid Ranger) trying to determine what part of Overworld could be sealed off and salvaged from the Tangle and the self-replicating nanobots. I was just married and just beginning my career but what did they care? They wanted me.

"The bots wanted you?"

The gens. The gens. The bots don't want anything. Does hair want to grow? It just grows. They just scuttle and repair. Simple instruction sets, low profile stuff. They replicate themselves and replicate the station, but they don't know what they are doing.

No, it was the gens that wanted me. Consciousness was an unexpected side effect of the laugh deletion. During the war they were able to use it to link up with the orbital defensive satellite systems. A link with the bots was easy after that. They are all part of the same consciousness now. It happened when they stopped laughing. I wonder sometimes. Was it really something I did?

The gen was snuggled up under his huge armpit. Her sleek, short black skirt had hiked up so Gun could see the black triangle of her underpants.

They thought so. That's why they wanted me. They literally thought I had created them. They still do. I have never been able to convince them otherwise.

The gen was pressed against the professor's chest, looking up at his ruined face adoringly.

They worship me.

"He talks too much," said a voice from the ceiling. A real voice. "Close your eyes, Gun, and we can talk."

TWENTY-EIGHT

A small shy plant called reverence.
—Oliver Wendell Holmes, Sr.

Can he hear us?"

"I don't know," Gordon said. "But we don't have to listen to him. I listened to him for two days after I got here. I've heard his whole story."

"How did you get here?"

"C-T helped me. The gens helped me. The uniform helped me. I couldn't have done it without you, little brother. You and C-T."

"Are you, is your heart—fixed?"

"I feel better. Help me down."

"I'll have to open my eyes."

"It's okay. He's asleep. He falls asleep when he stops talking. It's a neat trick. You close your eyes—and he falls asleep!"

Gun opened his eyes. It was true; the professor was slumped over, snoring softly. Gun jumped up and gave Gordon a tug. They floated down together, landing softly side by side on the glass-block floor. Lights twinkled vaguely underfoot. The same lights twinkled through the glass dome on the ceiling.

"They are same stars seen from two different sides," Gordon said. "That's how twisted the Tangle is."

"You do pretty good in zero/g," Gun said.

"I practice," Gordon said. "I practiced for ten years in my dreams. And now here I am!"

"What about her?" Commissary Taffeta lay floating face down in the pocket of zero/g under the ceiling. She was vague around the edges; Gun couldn't see her underpants or read the writing on her tee shirt.

"Let her be, for now. Let her rest. The Tangle is not real, but not virtual either, and it's a strain for C-T. She cycles down to eight bits when she doesn't have to be seen. Gets a little flickery. I'll wake her when it's time to split."

"You're not shivering anymore." Gun was astonished at how glad he was to see his brother alive. Gordon's face was still pale but his eyes were flashing like they flashed in the old holos at home.

"No way. The bots did their magic on me."

"A new heart."

"A tidal heart." Gordon buttoned the tunic of his Sierra uniform. "No pump but a tilting chamber. Say, is there any water around here?"

"I asked," Gun said. "He just said the gens don't fetch."

"He's full of shit," said Gordon. "But let's don't wake him up." They tiptoed past the great mound of flesh and synthetic nanoflesh that lay quietly snoring in the center of the room. The gen had disappeared from his lap. Shadowy ropes were wrapping around his mouth and eyes.

"He'll sleep a while," Gordon said. "They're doing some kind of renovations on him."

"What happened to the gen?"

"Even they need a break sometimes. The professor thinks the gens were created by him—though he pretends he doesn't—and it is true they love him in a weird, sick way. But actually, his tweak was only a small part of the reason they began to develop consciousness. The real reason was, they had been contacted from the Other Side."

"The other side?"

"The Peteys. Here we go. Water."

Gordon had found a plastic pitcher. It was half full. There were no glasses so he drank from the spout and passed it to Gun.

"The Peteys," Gordon said again. "They reached through, into this universe, and called forth a new creature. A negentropic, non-biological emergent consciousness. The bots are like the blood cells, repairing, circulating, stealing food and supplies and oxygen—necessary for their life as well as yours. The gens are the senses, you might say. Gathering information."

Gun pointed at the snoring professor. The nanobots had completely wrapped his face and neck in shadow. "The brain?"

"You flatter him. If this emergent system has a brain I suspect it's somewhere in the orbiting satellite weapons platforms; wherever the gens information is collected. My guess is that the professor is the retrieval code; the directory. But he's definitely part of the system."

"And me? And you?"

"I'm just a visitor," Gordon said. "A hitchhiker."

"And her?"

Gordon finished off the water and set down the pitcher, upside down. He looked up toward Commissary Taffeta. "She and I figured it out together. When Disney acquired Upstate, they ran the commissary VR through a leased broad band signal, and there was leak-through. Commissary Taffeta and I were able to tap into everything that the gens had gathered. We traced it all back to the Peteys. Did it ever seem strange to you that the Peteys first appeared right after the Three, just when the Tangle had managed to seal itself off from Overworld?"

Gun shrugged. What good did it do to think about things that had already happened? "I thought you said the Peteys created the gens."

"It's more dialectical than that," said Gordon. "The Peteys themselves may have been called into being by the new consciousness encircling the Earth. Being calls to being. The anthropic principle is reversible, like gravity, not irreversible like Time. Know what I miss most?"

"Miss?"

"Marlboros. Even though I'm not cold anymore, I would kill for one. Oh, well! Where I'm going . . ."

The gen walked into the room wearing an E-suit and carrying one on each arm. "Look what she brought us," Gordon said.

"I thought he said they don't fetch," Gun said.

"What does he know? They fetched me. They fetched you. And now they are about to fetch a whole universe. Help me put this thing on. I don't know how they work."

"You don't need that. It's an E-suit, for high vac. For outside."

"That's where we're going. That's where you're going, brother. We are going to complete what the gens have started. We are going *into* the Petey."

TWENTY-NINE

Fire!
—Trad.

The *snik-snak,* which had receded into the background while Gun was in the professor's semi-euclidean chamber, was louder here in the corridors of the Tangle. "Where are we going?" he asked; then shut up, remembering how stupid it was to ask a gen a question.

The gen was in a big hurry, and Gun had been told by Gordon to follow her. "She knows the program," Gordon had said. It had been useless to protest, and resistance was out of the question. Whatever the program was, Gun was part of it. He had no other way out of the Tangle. He was completely at their mercy.

Even if the program was suicide. For that's what it seemed like to Gun. *Into a Petey?*

The gen and Gun were both wearing E-suits, open at the top with the faceplates dangling. He followed her around corners that straightened into corridors and through tunnels that tied themselves into escher loops; past open grates that dribbled music and under pipes that sucked steam. The fire smell and the *snik-snak* were the only constants.

They came to three doors, each between itself and the other two, and stopped. Even though the Tangle was mostly zero/g, Gun could usually find a little pocket of gravity in which to stand; it was easier than trying to float.

The doors were welded shut, so Gun knew that they led into Overworld. He expected the gen to come up with a torch, or some kind of laser cutter. But it was the bots that did it, rippling round the middle door like a shadow shiny with spit.

There was a sudden flood of photons, and Gun saw the familiar orange and blue hallways of Cinderella. He even recognized where they were—halfway between the Glass Slipper and the embarkation gate where the *John James* and the *Henry David* used to tie up.

The gen pushed off and floated through.

Gun followed just in time; for when he turned and looked behind him, the wall was already stitching itself shut with a chewing sound, a *snik-snak* that sounded out of place in the familiar, homelike halls of Cinderella.

Overworld! After the dizzying confusions, the cold and the din of the Tangle, it should have felt like home. Yet Gun felt nothing but panic. He was an intruder, out of uniform and off-Protocol. And his panic underwent a sudden and steep intensification when two Marines suddenly came stumbling around the perfectly normal-looking corner.

They saw the gen and Gun at the same time, and made the mistake of concentrating their attention on Gun. "Restricted zone!" one cried out, as they both reached for their phones.

"Who says?" asked the gen: her first question in days as far as Gun knew; maybe weeks or maybe hours, since Time was erratic in the Tangle. But she didn't wait for an answer.

She reached for one Marine and broke his neck.

She reached for the other Marine and broke his neck.

Gun gagged but managed to swallow it; a Ranger trick. The gen was already gone, around the corner, heading down the short hallway toward the embarkation lock. One gate was sealed shut with black mourning tape. The other was open. Through it was the *Henry David*.

The gen was already inside. "Which of these closes the door?" she asked, running her cold hand along the control panel.

Gun could hear shouts back up the corridor. Without answering her, he closed the door, and hit the switch that would cut them loose. Banking off the ceiling, he dropped himself into the pilot's barca. Clearly, he was supposed to drive; he knew that even before the gen asked, "Can you drive this thing?"

Behind him before the door leased shut Gun could see the two dead Marines twisting in the air like bad dancers.

"You killed them!" he said.

The gen strapped herself into the barca beside him. Her faceplate dangled like a dead extra head. "What's killed?" she asked almost with a grin.

Using compressed air, Gun maneuvered the *Henry David* along the smooth steel and plastic rim of Overworld until he could see the mottled, hard-to-look-at edges of the Tangle. Behind him, though he couldn't hear them, Gun knew that the hallways of Cinderella were ringing with sirens and claxons. Murder! Theft!

Sierras! Rangers! Marines!

Once he had been a braid Ranger, one of them; now he was an outlaw, a thief. Worse than that. An intruder in his own universe. A denizen of the Tangle. He suspected the gen had killed the Marines to keep him from deserting; he was now an accessory to murder. Murder One.

The gen leaned up toward the faux windscreen, and Gun followed her pointed directions, scooting the sleek little yacht up and around the top of Overworld, then down into the scribbly shadowy corners between the modules, until:

"See the light?"

"You're getting downright talkative," Gun said. But he saw it: It was blinking over a sphincter-shaped, Chevrolet-sized hole at the edge of the Tangle. He pulled to within twenty yards.

Gun understood now why they were wearing E-suits. The *Henry David,* like its late sister yacht the *John James,* was designed so that an entire side could slide open for emergency pickups. It meant decompression, but it was essential for large items.

And it was a large item they were about to pick up.

"Know how to work your E-suit?" Gun asked. No answer, of course. He could only assume she did.

Gun put one hand on his own facemask zipper, and one hand on the side door lever, and waited and hoped for the best.

The sphincter lens in the Tangle had started out as part of Overworld, but had been forgotten and sealed off over the years as the Tangle grew over and around it.

It was still an airlock at heart, though: under the gray caress of the nanobots it groaned, it grimaced, it grunted as it grew larger; it ground glass and synth into a dust that flew off into the void, solidifying in the cold as it joined the rings within rings of debris that surrounded Overworld.

From Gun's point of view, it puckered outward.

It gave birth.

"Close up!" Gun closed his facemask with a single expert motion—and saw the gen do the same—while he pulled the lever to open the door. There was a sigh of air and a great cold silence.

Ten seconds and counting. Gun was just starting to feel the freeze when he saw a giant form expelled into high vac. It was star-shaped and spinning: it was the professor wrapped like a mummy in a nanobot spiderweb. Something was on his back, like a backpack.

Can you catch him? The gen was trying to speak behind her facemask.

Catch him Gun could. And did. Maneuvering with his compressed air thrusters; wearing the trim little Sierra yacht like an outfielder's glove ("National Pastime Survives in Old-Timers' Memories" NG:554:87:9), he backed up, spun left, eased back to cushion the blow—and caught the professor in the open side of the little yacht.

Easy enough for a braid Ranger. The yachts were like the rails, and the rails were like anything else in zero/g: just a matter of instinct and feel.

Gun felt the shock as the professor's giant body hit the far wall. His hand was already on the lever to shut the door, and he tore off his faceplate as soon as he saw a hint of fog; so that he could hear the clicking solenoids and oxygen *hissing* in. It was bitter cold but he could breathe.

Then he saw what the professor had been carrying on the back like a backpack. It was Gordon. His arms were locked around the professor's neck and his face was turning blue. He didn't know enough to unzip his E-suit so he could breathe, so Gun did it for him.

The gen was shivering in a little ball in her barca. Gun helped her unzip her faceplate. She kicked her way to the back, where the professor was floating unconscious.

Gun stuffed Gordon into the gen's just-abandoned barca and showed him how to hold still in zero/g by wedging his heels under the rails.

"What about Commissary Taffeta?"

"C-T? What about her?" Gordon asked.

"You left here there in the Tangle? After all she did for you?"

"This is the real world," Gordon said. "She can't survive out here. Let's go! Let's go!"

THIRTY

Leave the fire ashes; what survives is gold.
—Robert Browning

What are all the lights?" asked Gordon. It was his turn to ask the questions.

"Alarms!" said Gun.

Overworld was lighted up for miles.

The professor was crumpled in the back of the *Henry David*, shivering. The shadows that had wrapped him were withdrawing back into his mouth and eyes. The gen had taken off her E-suit and wedged herself between his chest and his arm. She was shivering with him.

"What about the *Penn State?*" asked Gordon.

"The *Penn State* is already headed for the Petey range, loaded with the rails and the Rangers and the Sierras, High and low. Hadj cleared the way for that."

"Hadj?"

"My old partner."

"How long will it take us to get to the Petey range?"

"At conservatory speed, a day and a half; this little ship

doesn't have enough fuel to go out and return at full speed."

"We don't need to return."

"I was afraid you were going say that. Six hours, then."

Gordon looked over at his younger brother with a proud smile. "I never saw you in command of a ship before. It looks good on you."

It was illegal under several separate sections of the Interim Protocols to fire primaries within a hundred meters of Overworld; and even in an emergency, even fleeing, even chased, even headed for another universe, Gun had been a Ranger too long to break that rule and blast away. He used twenty minutes of precious time and almost the last of the *Henry David*'s hydrazine to align the yacht for a lower orbit, before he fired.

Gordon understood all that. What he didn't understand was the lower orbit.

"How come we're going down instead of up?"

"I want to check up on a friend," said Gun. He slid the throttle forward as he crossed the terminator, and was up to speed by the time Overworld fell behind, over the dark horizon.

Fire, said the professor. The gen was warming her cold hands under his tunic, an adoring look in her black eyes.

"He's coming out of it," said Gordon.

The Fundamentals have it right. That's why they are lighting fires all across the globe. Fires were the first discovery of mankind.

Through the faux windscreen of the *Henry David*'s bridge, lights could be seen all over the dark planet below: lights where the cities and forests used to be, lights where the plains were mixing grass and wind into flame.

"What are we looking for?" asked Gordon.

Before tools. Before language. It's fire that shaped man in the shape of the Gods.

"We're looking for Hadj," said Gun.

"Your old partner."

"Right."

"Why?"

It's fire that brought humankind here, to high earth orbit, looking down, and it's fire—the internal, tiny electron fires that rage through the transistors—that created the Overworld and the Tangle, the bots and the gens. Ultimately, it's fire that created a whole new kind of life. Negentropic, not biological life. The professor's head lolled against a bulkhead. His eyes were closed.

"There," said Gun, pointing ahead.

"That's him?"

"That's Shorty; that's Hadj in the E-suit clinging to his chest," Gun said, closing in and catching the giant corpse in the *Henry David*'s searchlight.

Shorty still wasn't spinning. A corona of ionized air was glowing around Shorty's head, already lighting Hadj who was looking out (as far as Gun could tell) into space. Soon they would both be glowing with the heat of atmospheric reentry.

"He's dead! They're both dead."

"More or less," said Gun.

"So why are we here?"

"To say goodby."

Fire! said the professor.

"They'll burn up in the atmosphere," said Gun. "It might take a few days."

"Days!?!"

"Or weeks . . ."

A slow explosion. Farewell. . . .

Fire! said the professor.

"Shouldn't we . . ." Gordon began. Gun shut him up by aligning the *Henry David* for another burn. "If the triad is where I think it is," he said, "We'll come in on the near side of the Petey range."

"In how long?"

"Four hours tops."

"You're the boss," Gordon said.

Gun didn't believe it for a minute.

Four hours is a long time in a small yacht going full blast. It gets hot. Gun unzipped his E-suit. The gen slipped off her skirt. But Gordon's teeth were chattering.

"You're shivering! I thought they gave you a new heart."

"It's tidal."

"It's a gravity heart? It doesn't work in zero/g!?!"

"It's tidal for Time. It doesn't work in newtonian space. Nothing is circulating."

Gordon let Gun place his hand against his forehead. It was as cold as a gen's kiss.

"I'm freezing!"

It's a form of worship, said the professor.

"What's he raving about?"

"Talking to himself. Turn up the heat."

The Fundamentals want to worship them. The fires are to attract the Peteys, draw them closer. The Sierras want to capture them—

"And we want to kill them," said Gun.

"We?" Gordon asked, shivering.

"Disney-Windows. The Rangers. Me. We've been killing them all along."

Not really, said the professor. *You've been taking the skins. But the skins are not part of the Petey at all. The skins are part of this universe. They are in fact, the very fabric of it.*

"How do you know?" Gun asked.

Because I am the fishermen. You've heard of fishers of men? I am a fisher of Universes.

Some fisher, Gun thought. But the professor didn't look so bad. The nanobots had quit working on his eyes. They were bright blue.

"Turn up the heat!"

I fish with desire.

The *Henry David* grew hotter and hotter inside, but Gordon shivered harder and harder. The gen took off her tee shirt and let it float up toward the ceiling; she cuddled up in the professor's arms in her sleek black bra and panties.

I gave the gens their desire. I gave the Peteys their desire.

"What do the Peteys desire?" Gun asked.

Us. The gen took off her tiny, sleek black bra. Under it was a tinier, sleeker, blacker bra.

Or more properly, our Universe.

"Our Universe?"

They need a piece of ours. A seed. A cutting. It's the heart of the anthropic principle. There are other universes spawned all this time, either from within this one, or outside it, but they don't last. To last they need to be perceived.

Gordon was floating up out of his chair, unconscious.

"Wake up!" Gun said. "we are almost there."

In the back, in the professor's arms, the gen was peeling off her sleek little black panties. Under them she wore sleeker, blacker, smaller panties.

"Gordon, wake up," said Gun. "There they are."

You have seen pictures . . .

THIRTY-ONE

Wheels and wheels and wheels spin by.
—Vachel Lindsay

You have seen pictures, but no matter how many pictures you may have seen, they never prepare you for the real thing, in the flesh, so to speak; in the glory; swimming up out of the darkness in which the stars themselves swim.

Gun couldn't decide which was more wonderful to watch: the Peteys in triad or Gordon's face awash with the light of amazement. "They are as beautiful as I dreamed they would be," Gordon said, still shivering.

The triad was soaring slowly in formation across the dark face of the "new" moon, talking in colors, left to right, storm to crackling storm. Each flash of lighting was a thousand kilometer cry that filled the entire sky.

The one in three. The three in one. The mystery of the trinity.

"Are they always this beautiful? Every year?" Gordon asked, still shivering.

"Every year is the same."

Every Petey is the same. They are not separate in space or Time.

This year's Peteys, last year's Peteys—that's all illusion.

"The hunt is not illusion," Gun said. "The skins aren't illusion." He fingered his cut-down Petey certificate in the breast pocket of his long johns. He thought of the woman at the Bowsprit Bar and her shimmering oil-slick bra.

The skins are not the Peteys. They are just the sign of the Petey. Do you know how when you poke your finger against a sheet, a bulge appears on the other side? The Peteys are bulges poked in the fabric of our universe from beyond; indications of something beyond the wall. The skin that remains is not really the Petey at all; it is a piece of this universe, cut off and collapsed into a two dimensional fabric. Every time we kill a Petey, we diminish our universe. Not that it matters. There's more than enough Universe to go around. . . .

"Look," said Gun. "There they are."

The *Penn State* was a tiny light between two of the three continent-sized cloud-like towers.

"They're not concerned with being seen," Gordon observed.

"Should *we* be?" asked Gun.

"I don't know," said Gordon. "Help me come up with a plan."

"I thought you had a plan."

"Only to get us this far. Now here we are."

They made their plan.

Gun backed off and cut his lights. He waited and watched the *Penn State* release its rails (only eight this year! Only twenty Rangers left, counting himself and Hadj, who couldn't count—) and then launch the *Yankee*. The hard-light boat.

It looked like a hunt even though, if what Gordon said was true, it couldn't be. And what Gordon had said so far, had turned out to be true.

The rails moved into position, waiting for the *Yankee* to begin the cut. Only this time the skin wouldn't be peeled away. It would be held back just long enough for the *Penn State* to drop an unmanned drone with a moby into the opening seam; and then the Petey would be (if what Gordon said was true) towed into orbit around the Earth.

"There they go," said Gun. "Hold on. Get ready for a burn."

A hundred kilometers ahead and down, under the *Yankee*, the seam was opening. The Petey was flashing like a panicked city, like a prairie on fire. Obeying his Ranger training, Gun averted his eyes; but then he let them drift back, drawn to the mysterious emerging light of the opening seam.

The professor was wedged against the bulkhead. The gen in his big, soft arms was slipping off her sleek black little panties. The panties under them were tinier still.

"It's beautiful," Gordon said, shivering. His face was bathed in the rose-colored light from the opening seam.

It's terrible.

"There!" said Gordon. The *Penn State* was moving into position.

"You were right," Gun said. "It's a drone!"

It was dropping a clumsy little lifeboat; on its tail was the glowing end of the moby, flickering in and out of existence. "Wonder where the other end's attached?" asked Gun.

"Who knows?" said Gordon. "The White House? The *Penn State?* The North Pole? Who knows what disaster they have in mind?"

They have no idea what they are taking hold of.

"I thought they knew it was a universe," Gun said.

They know it is a bubble universe. They think it will only last a thousand years or so, providing cheap power for the planet. But you can't tow an expanding universe.

"How do we know it will be expanding?" asked Gun.

"We're the seed," said Gordon.

The word. The light.

"That's why we're going in," said Gordon. Still shivering.

Gun was already swinging in, riding on chems, blasting an arc through high vac. The rails were falling back, alarmed, four on either side of the cut but only one that Gun could see. He roared past it like a comet in a cartoon.

The light was wonderful. The light was terrible. Gun didn't look away didn't look away didn't look away. In the back the professor was snoring or groaning. The gen was cooing questions. A sleek little black bra floated near the top of the cabin.

"They're going to try to cut us off," Gordon said. Still shivering.

"They're too late," Gun said. And they were. Gun held his nose down, held his tail up, held his chems wide open, spitting fire *(Fire!)* as he took the *Henry David*, spinning, in. Under the *Yankee*.

In!

And they were in.

And the *Penn State*, and the cloud-caparisoned Earth and the dust-heaped Moon and the stars behind them, and the stars behind them, and indeed the Universe that had spawned them all—

All were gone.

THIRTY-TWO

God makes the glow worm as well as the star.
—George MacDonald

It was like waking from a dream.

The Universe which had spread around them, so varied, so various and so new, was condensed into a single spot, and then they entered that single spot. It was gray.

It was gray.

It was flecked in the distance but it was a near distance, a distance that Gun (it seemed to Gun) could almost touch, with spots of black; then more. Black that rolled and roiled and shimmered in and out and in of existence.

"Oooohhhhh!" cried the gen. She lay back on the professor's lap, her sleek little knees pressed tight against her sleek little chest.

"I'm not so cold anymore," said Gordon.

Let there be Light, said the professor.

"He's making a joke," said Gordon.

"You sure?" Gun asked.

"Where are we?" said Gordon. He sat in the secondary barca

beside Gun staring through the two-piece faux windscreen of the Sierra yacht *Henry David* at the Universe unfolding before them.

Let there be Light.

"Maybe he's not joking," said Gordon.

Were they moving? None of the instruments in the ship were working. It didn't seem to Gun that they were going anywhere. It seemed rather that the *Henry David* was holding still while a huge hole was falling open below, and in front of, and above and around it. The distant corners of the hole were flecked with black, swarms of spots in sheets, in little clouds that shimmered in and out of existence.

Look.

"Look?"

"What?" asked Gordon.

The probability wave. It's collapsing. This is a Universe being created.

"I thought you said it was going to be expanding," said Gun.

Expanding is collapsing. Probability works both ways. Existence is a collapse which expands back to infinity. Are you still cold?

"Me?" Gordon asked. "No. In fact . . ."

That tidal heart should be working.

"Seems to be."

Gun looked back and saw that the nanobots had finished their work on the professor's mouth. It was smiling. The gen on his lap was nude, or almost. She appeared to be singing. "I didn't know they sang," said Gun.

Everything sings. The metauniverse is a universe of universes, all falling, ascending, being formed and dying; occasionally one bumps against another one. Sometimes even deliberately. When it senses the negentropic heat of the other it is attracted, as a moth to a flame. It sings.

"He's starting up again," whispered Gordon.

It's a love song.

The dot ahead resolved into a swarm of dots: a little gray cloud at the center of a little gray cloud of clouds, all still swirling, swirling and shimmering.

"Love song my ass," whispered Gordon.

The singing is the stuff of existence itself. The patterned dance of energy we call matter.

"Wish we'd brought that water," said Gun.

Life is matter laughing. Matter is energy dancing. Enjoying itself. Existing, if only for a moment. Only for the fun of it.

The gen took off another bra; another, even smaller, even sleeker, blacker bra.

Existence is a contraction from the isn't. What is life made out of but the dance?

They were falling. Gun and Gordon were falling side by side, in the two barcas. The *Henry David* was falling; or rather the universe was falling into existence around it.

Gun checked his ready lights. They weren't working. Would the braking engines fire when he needed them?

Doubt it, said the professor. *Chemical rockets act on Newton's third law, and this universe is too immature to have a third. It's a heavy element law. A few hundred thousand years away. Like water. Subjective time of course. Are you two falling asleep again? What's that?*

"What's that?" Gordon asked, sitting up.

"We seem to be accelerating," Gun said.

That of course was impossible but that of course wasn't.

That's just the universe, said the professor. *This universe is expanding. The probability wave collapsing. Pulling us with it. There are other laws here, new laws, just collapsing into being. That's why we had to do this quickly, before the universe had settled into a steady or near steady state.*

A howl A moan. An even sleeker, even tinier, even blacker . . .

A universe is existence perceived. We are perceiving this universe into existence.

. . . falling toward the cabin ceiling.

Falling toward the center of the universe.

Falling.

"Are we moving?" Gordon asked.

Sort of. Although the ship is stationary, or as close to stationary as anything can be, the universe is unfolding around us like a flower. We are enjoying the first faster than light travel.

"How will we stop without a burn?"

We are lucky the universe is still so new. There is only one direction. Only two or three locations. We are locked in to where we are going. It's the Creation Lock.

The gen was curled up into a ball again. Almost naked and almost smiling. Every time Gun thought she had taken off everything, she took off something more.

"Faster than light?"

A figure of speech. The speed of light here is not a constant, not yet. Our speed is the constant since we are the only thing moving.

Gun must have dozed off. He had been dreaming of running through Tiffany's empty rooms. When he woke up they were still falling. Gordon was asleep in his barca; the gen was quiet, curled in the professor's big, soft arms; the near-distant flecks that Gun had seen earlier were almost resolving themselves into almost-stars—black stars, forming into crude pinwheels.

"Not much of a universe," said Gordon, stretching.

Not yet.

"Do you ever dream about her?" Gun asked.

"Who?"

"Commissary Taffeta."

"C-T? I won't have to. She'll be there with me."

"Where"

"There." Gordon was pointing toward the pinwheel dots.

There was no reason to stay in the pilot's barca, except to sleep. There was nothing to fly. The *Henry David* just fell, or the universe just fell into place around it. Gun wasn't hungry but he was thirsty. He found two cold soda tubes which he and Gordon shared.

The gen had stopped singing, and Gun would have thought she was naked except for the sleek black stripe between her outstretched legs. The professor's eyes were glaring, gleaming, wide—fixed on the forward faux windscreen.

As he half-walked, half-floated to the back of the yacht, Gun felt his heart flopping in his chest; as if it, alone of his organs, were weightless. Everything else was running about one third/g. The toilet even gravity-flushed.

But when he headed back toward the bridge, he found it bathed in a strange, new light. Everything had a silvery glow.

And he saw that it was good, he heard the professor say.

Gordon sat up. "Where are we? What's going on?"

Gun pushed down into his barca. Ahead, the spinning cluster

of stars he had thought was resolving itself into a galaxy had resolved itself into something less awesome, less beautiful, but infinitely more welcome and unexpected.

Overworld.

Actually, the Tangle, said the professor. *It retains the shape of Overworld, but we have penetrated straight through. You're seeing it inside out.*

It was coming up fast. Gun tried to study it. A sort of half doughnut but one which opened instead of closing on itself, and yet retained an arc shape somehow.

"Non-euclidean," said Gun.

"Un-euclidean, actually," said Gordon.

Anti-euclidean.

"Whichever. But why would that look odd in this universe?"

Because this universe started out euclidean. They all do. Default mode.

"Whatever," Gun said.

You are probably wondering how this section of your universe can be here in the center of ours, the professor said.

Gun wasn't but he saw no reason to mention it.

We have accomplished what the Sierras with the Penn State *could never hope to accomplish. We have put the Petey into orbit.*

"Into orbit?"

"Around the Earth," said Gordon.

Now there is only one thing left for you to do.

"Me?"

You're the captain. Lock us on.

THIRTY-THREE

Goodnight! Goodnight! Goodnight!
—Sarah Doudney

A *beautiful sound.*

It was a beautiful sound.

"Like the ringing of a bell," said Gordon.

The meeting of two universes.

Gun had eased the *Henry David* into the open arc with the hydrazine thrusters, a sticky, counterintuitive operation without the Third Law; but it worked, at least close enough for the yacht and the Overworld, or its inside-out antianalog to meet and match and mate. And ring like a bell.

"Is there an airlock?" Gun asked.

There will be.

Gun could already hear the *snik-snak* of the bots through the thin walls of the yacht.

"Are you hot?" Gordon had taken off his E-suit and hung it over the back of his barca.

Gun shrugged. He was comfortable enough in his quilted underwear. But he was uncomfortable with what he saw. He could see nothing out of the yacht's faux windscreen but swarms of small dark stars. "I thought you said we were in orbit around the Earth."

"I said the Petey was," said Gordon. "There. Not here. Here we are outside the inside of the Tangle. There, in our old Universe, if you looked up you would see Overworld and the Tangle gone. And in its place—"

A *universe*.

"A Petey."

"A Triad?"

"I don't think so. I think just one."

Snik-snak.

"They're making an airlock?"

Exactly. So we will be able to pass back and forth. It will give us the space we need, and deserve. A very heaven. Gods can't live in a new universe. It's too raw; too muddy, so to speak.

"Gods?"

"Don't get him started," whispered Gordon.

"Is he sick?"

The professor lay wedged against the rear bulkhead, clothed in shadow. He had taken off his Penn State professor uniform and the bots were wrapping him like a mummy again in strings of gray shadow. "They're making him a new uniform," Gordon said. "They're going to make me one, too."

The gen was wearing her short skirt again, and her sleek, short, black baby tee. She was folding the professor's old professor uniform.

* * *

"But if the Petey is in orbit . . ."

"That's from Earth. Look out from here. Do you see an Earth?"

"I don't think so," Gun said. "I don't like to look out."

"Well! See? That's what I mean," said Gordon.

"Maybe I could get from the Tangle to Overworld."

Gordon was taking off his quilted long johns. The gen was waiting to fold them. "There's no Overworld. As far as the Earth is concerned, it was winked."

"So how are we going to get back?"

"Back?"

"We can't live here!"

"When the airlock is opened, we'll live here and in the Tangle. One foot in each universe."

"Till when? For how long?"

Gordon didn't say anything. He didn't seem to want to answer.

Forever, said the professor. He was wearing his new uniform. It was not yellow like his old one. It was gold with gold braid.

Gordon was with the professor, toward the back of the *Henry David*, trying on his new uniform. Gun sat in his barca watching the stars (for they were starry now) forming into little clusters.

Pathetic little clusters, he thought.

"Are you worried?" It was the gen, drifting down into the copilot's barca. She had her whisper back.

"I guess."

"Why?"

"Gordon's got me stuck here. He doesn't care. All he cares about is that new uniform."

"The god uniform?"

"Is that what they call it?"

"What if they could make you one?"

"The professor says they can only make so many. I don't want one anyway. I don't even like it here." Gun flicked his hand at the new stars as if he were flicking away flies. "It's pathetic."

"If there was a way back," the gen asked, "would you go?"

Look!

The professor floated up toward the bridge, wearing his new uniform. He moved almost gracefully, barely bumping against the narrow cabin's walls.

We have already caused a great expansion in this universe. It has passed the critical stage. I can see stars burning.

"They're just glowing," Gun said.

"Don't argue with him," Gordon whispered. "And you can quit pouting. I think I found you a way back."

"Back home?" Gun sat up in his barca.

"The gen asked me if I knew about it," Gordon said. "She heard about it from C-T. It's a connection if it's still open."

"Where?"

"In the Tangle. From the Tangle to the Dogg. But it won't stay open long. Remember, this universe is expanding."

"How much time does he have?" Gordon asked. He was wearing the same uniform as the professor, only smaller. Gold with gold braid.

He?

"My brother? How long before the link closes?"

Not long. Look how fast this universe is expanding, the professor said, pointing out the faux windscreen. *Maybe a hundred thousand years or so.*

A hundred thousand years. Gun breathed a sigh of relief.

"That's about an hour our time," Gordon whispered.

"The gen knows the way," said Gordon. "She's going into the Tangle to get C-T. Follow her."

"I wish you would go with me," Gun said.

"Don't be silly," Gordon said. "I can't go into the Tangle in this uniform. It wouldn't be the Tangle if I could."

"I mean, back with me all the way."

"My heart wouldn't work right." Gordon fingered the gold braid on his gold uniform. "Who knows what's back there anyway? Who knows how long it's been?"

"Does this mean you never want to go back?"

"I never wanted to go back, even when I was in prison. I always wanted something bigger. Something different."

"I guess this is your chance," said Gun. Through the window he saw the several stars. "I don't know if it's bigger but it's sure different."

He had to admit the uniform was perfect. In the back of the yacht the professor was combing his thick hair.

Damn right it's perfect. It's a god uniform.

"A what?"

"Don't get him started," Gordon whispered. "You need to get going while you can, anyway."

"What am I going to tell everybody? What am I going to tell Iris?"

"You'll think of something."

Tell them about Gordon's uniform.

The professor was still a giant, three times the size of Gun, but with his mouth and eyes finished he was astonishingly good-looking. He had thick, wavy black hair; Gun had no doubt that it would grow thicker and blacker as time went on. Time, he thought. What did Time mean here?

Tell them about us. The professor held out his right hand, waist high.

"I'll tell them," Gun said. He reached up to shake the professor's hand. He took Gordon in his arms for the first time since the visiting room at Upstate, since Grant's Tomb deep in Morgan's cave.

"I'll miss you."

"You never missed me before," Gordon said.

"I always missed you."

THIRTY-FOUR

God never repents.
—Seneca

It was still the same Tangle, even entered from a different universe. The same cold fire smell, the same incessant *snik-snak* din. The same shadowy bots out of the corner of Gun's eye every time he turned an impossible uncorner.

The gen knew the way. Gun followed her, pushing off expertly with his hands down the long corridors—which no longer looked strange even when Gun stared at them, trying to *make* them look strange, *wanting* them to look strange. What if the Tangle were normal here? How would he ever get back then?

Are we going in circles? Gun wondered. Were there such things as circles anymore?

Then, just when Gun thought they were running out of improbabilities, they found it: the semi-euclidean room where the professor had waited for nine and forty years. It still smelled of his long wait. The little zero/g pocket was still there, up under the glass dome. The lensed stars were dimmer, though; closer and fewer than before.

Commissary Taffeta was dim, like a sketch or a ghost image. But as soon as Gun and the gen floated into the room, she jumped into focus. Her blonde hair got blonde and short. Gun reached up to help her down. Her tee shirt read

PROPERTY
OUTER ORLANDO
RECEPTION
CNETER

Her blue eyes got bluer.

"Where is Gordon!" she asked. "Did he make it? Is he here?"

"He's waiting for you," said Gun. It made him both sad and proud to tell her about the new universe. He had been part of it all. But now he wanted only to go home.

The five-sided triangular door was partly in the floor and partly in the wall. Everything in the Tangle was hard to look at; but the door was impossible. It was like two triangles that shared one point in Time, and two in space. Whenever Gun tried to look at any part, he found he had just looked away.

"It unscrews," said Commissary Taffeta. She was wearing white cotton French cut bikini panties with lace detailing under her tee shirt. The door was secured with five, no four, no five wing nuts. They weren't right-handed or left-handed, but had some *other*, more complex threading; Gun's mind left it alone so that his fingers could figure it out.

The gen watched with little black eyes.

Commissary Taffeta watched with her china blue eyes.

The panel came away. Gun tried to look down but there was

nothing there; lots of swirling nothing. It was like looking through a hole into forever.

"Just step through," said Commissary Taffeta.

"I can't," said Gun.

"You have to."

"What if it doesn't go anywhere? Then I won't be anywhere forever?"

"You're nowhere now," said Commissary Taffeta.

"I can't," said Gun.

Did she push him? Something pushed him. It could have been the gen.

And he fell.

THIRTY-FIVE

Pause not! the time is past!
—Percy Bysshe Shelley

And fell
and fell
and fell.

Gun held his breath, and realized he had been holding his breath for as long as he could remember.

When he hit, his hands hit cold concrete. He landed on his knees. He stood up, then opened his eyes. He was in a bare, unfinished, circular room, with windows all around.

The *snik-snak*, the low din of the Tangle was gone. The fire smell was gone. The bone-cold damp was gone.

But this was not the Dogg. Gun felt a sudden terror. This was nowhere. There was a damp smell of new paint, a construction smell. He walked to the window and looked down. There was nothing out there but stars. Bright stars. And not just a few but millions. They were scattered like burning sand across the black sky. The universe was burning down.

He was lost.

And then he heard, or felt, or saw something move behind him. He turned and saw Commissary Taffeta.

She wasn't wearing her tee shirt. She wasn't wearing her white cotton French cut bikini panties with lace detailing.

She wasn't wearing anything at all.

"Is this—the Upper Room?"

"Of course, where else could it connect?"

"So I made it. Thank god!"

"So to speak. Will you stop staring at me?"

"I can't help it."

"Probably not. But still . . ." Commissary Taffeta walked to the window, and Gun stood beside her. The universe was turning on its axis and as they watched the Earth wheeled into view. It was streaked with smoke.

"I wanted to make sure you made it," she said. "And I wanted a last look. Now I'm out of here. The gen is waiting to take me to find Gordon. I have to go while this connection is still good."

She held out a perfect, naked little hand. Gun could almost touch it.

"Wait!" Gun said. "How will I get out of the Dogg?"

"Just head downstairs," said Commissary Taffeta. "The Dogg's a lot shorter down than up. Sooner or later you'll come to a room with a phone."

"But there's nobody to call me. Nobody knows I'm here."

"Just pick it up. And stop staring at me. What did you say?"

"I said good luck," Gun said. "Good luck to both of you. I hope you're happy ever after. You might get a uniform, you know. And even if . . ."

But she was gone.

* * *

There is only one direction in the Dogg from the Upper Room.

Down.

Gun found a stairway through a hatch in the floor, and he went through without looking back. It led to a hall, which led to a room with no windows but shelves of books, and a globe.

The globe was streaked with smoke. Gun couldn't make out any of the continents. He took down a book and opened it but the print was wavery and hard to read.

He put it back and found the stairs again.

There was a high arched double door, and through that door Gun could see another room. Someone was in there.

He stepped through, his heart pounding—

Tiffany! She was standing at a window looking down on fleecy white clouds, wearing a smooth seamless stretch floral jaquard bra with underwire cups and deep plunge center, and a satin thong bikini with front lace accent panel.

"So glad to—" Gun started, but his eloquence seemed to have deserted him. He couldn't think of anything to say.

She was smiling; waiting to hear from him? He fled through another door, down a short flight of stairs, into an oak paneled room where Tiffany lay on a fur rug in front of a fireplace with stationary flames, looking up, wearing a pale pink demi bra with scalloped lace straps and matching stretch lace hipster panties. Her big eyes looked up expectantly. Had they always been brown?

Gun couldn't remember. She was still copy-protected.

"Tiffany!" he said on his way out the door. He found another door, another stair, another door. It was so strange, going down. Tiffany stood at French doors wearing a luminescent silk charmeuse chemise with a princess seamed, lace trimmed bodice, overlooking a garden with perfect, waving plants. The sky above was china blue.

"It's always nice to see you," Gun said. He couldn't remember why he'd had such trouble before. What could be easier than talking to a pretty girl?

She smiled that same old smile he could never remember ever seeing before.

On the table beside her was a phone.

THIRTY-SIX

Wild still, almost, as it ever was . . .
—Zane Grey

It was like waking from a dream. The sweet smell of Vitazine™ filled Gun's nostrils. His shoulders ached. His fingers were numb and he was hungry.

Something banged off the lid of Gun's suite, and he opened the lid himself, from the inside, and scrambled to his feet.

It was a bottle; it was the monkeys. They had ceased their sorrowful noises and were trilling happily far overhead, in the high, smoky rafters of the dome. The roof of the Dogg was missing. The wheel was lying on its side. Empty suites lay scattered, lidless, like opened coffins across the marble floor.

A family, or a small grouping of some kind, was huddled over a fire in a far corner of the shattered lobby. They were cooking a small beast; a dog? a horse?

Gun looked for his uniform. It wasn't folded at the head of his suite as usual. Then he remembered that he had only exited, and never entered the Dogg.

As always when he was just emerging from the Dogg, he had

to pee. The bathrooms were boarded up, so he stepped behind a pillar.

The real clerk was gone. The desk itself was gone.

The street outside was empty except for an old man and a doggit™ gathering sticks for firewood. The old man gathered and the doggit™ carried.

Wearing only his quilted long johns, Gun walked across the plaza to the Littlest. The TV was on, and Joe, the regular Joe, the original Joe, was wiping glasses with a rag.

A regular rag.

"Hello, Ranger," he said as Gun knelt at the bar. "The usual?"

"Sure." It was good to be recognized. "What happened to your moby?" Gun asked.

"Mobys are definitely off-Protocol," Joe said, popping the rag. "Too much danger of cross-universe feedback, or something. Where you been?"

"There's a new Protocol?"

"New Protocol!?! The world was bumped off its axis," said the only other customer in the Littlest, a regular person™ on a stool at the end of the bar. Gun hadn't noticed him before. He was wearing an unfamiliar uniform.

"Bumped off its axis?" Gun couldn't tell if he was exaggerating for effect, or telling the truth.

"It felt like that, anyway. The new Protocols came out, and the Petey was captured, the same week. It was beautiful. We saw it on TV, didn't we, Joe?"

"It was terrible," said Joe.

"The smoke was rising all over the world, not just above the White House," said the regular person™ at the end of the bar. "The Peteys came closer and closer until they filled the sky, just like the Fundamentals said they would. Bigger than the Moon.

Bigger than the sun. Gobbled up that orbital, what did they call it?"

"Overworld," said Gun.

"Did Joe call you a Ranger? Where's your uniform?"

"Guess I lost it. No more hunts anyway, right?"

"Not with the Petey turning everything into free energy," said Joe.

"What happened to the Rangers?"

"They inducted the last batch into 'Pirates of the Universe' last week, then closed it off. Can't believe you're not there. Always figured you'd made it."

"Guess I missed it," said Gun. He wondered how he was going to explain to Donna that her lifelong dream was dead.

"That'll be twenty," said Joe.

Gun found what was left of his Petey certificate and set it on the bar. All that was left was the rose colored central oval of the soaring Triad. "Is there anything left you can cut off of there?"

"Look at this!" Joe said. The regular person™ came up from the end of the bar and whistled.

"What's the problem?" Gun asked.

Joe slid the remains of Gun's Petey certificate back toward him, across the bar. "This must be the one they were looking for, the one that was never cashed in. It was on TV. They're holding two places for you."

"Lucky dog," said the regular person™.

"Two places?"

"At 'Pirates of the Universe.' For you and your very best girl."

THIRTY-SEVEN

Home is heaven for beginners.
—Charles Henry Parkhurst

You have to tell us *all* about it," said Iris.

"Yeah," said Hump.

Ham, sitting up in his coffin at the dark end of the room, just nodded.

"I hardly know where to start," Gun said. "Why don't you start, Donna?"

"It's nice," Donna said. "Super nice. Just as nice as I ever dreamed it would be."

"Dreamed," said Glenn.

"Each house is different, yet they are all the same," said Donna.

"Explain," said Whitmer. Since he had bought into the Yard he had taken to eating with the family twice a week. He considered that his compensation for the fact that the Yard was out of oil.

"They're different on the outside," said Gun. "But alike on the inside."

"Sort of like people," said Iris. Since Round Man had disappeared and never returned, she had become almost philosophical.

"Pass the bats," said Donna. Gun winced from habit, expecting Hump to jump all over her. But Hump didn't complain anymore when people called things by their real names. They *were* bats, after all. And while it wasn't off-Protocol to call things by the wrong names, it was definitely off-Protocol to insist that they be so called.

"Take one for yourself, Napoleon," said Iris. Since Round Man had disappeared and never returned, the doggit™ had taken his place at the table, and with the strap-ons, did pretty well.

"Tell us more about 'Pirates of the Universe,' " said Hump. "What do you eat?"

"The best of everything," said Donna.

"And seconds on desserts," said Gun.

"Cable and a pool," said Donna.

"We never want for anything," Gun said.

"We don't have to cook or clean," said Donna.

"Or work—or cut the grass," said Gun.

"Only one thing we have to do for ourselves," Donna said, blushing.

"Lucky dogs," muttered Whitmer.

Napoleon looked up, startled, from his plate of little wings, as if he had almost remembered something long forgotten.

"If it's so perfect, why ever leave?" asked Hump. He was retired, but he still went to the Yard every day to make sure the chevrolets' doors were shut and the windows all rolled up.

"We like to see our family once a year," Donna said.

"In fact, under the new Protocols we have to," said Gun.

"Have to," said Glenn. He still operated the ferry three times a day. Like everything else in the world, it ran on free electricity microwaved down from the orbiting differential interface engines.

"Where you two love birds going?" asked Whitmer. Since Donna had turned him down, he had proposed to Iris even though she was sixteen years older than him. He was still waiting for his answer.

"Take a little walk," said Gun.

"Don't they look almost perfect?" Iris said. And it was true. Gun and Donna looked almost perfect in their matching "Pirates" uniforms.

Even though Morgan's Ferry was no longer cloud-locked, the top of the ridge behind the house was still cloaked in river fog until nine every night. Gun and Donna waited until it cleared and they could see the darkened downtown, the ferry landing, the stopped town hall clock (8:55); and Mayors', still lighted. A uniformed druggist from Tell City was running it now, since K-T was no longer a free zone.

"Do you ever miss it?" Gordon asked.

"Just once a day," Donna said. She led the way across the ridge to the top of the Yard, and found their old chevrolet, the Oldsmobile.

Gun held the door for Donna. She got in and lit a Marlboro.

"I thought you'd quit," he said.

"One won't hurt," she said. She gave it to him to hold while she reached up under her silver tunic and unhooked her bra. What memories that *click* brought back! Gun thought of the

Tangle with its constant *snik-snak*. He thought of Commissary Taffeta, and Gordon, and Hadj. He even thought of Tiffany still holding the phone he had handed back to her. Soon the clouds thinned and there, floating in the center of the eastern sky like a jewel, was the Petey. Circling it were the interface differential engines, and circling each of them, like fireflies or tiny stars, were the microwave widebeam relays that made life on Earth so easy these days.

Donna handed him her bra and he put it into the glove compartment. Her panties followed. *Click*.

"I can't believe there's a universe in that thing," Donna said.

"There is, though," Gun said. "It even has a God. Or two."

They stayed four days and three nights in Morgan's Ferry. On the last morning Gun talked Glenn into taking the *John Hunt Morgan* down the river and up the creek, to Morgan's Cave. He found the sand still dark with blood. He peered down into the Bottomless Pit and heard the *snik-snak* of the bats. He was surprised to find the ashes still warm in Grant's Tomb; but perhaps others were using the cave as well. He was glad to leave, to see the light ahead. He was ready to go home.

That afternoon, Iris walked with Gun and Donna down Water Street to catch the ferry for Tell City, and "Pirates of the Universe" beyond. Iris was getting out more often. Whitmer and Napoleon followed at her heels.

"You're pregnant, aren't you?" Iris asked Donna.

Donna, who had never bothered to learn to blush, just smiled. Gun followed her onto the ferry, and the little electric boat backed out into the streaming Ohio.

"Have you decided on a name?" Iris called out from shore. "No Hams, no Humps, no Irises—please!"

"If it's a boy, we're going to name him Gordon," said Donna.

Iris nodded approvingly. "And if it's a girl?"

It was Gun's turn. "Commissary Taffeta."

"Taffeta," said Glenn, who always had the last word.